CRIPPLED EARTH

CURVE

OF

HUMANITY

BOOK FOUR

MAQUEL A. JACOB

Cover art by:

Keith Johnston

https://keithdraws.wordpress.com

Edited by:

Rhiannon Rhys-Jones

Published by MAJart Works

www.majartworks.com

Hillsboro, Oregon

ISBN: 978-0-9979564-8-1

BOOKS BY MAQUEL A. JACOB

THE CORE SERIES

CORE OF CONFLICTION: BOOK 1

SEEDS OF CONVICTION: BOOK 2

BONDS OF CONTRITION: BOOK 3

WELCOME DESPAIR

A COLLECTION OF SHORTS

BLOOD DOCTRINE

BLOOD DOMINION

*****COMING SOON*****

CURVE OF HUMANITY

BOOK FIVE: AFTERMATH

BLOOD DESCENSION

(BOOK THREE OF THE BLOOD SAGA)

ACKNOWLEDGEMENTS

Thank you for taking a chance on my new six book series Curve of Humanity. My great passion is to find the good in humanity and show we can combat corruption within our societies. This book series is a lesson of hope in the face of futility.

Or so I would like to think.

For those who encouraged me to keep going when it all seemed too daunting, I appreciate you all.

A huge thanks to NaNoWriMo (National Novel Writing Month) for supporting writers' creative juices. My peeps at NIWA, you all keep my humble and showed me to put myself out there with no fear.

To Blaze Ward and Leah Cutter for being awesone cousins who believed in me and helped guide me to hone the business side of the craft.

Keith Johnston: Your talent is mind blowing. I never thought the covers would turn out so awesome. Look forward to working with you again on future projects.

A Sonnet for Humanity

-Blind Sheep-

I had hope for some sense of sanity
It being the 21st century of man
But, it seems we are losing our humanity
With no way of fixing it- If we can.
The end is near, or so they say
They, being the prophets and pessimists
Salivating at the promise of doomsday
Even as society and everyday life persists.
Let us not fall in line
Marching towards our own annihilation
And read into the inevitable sign
Of our final destination
Lest we forget an important note
We all wear the same human coat.

- Rachel E. Robinson 2012

Chapter One: Progress Reports

CONTINGENCY PLAN

The London World Conference arena was stuffed to the gills with each country's government, military, and science leaders in attendance. By the looks on their faces, they were bracing for the worst-case scenario. A small transport ship appeared above the field and descended onto the turf. Its ramp came down and the two Interfacers Sspark had loaned out to Darnizva entered the center stage. They had been connected to the world database over the past two years calculating population loss percentages for the duration of the war.

The numbers so far weren't looking good. After weeks of estimations and crunching data they came to a grave conclusion. Seeing the dour looks did not give them much confidence. They stepped onto the raised platform to present their findings.

"Have they no faith in their kind's capacity for survival?" the red head, Sugil, asked.

"Would you?" Nellan, his dark haired counterpart answered.

"They are a bit behind, but all civilizations have to start somewhere."

"True." His companion nodded. He saw Darnizva give the signal to start. "Let's give it to them without filters, shall we?"

He hit the commlink attached to his ear connecting it to the wireless amplifier system.

"Good morning, humans. As you may have heard, we were given the task of determining your survival rate in the upcoming war. Our research was based on inhabited areas, trajectory of weapons from the Relliant ship, friendly fire incidents…"

"Enough of all that!" A French general shouted. "Tell us the numbers!"

A din of voices concurring with him filled the arena. The two Interfacers glanced at each other then Darnizva, who shrugged before nodding.

"Very well." Nellan continued. "Based on our research and the data available, we have concluded that seventy two percent of your planet's population will die from a multitude of events. Disintegration, exposure to alien biochemicals, starvation, and shock. I believe one of the common failures is what you call a massive coronary."

He happened to see Darnizva's face and realized he had been trying to stop him from talking. The entire arena had hushed. No one was moving. They all sat awestruck.

"You should have warned them first, I think," Sugil stated.

"Hmm…not sure that would have done any good." He whispered back, despite his commlink still on.

Slowly, the audience began to show signs of life as one by one they turned to their colleagues and started to argue. The Interfacers were baffled at the humans' anger towards each other for something completely out of their control.

"I don't understand. What's going on?" Sugil asked.

Since their arrival on Earth, they had sensed an imbalance in the humans' psyche. Mankind seemed to be a civilization on the brink of madness. Their eyes darted back and forth as they caught snippets of hostile words being thrown around. Darnizva stepped up onto the platform.

"You see, humans can be quite selfish, and each faction had their own agenda instead of one that benefitted their planet, or race for that matter."

"Ahh," they both exclaimed.

"Now they realize all their separate agendas mean absolutely nothing if their race will be practically extinct."

"Why? I still don't understand this divide. Are they not all the same race?" Nellan asked.

"Their logic of race is complicated and makes no sense, so I won't attempt to explain it."

"Well, it's too late now, isn't it?" Sugil surveyed the humans with pity.

"Indeed." Nellan replied.

"I believe it may be time for a short break." Darnizva announced through the amplifier system via his own commlink.

Every top military leader assembled in the conference room positioned under the bleachers brainstorming on how to save humanity. The original scientists still in play had been tapped for suggestions earlier and the results were frightening. No one wanted any of their ideas implemented and made it clear, would not be tolerated. They did not have the same clout they once did decades ago.

"The only option left is to find another planet and start shipping people out," one general said.

"Yes, but that would take another fifty years. There's no way we could find one so quickly that could sustain human life," another one stated.

"Well, we better check out every map of the solar

system ever made and come up with something," a third general piped in.

"Oh stop! We have plenty of options when it comes to planets. What do you think was first on those scientists' agenda after dissecting those aliens?"

"That's great and all but the question is if any of it is applicable given our level of technology?"

Another general jumped in.

General Rubio Perrara was not really listening. He got the gist of what they were trying to do. It seemed daunting at best, nearly impossible. With less than two decades left, humankind had run out of time. Evacuation was inevitable. Where, was a mystery. To his left, General Takayama also stood staring out the window, a whimsical smile on his face. He walked over to stand next to him.

"You know, the cherry blossoms are blooming in Japan right now." Takayama said.

"Is that right? I'd love to see them again. Been a while since I visited."

"Yes, you should," Takayama turned to him, still smiling. He made a full turn to face the door and headed towards it. "Look me up when you come. I'll treat you to the best Sake on Earth." He waved a hand as he left the room.

On the main deck of Sspark's battle ship, the crew prepared for departure. There was a flurry of activity as each station was being manned. Darnizva stood out of the way near the entrance. Sspark gave orders in his usual passive aggressive tone. When he felt all was in order he turned towards the entry and motioned for Darnizva to follow. They entered the corridor with Sspark's Cybok, Ballamian, taking the rear.

Darnizva glanced back at the soldier who stood a little over seven feet tall, wearing an all black body suit. Electric blue eyes were in contrast to his pale skin and jet black hair that hung past his shoulders. Cyboks were deadly, and expensive. He felt a twinge of disgust, knowing the only reason Sspark had one was due to his mating status with the general.

"You can't have him," Sspark said.

Darnizva turned his attention forward. Beside him, Sspark's hips swayed with every exaggerated step. In a shiny white bodysuit that glittered like starlight, it was again hard to tell whether he was in male or female form. The crew members passing by lowered their heads in quick acknowledgement of their superiors.

"I wouldn't ask for him. I am grateful for the Interfacers."

"As you should." Sspark smiled. "We are leaving."

"I see that. Why? Training of the humans is not yet complete."

Sspark stopped at an intersection and turned to him.

"I will not waste any more of my time on that inferior race."

Darnizva's face scrunched in anger.

"You agreed to do it!"

"And I was wrong. They have no appreciation for my skills and will be annihilated regardless of our efforts. Or theirs, for that matter."

"I promised not to abandon them."

"Exactly." Sspark resumed his walk by turning down the left corridor. "I'm sure you'll do just fine without our interference in your pet project."

Darnizva slammed Sspark against the bulk head and locked eyes. Ballamian's hands receded into his wrists, displaying the arm cannons.

"Let go of me, Darnizva," Sspark hissed.

"This is not," Darnizva said heatedly, grabbing

Sspark by the arms and slamming him into the wall again, "some pet project!"

His eyes glowed red and Sspark's narrowed. Sspark raised a hand signaling Ballamian to stand down.

"No need to get nasty. I will retract my statement on that. The rest." Sspark pushed him off and moved to the center of the corridor. "I stand by. You shouldn't have run."

He walked away with Ballamian in tow, leaving Darnizva to seethe.

I know that!

Darnizva regained his composure and caught up with Sspark. They continued towards the ship's exit, Sspark wanting him gone. He needed to get back to his own ship and map out a new strategy. The only other option would be Celestial Mother, and he wanted her to be a last resort.

While traveling back to his ship with the fight cruiser on auto pilot, Darnizva sat casually in the cockpit mulling over his situation. There would be no help coming from his home world. The dash console lit up and the communication icon blinked. He stared at it for a long time, contemplating on if he should answer. As it went through a second round of its sequence, he tapped it.

"Captain, I was getting worried." His second in command's voice was terse as his image appeared on the small screen.

"I was seeing Lieutenant Sspark off. What is the urgency?"

There was a pause. He knew what his second was thinking by the instant frown that formed. Sspark rubbed everyone the wrong way.

"Celestial Mother wishes to speak with you." Darnizva winced at that. His second continued. "General

Perrara and Hana would also like to set up a meeting at your earliest convenience."

"I will talk with Hana first. The general can wait."

"And her?" His second asked.

He remembered the sly smile on Celestial Mother - Telia's face the last time they met. She was up to something and it didn't bode well for his agenda.

"Sooner than later. I will let you know. I am on my way back."

He disconnected the feed and the screen went blank. The viewports gave him a one hundred and eighty degree line of sight as the scenery passed by. Dense forest lined both sides of the pathway that stretch wide to accommodate the alien ships coming through on a regular basis. A closer look through the trees found remote cameras attached to floating drones. In the past few decades, Earth had not change much.

…And there lies the problem.

At the edge of the forest, the landscape revealed a bustling city up ahead. Darnizva sat correctly in the cockpit and tapped the icons to engage the secondary engine. The cruiser went from hover mode to flight and lifted into the sky above the city. It shot over in seconds and arrived in the other forest where his ship sat idle emitting a soft hum that vibrated the foliage.

Human military soldiers on guard duty walked around its perimeter, keeping clear of his own guards. They were Cyboks except of the lower tier. He had negotiated for them personally despite the discouragement from his father. He was of a higher rank than Sspark and Zanzibar, yet they had high level Cyboks. There was no logic in his father's blatant favoritism and lack of respect for him.

The ship's guidance system took over the cruiser's and it sailed effortlessly into the docking bay. Crewmembers rushed over as the clamps grabbed hold to secure it. Darnizva leapt out once the cockpit opened.

"Captain," his second greeted him as they met halfway.

They made their way to the lift and let it take them to the bridge level. Entering the corridor, Darnizva paid attention to his stride, avoiding the heavy traffic of soldiers going about their daily routines.

"Where are we on the timetable?" He asked his second.

"There are still some glitches, but nothing that can't be remedied," his second replied while keeping up.

"Did you get a hold of Hana?"

"Do you want to have a video chat or face to face? That was his question."

Darnizva thought about it. On one hand, less travel was ideal. Some humans were dead set on taking their frustrations out against any alien they encountered. It would also mean being caught on radar heading into the desert compound. On the other, real time deliberations where both parties could gauge each other's reactions was best.

"Tell Hana we need to find a better location. Too many eyes focused on our movements."

"Of course." His second reached the bridge entrance ahead of him and turned around. "Is it worth all this?" He stared Darnizva down. "No one on this ship blames you for anything. If you hadn't made the jump, we would all be dead. So, I am asking, on behalf of the crew. Is helping this race worth it in the end?"

It was a valid question that deserved an honest answer. Darnizva walked past him and entered the bridge.

"I do not know. But, I will not go back on my word."

"That's good enough," his second said as he followed.

∽

The entrance to Metropolis emerged as a shimmer in the landscape. Three military jeeps traveling on the dirt road sped through it and came out on the other side to a false blue sky. Looming ahead was the main building that ran all its regions. A multilevel stark white structure built into a mountain. In the first vehicle, Kevin sat in the front passenger seat, one leg propped up against the dash and his head resting in his hand along the window. He stared up at the building and instantly connected telepathically with Terence.

"Why have you come here?" Terence's message was at a high volume in his head.

"If you didn't want me here, you shouldn't have let me in," Kevin answered calmly.

There was a long pause.

Kevin laughed inwardly. *Hmph!*

"Whatever it is, the answer is no," Terence finally sent.

"I'm still going to try and convince you."

The lower docks of the building opened, and the vehicles went down the ramp, deep into Metropolis. Overhead lights flickered on to guide them through the underground maze. They parked in designated stations and their passengers were forced out by armed security guards. Kevin found that to be unnecessary.

"I don't like uninvited guests," Terence snapped.

"This way," the transport operator closest to him ordered.

Seeing the strange purple glow of its eyes and the internal microphone protruded from behind its ear made Kevin shudder. He never liked them. As his group moved, the security detail raised their weapons.

"Just you, per his instructions," the transporter said.

Kevin sighed in defeat. He turned to his entourage. "Wait here."

"We don't seem to have a choice," said one operative.

"I will talk with him and get him to see reason," Kevin said.

"*Oh?*" Terence asked playfully.

"*Stop being a snot! You're too old for that shit.*"

When Terence didn't retort, Kevin nodded at the transport operator.

"Lead the way."

Kevin followed the operator down the massive corridor. It was nearly fifty feet wide and he wondered what it was accommodating. The two men walked for another ten minutes and came to a small enclosed vehicle set on a railing system. The hatch opened and the operator waited for him to get in. Once he saw Kevin was settled, he got in the front section and hit a button. The pod lurched forward at high speed and didn't let up until it reached the end of the rails in front of cargo bay doors.

"Forward, please," the operator said.

The doors swung apart like a giant readying itself to devour a meal. On the other side was lift. As Kevin walked to it and entered, he stared sideways in an upward glance at the tiny camera in the corner.

"*Really? Just how many transits are there to get to you?*"

"*I like to keep my guests on their toes,*" Terence laughed.

The lift dropped down many levels before stopping. When it opened, Kevin found himself on the command deck. In the center, wearing military dress and standing at ease, arms behind his back, was Terence. His dark hair flowed freely down the middle of his back.

"The answer is no," Terence said.

"I haven't asked you anything yet."

"I know why you came here. This has nothing to do with us."

"You're wrong," Kevin replied. "This planet is your home just like everyone else's."

Terence turned around to face him. They locked eyes. Kevin let his arms drop loosely to his sides. That look. He knew it well. A longing he could never fill. He averted his gaze and heard a soft tsk from Terence.

"Ask your question." Terence's tone was harsh.

"We need the Terrors to join the ranks of fighters."

"And you know my answer."

"Then what about the other ones?"

He gestured towards some of the transport operators.

"You think I created them to be sacrificed? Absolutely not!"

"Why?" Kevin stepped to him and grabbed hold of his shoulders. "Why are you being so stubborn about it?"

Terence brought his arms in, knocking Kevin's away.

"They need to learn how to fend for themselves! We were used, tortured, and hated all our lives, doing their bidding. We're done!"

Kevin got hold of him again and didn't let go when he tried to push away. "Tere, please."

Terence's eyes went wide and he leaned as far away as he could from Kevin.

"Don't act like you suddenly care!"

"*When have I not?*" Kevin asked telepathically.

Terence wrench out of his grasp and stepped back.

"Tell them what I said." He turned away and headed towards the main console.

"What, no grand tour?"

Without turning back, Terence said, "You need to leave."

"I'll be back."

The operator had been waiting at the lift doors and gestured for him to get in.

"*Wait for me,*" Kevin sent to Terence. Before the doors closed, he saw Terence's body, back in his military stance, go rigid.

UNATTAINABLE GOALS

The facility chairman sat with his chair positioned sideways at the end of the large oval table while he scanned the faces of the world leaders and dignitaries sitting around it. Not one of them had cracked even the slightest smile. Dead silence filled the room, making the atmosphere uncomfortable for most. He swung in his chair so that it was straight forward.

"I understand the frustration, but what are you all so worried about?" He asked.

Former Army General Bradley Hoskins leaned towards the table's edge.

"I had proposed decades ago when we found out about the timeline that we should shoot for twenty percent of the population to be in military service as the needed goal."

"Based on what?" George of Homeland Security shouted. "What good is that when we are up against an alien race that uses eighty percent of its adult population as a military force?"

"Hmm." The Chairman raised a finger to his lips. "True. The human race is outmatched. But, twenty percent is the best we can do. Hoskins is indeed correct."

"It's unprecedented and nearly impossible," Neil Shannon added. "As much as we recruit each generation, there just aren't enough people willing to fight."

"Let me off this rock. I'm not dying with these fools," a scientist said.

"That!" Hana yelled, standing. "That is one of the reasons why we can't reach our goals!"

Everyone leaned back from the table at his outburst. The scientist frowned and looked away, not making eye contact with anyone. Hana sat back down, his face flushed pink.

Hoskins nodded. "The little twit is right. Can't argue with that." He turned to the chairman. "That purge stunt you all pulled did us no favors."

"Then what do you propose we do now?" Another general asked.

Further down at the table, President Lynmore remained silent with a pained expression. When she finally looked up, her gaze fell on the chairman.

"You have Bi-Genetics with untapped talent sealed away in the facilities. I want them."

"Wanting is always encouraged. Getting is another matter," he replied.

"I will reinstate the draft," Lynmore seethed as she stood up, planting her hands on the table. George set one of his hands on hers. She slipped hers from under it and smacked his away.

"Let's not get too hasty," the chairman said angrily.

"I will not be made a fool out of." She turned to Hoskins. "Do you agree? Or are you also going to roll over and let them dry screw us?"

Hoskins also became angry and stood.

"Now, hold on, Miss Brass Balls. I don't roll over for nobody!"

"We are not trying to screw anyone," the chairman said. He was barely able to contain the rage he felt. None of this was the facilities doing. Humans had brought this on themselves. "You asked for assistance and we obliged."

"But, you won't contribute to the cause," Admiral Perrara added. He was the picture of calm with his arms folded while he stared at the ceiling. Looking down at the others at the table, he shifted in his seat. "There is no negotiating. We need to reach twenty percent. Period."

The chairman leaned back and stared at him.

"This is not something I can authorize on a dime," he began.

"The draft, it is." President Lynmore turned away from the table and walked towards the door. "Let's go, George."

"Madam President!" The chairman's assistant cried out. "This is unacceptable!"

Hoskins glanced over at Perrara who closed his eyes in defeat. As she stepped out into the hallway, Lynmore halted.

"You left me no choice."

The doors closed behind her and George, leaving the rest of the room gawking in awe. After a few seconds, the chairman regained his demeanor and cleared his throat to get everyone's attention. He was met with hostile stares.

How dare they ask such a thing of us! He thought.

"Again, I understand. You also have to acknowledge what that would mean for the facilities."

"This is a war!" Another President shouted. "Did you not hear what we are saying?"

The telepath, Aleem, swung his chair towards the chairman and gave him a strange look. Before he could ask what was on the man's mind, he heard his voice in his head.

"Do not cave. Let the draft happen."

Stunned, the chairman immediately made his face void of emotion. Aleem continued.

"Play their game. We have a plan of our own."

"We will also implement a draft," a different country's

President said. "I am sure other countries will follow." He stood from his seat. "There is no reason to continue this meeting."

He gave a bow then headed out the room. The rest of the world leaders and most of the scientists did the same until the only ones left were Hana, Perrara, Hoskins, the telepath and the chairman.

"You need to make her see reason," the chairman said to Admiral Perrara.

"I will do no such thing." Perrara uncrossed his arms. "I can guarantee, Darnizva probably thinks the same."

Those damn aliens, the chairman chided himself.

Inside his personal chamber aboard his ship, Darnizva watched news from all over the world on multiple holoscreens before him. He couldn't wrap his mind around the images and articles flooding his senses. With everything that happened with the Grid City and the purge, humans were no closer to salvation.

What will it take?

The notification on his entrance chimed and he looked up to see the two Interfacers enter. He saw their grim expressions and let out a sigh. Both stood near the door, not daring to move further in.

"Sit down," Dranizva ordered.

They hesitated then went around him to sit on the window seat.

"What is it?" Darnizva asked.

"We may be recalled soon and wanted to make sure you had everything you need."

Darnizva glanced over at them confused.

"What do you mean? Why would you be recalled?"

"Lieutenant Sspark is leaving. Since we are his

interfacers, we assumed," Sugil said.

"Do you wish to go?" He watched them appear to struggle inwardly. "I won't force you to stay on this planet and fight for me. I am not your Captain."

Nellan leaned forward.

"We don't want to leave our work unfinished."

"Then it's settled. You stay."

"What about the Lieutenant?" Sugil asked.

Darnizva didn't have the heart to tell them Sspark couldn't care less. When they were loaned to him, he got the impression they were expendable. There were already four new Interfacers at the helm of Sspark's ship mainframe. He concluded it was because of their age. They were still quite young, like his own crew, and he didn't have Interfacers for his ship.

Their conversation was disrupted by a new notification on one of the holoscreens. Darnizva read the message outlining the details of the meeting at Facility HQ. He felt his face twitch as he forced down disappointment and rage.

"I have a meeting with Hana soon. So, I must leave for Earth side."

"As do we," Nellan said. "The cannon needs another tweak. We can take the same transport, if that is acceptable."

"Let's go."

Darnizva waved his hand across the holoscreens and the messages disappeared. He grabbed his outer robe and put it on, securing it with the sash. The Interfacers left first and he followed. His mind raced while they walked down the corridor. Although he despised the person who popped up in his mind, there was no one more suited. He would need to meet with them after his talk with Hana.

The small café on the quiet suburban street was

wedged between two bigger shops. At midday, the sky was partly cloudy and the temperature mild, making Hana feel slightly overdressed. He walked into the empty space that prominently displayed the occupancy capacity at twenty five. There were six small round tables and four stools at the bar. No rack of liquor bottles, only five taps.

He sat down at the farthest table and unbuttoned his sweater coat. His hair, temporarily colored black, was pulled back in a severe ponytail, making him look more Asian. A man appeared from the back through the heavy curtain separating the area. Hana was taken aback by the man's hipster vibe. Wearing a tight V-neck t-shirt, skinny jeans, messy hair, and a short beard, he was like an ad from the early two thousands.

"What can I get ya'?"

"Just an IPA. Waiting on a friend."

"Starting a tab?"

Hana sat back stunned.

"Places still do that?"

"I still do that," the man replied. "Don't trust technology. Especially with all this new bullshit going down in the government. But I gotta' use it. Tabs are easier than a shit ton of single payments."

"Can't blame you there." Hana held out his wrist and the man pulled a scanner from his back pocket. "I'll pay for my friend too."

"Gotcha."

The man nodded as he held the device over his arm. There was soft beep. As he went through the curtains and reemerged behind the bar, the tiny bells above the main entrance jingled.

The tall man straightened himself from ducking down to enter. His hair was up in a messy bun and he wore dark shades. The button down shirt was untucked over black jeans. A full length tan colored trench coat lay open. He pulled the shades up and positioned them atop his head. Hana stared gawking at him in surprise.

"Umm," Hana stuttered.

"David," Darnizva said.

"Is that really you?"

Darnizva walked over and pulled the chair out further so he could sit comfortably across from Hana. He smirked at the shocked stare.

"Seriously, Hana. What part of blending in for decades had you confused?"

The bartender came back with Hana's beer and set it down along with a coaster. He turned to Dranziva.

"Whatcha' drinking?"

He glanced over at the taps behind the bar.

"I'll take the stout."

"Good choice." The bartender left.

"I guess David could have paid for his own beer then," Hana said.

"True. I do have my own money."

When his stout arrived and the bartender went back through the curtain, Darnizva took a sip before starting the meeting.

"I saw the feed from facility headquarters."

Hana paused lifting his beer halfway then took a big swig.

"It was sort of disgraceful. My part, anyway."

Darnizva shook his head.

"No, you were right on target. I fear you were the only one with open eyes."

Hana grimaced, nodding in agreement.

"Which is why I wanted to speak with you." He watched Darnizva sit back and let his body lounge freely. His demeanor oozed sex. It was done so nonchalant that Hana realized that may have been how he managed to stay under the radar for so long passing as a human.

"How feasible is evacuation and can we withstand the onslaught if not?"

Darnizva tilted his head back and stared at the ceiling for a while.

"Getting every human soul off this planet is unrealistic. Maybe sixty percent at the most."

"And yet, you won't tell the world leaders this."

Averting his gaze from the ceiling, Darnizva locked eyes with him.

"They don't listen to reason!" He seethed.

The door bells jingled and a group of four women stumbled in laughing. They all slammed against the bar and giggled at the bartender as he came out. Two of the women turned towards their table. Their eyes nearly bulged out their sockets as their sights landed on Darnizva. He gave them a sideways glance, the sun glinting across his cinnamon red eyes still full of anger.

One of the women smiled while the other sized up Hana, assessing him as a non threat. She tapped the other two who were trying to butter up the uninterested bartender. All four women zeroed in their new prey regardless if he was perceived to be already taken.

Hana sighed. Searching mentally for Darnizva, he sent out a thought.

"Guess our serious conversation is taking a back seat."

Darnizva's gaze changed to astonishment as he turned to stare at Hana.

"I didn't know you could tap into another's mind like that." He replied.

"Hey, sexy," the first of the women sang as they neared the table.

They sat down, beers in hand, surrounding both men.

"We skipped out of work early," the second one said. "We're bad."

"This your girlfriend?"

The third asked, pointing at Hana.

"I'm a man," Hana retorted.

The fourth woman shrugged. "Boyfriend?"

"Would it matter?" Darnizva asked.

"Depends," the second woman replied. "How kinky are you?"

Darnizva sat straight in the chair then leaned forward, his coat laying behind him in perfect symmetry on both sides. His fingers clasped loosely together he let his eyes glow softly.

"How about, we go somewhere private. I make sure you're all bound and incapacitated then tear each one of you apart while I desecrate you; sexually. Or, you can take yourself to another table and enjoy your freedom together instead of harassing others?"

Hana blanched along with the women as an eerie silence filled the café. From the look in Darnizva's eyes, he knew the alien was not joking in the slightest. With swift ease, the women stood and went to another table closer to the doors. They didn't look back. The bartender let out a soft grunt as he wiped down some freshly washed glasses.

"That was…" Hana didn't finish.

"Genius?" Darnizva sent, smiling as he leaned back with his beer in his hand.

"Frightening," Hana replied.

Darnizva took a long drink, his stare unwavering.

Hana got the impression the alien had done something like that before. For the first time, he saw the captain as a potential threat. As if understanding his change in demeanor, Darnizva sent him another thought.

"As you should have from the beginning."

~

Seagulls circled above the deserted beach, their cries

piercing in the early hours of the day. The waves swished loudly as they rolled up halfway. Hoskins lay on a lounge chair with his eyes closed, letting the sound lull him into submission. Back at his beach house, located two states over from the Grid City, he relished in the coastal town's solitude. His right hand man stood nearby with a tablet checking for updates. He glanced over at him. The dark suit with an opened white dress shirt made Hoskins feel uncomfortable. For once, he would like the man to relax. He deserved it after the shit storm they went through.

Hoskins sighed and adjusted his body into a more pleasing position. He was about to close his eyes again when he caught a glimpse of something off in the horizon. His right hand man raised his shades and pushed them atop his head. Both men squinted at the dark shape as it got closer, taking form.

"I'll be goddamned," Hoskins exclaimed as he swung his legs off the chair and stood.

He too removed his sunglasses for a better view. The ship was by no means small and by the sleek architecture, Hoskins knew it to be a Karysilan craft. It slowed down a quarter mile from the shore and hovered before landing in the water, causing large swells to rush almost to Hoskins' feet. The ship opened to let the ramp extend out and out came Darnizva strolling down it with a stern look on his face.

Darnizva approached him, standing not five feet away and Hoskins was barely able to crane his neck to look the massive alien in the eyes.

"You're not hard to find," Darnizva said.

"And, you could have at least called."

"I didn't want it tracked."

"Oh?" Hoskins lifted an eyebrow at that. "What is so secret that you can't let anyone know we're talking?"

"I saw the recap of the meeting."

Hoskins snorted. "That shit fest! Yeah, it was not a meeting of the minds." He turned to his right hand man. "Get the man a seat, will ya'?"

"Sure thing, boss." He disappeared into the house for a moment then came back with another lounge chair. It was set next to Hoskins' and the two men sat. The lounge chair creaked as Darnizva settled down on it, the frame bowing slightly from his weight and size.

"Want a drink?" Hoskins asked.

"It's still morning," Darnizva said, frowning.

"Well, I'm having one. Got a feeling this ain't no social call." His right hand man nodded and went back inside the house. "So, what gives?"

"I need to know how solid your contacts are. If Lynmore actually implements this draft, there has to be a filter in place. Your race is not set up to have its population as a full militia."

"Oh, there's no if on her part. She'll do it. And I gotta' agree, we would have had to establish that system centuries ago." The drinks came, a whiskey neat for Hoskins and lemonade for Darnizva. "I can't really manipulate her system until she goes green on it."

"I understand that. Maybe get someone inside to influence her decisions."

"Woo wee!" Hoskins smacked his lips after taking a sip. "You got a real audacious plan there, alien." He swished his drink. "That broad ain't letting no one she doesn't know anywhere near her circle."

"Yet, it's been done more than once."

"I think she's caught on by now." Hoskins pointed his pinky at him. "What do you have in mind?"

Darnizva shifted in his seat, causing the frame to protest a little more.

"I'm not completely distrusting of your kind. My fleet and I have gone far beyond our comfort zone to assist humans. But, I am frustrated with the outcome."

Hoskins nodded. He felt the same and time was a major factor. He looked up and saw those blood red eyes flash bright for a split second as the alien took a swig of his drink. Darnizva was more than angry. Trying to help mankind was like beating your head against a brick wall.

"I just need some assurance this is all not in vain," Darnizva continued.

"I may know a guy." Hoskins tilted his head sideways. "This is between us, huh?"

"You're a pariah, but patriotic. You love your country. Although you despise certain nationalities, you still want the human race to survive. I admire your convictions."

"Yeah, well, I wish more people appreciated my contributions."

Darnizva turned towards the shore and stared out at the ocean. There was a deep sadness in his expression.

"Homesickness," Hoskins blurted out.

Darnizva turned back.

"What did you say?"

"That's what you got. Don't think for one minute we don't want you all to go home too."

"I noticed." Darnizva drained his glass and toyed with it for a while. "It won't be long."

Both men stood, Hoskins still holding his drink. Darnizva handed his glass to Hoskins' right hand man and walked back to his ship. When he was up the ramp, it retracted, and the ship lifted off. Once the dock was sealed, it shot off into the sky.

"Find Kevin. I think he's the best one for this gig," Hoskins ordered his man.

"Right on it, boss."

∽

Kevin sat in the tiny office space of his new hide-out staring at the message on his laptop from his back channel feed. The video of the secret facility meeting with all the world leaders had preceded it and his mind seemed to freeze afterwards.

They've learned nothing.

He finally shook off his astonishment and thought about the situation at hand. A draft had its pros and cons. It would increase the number of soldiers. On the other hand, most would burn out during training, leaving an even worse gap. He needed insiders who could get in the heads of those authorized by the president and a super hacker.

A knock on the door pulled him out of his deep thinking.

"Dad," a young man's voice called out. "Open up!"

He exhaled slowly while closing his eyes. When he opened them, he hit the release button on the side of his desk. The door clicked and his oldest son, Otto, entered carrying a shotgun resting against his shoulder in one hand and a tablet balanced on the palm of the other. He was tall with sandy blonde hair that touched the nape of his neck and dark blue eyes. His well shaped lips were stretched in a smirk. The graphic tee shirt had seen better days and his sweatpants had stains on them.

"I got in!" Otto said in excitement.

"What are you talking about?" Kevin frowned in anticipation of something bad.

"Remember when you said if we could fix the database, we wouldn't have to go underground anymore?"

"Yes," Kevin answered slowly. *Uh oh.*

His son tossed the tablet on the desk and pointed down at it.

"Voila!"

"Seriously, that doesn't suit you and it's annoying."

While his son gave him a dirty look, he straightened the tablet so he could see what it was displaying. Multiple tiny screens overlapped each other and were linked. One was from Grid City, two were from the facilities he was raised in, and another was a separate database he had never seen before. He scrolled on the main screen and saw his entire family's registry being changed in real time. Looking up, he saw the wide grin on his son's face.

I did say I needed a hacker. Shit. Fuck you, fate.

Otto was at a genius level and had a knack for information technology. The last thing he wanted to do was involve his own kid. Only problem, his son was better than most of the hackers he had on standby.

"How long did it take you?"

"About six months."

"Too slow." Kevin watched his son's expression go from pride to anger.

"I worked my ass off to get this done for all of us! This was not easy!"

"Calm down. Don't ever yell at me again." Kevin's eyes flashed bright and his son stepped back, afraid. "Listen to me," Kevin said in a soothing voice. His son came back and stood silent before him. "If you feel you could have done this faster, tell me now."

"Well, yeah, sure. If I was in a hurry, I guess."

"You guess?"

"I could," Otto replied vehemently. "Definitely."

"Good. Just so happens, I have a job offer." Otto's eyes widen with joy. "And don't carry that damn thing around the house like it's an accessory. You're scaring the young ones."

"Right," Otto snorted. "Cuz, even my baby sister has no idea how to snap a man's neck. Really, Dad. We figured out what you were a while back. You gotta' trust us a little."

He backed out of the room then turned to walk down the hallway. Kevin sat stunned. When Otto was halfway down, he snapped out of it.

"I'll send you the details later," he yelled to him.

His son gave a short wave without looking back. The shotgun barrel swayed, nearly touched the ceiling.

Saw it down, at least.

He drew his attention back to the tablet, watching the progress bar inch closer to the one hundred percent icon.

KEEPING TABS

The Relliant training grounds hidden in the Rocky Mountains was at full capacity with soldiers dedicated to Earth's cause honing their combat skills. Gragor watched from the observation deck of his private quarters. He scanned the mass of bodies in motion below and found his two commanding officers. Bree was back to being deadly, his quiet demeanor making him more so as he struck down his opponent. Craig held his own but was trying a little too hard to impress his sparring partner.

"Hmph!" He tapped the commlink in his ear. "Get up here," he ordered. They were required to wear their earbuds during training sessions to receive his directions. The two finished their sessions and waded through the others towards the compound.

Within minutes, they were entering his chamber door and standing behind him. He turned to see them both at attention, arms folded behind their backs.

"Sit down! We can leave the formalities for later."

"Yes, Commander!" They answered in unison then plopped down on the sofa.

"Rehydrate yourselves before you both pass out."

"We're fine."

Gragor stepped before them and looked down. They had been fighting for three days. He could tell their stamina was nearly depleted.

"I see differently. Do as I say."

They lumbered off the sofa and went to the drink station along the wall. Cold mineral water for Bree and fruit infused water for Craig. Sitting back down, the two drank half of it.

"Now," Gragor said. "I need the two of you to check in with the Command Fleet and make sure we are on track."

"When?" Craig asked.

"End of the week. I don't need to stress evading contact with General Tartha."

Bree frowned and took a sip of his drink. He was a great soldier, obeying commands without question, until recently. The past two centuries, Gragor found him casting doubt on his role in the militia. That was of no fault in him. Many of those in command were not fans of General Tartha's way of battle. Even this incident, where they chased down a small fleet of The League and now involved with an alien planet of noncombatants who had nothing to do with their war.

"I'll see to it," Bree stated.

"Report to me as soon as you can in case there is a shift in loyalty."

"Shift in loyalty?" Craig blurted. "There better not be! The Command Fleet does as it pleases. We do not take orders from General Tartha unless it benefits us."

"That being said, some may start to see otherwise."

"Do you want us to go through another round of training sessions?" Bree asked.

Gragor went to the windows and took a quick look at the mass of soldiers giving their all.

"No. I believe you are fit for full duty." He turned his head sideways. "Do not engage our people unless it is absolutely necessary."

"Yes, Commander!"

Draining their glasses they stood. After returning the empty ones to the drink station, they saluted and left. Gragor let out a sigh and went back to observing the grounds.

On the transport headed to the Command Fleet, Bree sat in silence watching Craig give orders to the handful of soldiers accompanying them. The group was ten strong, enough to break free if needed, and ready to face whatever happened next. His goal was to get every-one on board with Gregor's plan. It all depended on if the Fleet had something else on its agenda. They could decide to leave their Commanders stranded and go on a new expedition in the galaxy. From the port hole he could see them approach the gigantic main ship and head towards the docking bay.

The main ship was the size of California laid straight. Its white exterior was covered in various squares making it resemble a life sized building block project. The bigger squares housed cannons and there were hundreds of them. A raised panoramic section was set three quarters down its length. Soldiers could be seen going about their duties on the main deck.

As the transport entered the bay, the overheads dimmed, and the engines cut off. It came into a flood of lights revealing other ships being serviced. A giant robot arm swung into view and grabbed hold of the small ship. It was guided into an empty station that clamped it in place. The ship opened for the ramp to engage the inner hull and the group walked down. Inside the main corridor, four soldiers awaited them. They gave a salute.

"Lieutenants Bree and Craig. Welcome home."

"Thank you. At your leisure." Craig said.

The soldiers relaxed their stance and started walking. As the group moved, two of the soldiers took up the rear while the other two led.

"Who's taken charge in the Commander's absence?" Bree asked.

The soldier in front on his left glanced back.

"That would be Captain Fravral. He is in the process of assessing our fuel and supplies."

"Going somewhere?" Craig asked curtly.

"That remains to be seen. We have no desire to take part in this farce with Earth."

"I concur with your sentiment," Bree said. "But you do understand, this fleet is the only thing that can stop General Tartha's if it comes to be."

The two leaders stopped, halting the entourage.

"What are you suggesting, Lieutenant?"

The first asked, eyeing him with suspicion.

The doors before them opened and Captain Fravral stepped into the corridor.

"Yes, what indeed."

He was followed by four Cyboks. By their black pools for eyes, Bree knew them to be true blooded Relliants grown from ancient DNA in the labs. Monsters.

"There is no reason to bring them," Bree gestured to the Cyboks.

"Oh, don't mind them. They are merely my guardians. I dare not travel without them." Captain Fravral gave a small, devious grin and turned down the adjacent corridor. "Come, let's continue this discussion on the command deck."

The entourage resumed moving, following the Captain with his four Cyboks blocking the view and the corridor itself. The command deck was sparsely manned, each crew member working silently. Bree couldn't hear their boots striking, their steps so light. He had forgotten how serene the fleet environment was. His entourages loud marching made some of the crew's lips curl.

"So," Captain Fravral began. "You have come to see if we are on board. If we will aid in the fight. To go against our," he waved a finger in the air. "Not so beloved General," he finished sarcastically.

"And your answer?"

"What would you have us do, exactly?"

"Should our general decide to use his own ship in this mess, you will disable it," Craig replied, stepping forward.

Captain Fravral raised his eyebrows in bewilderment. Some of the crew stopped what they were doing and stood still.

"You want to blow a hole in the flagship, possibly killing our General?"

"I never said that!"

"But, that is what would happen if we 'stopped' him," Captain made his fingers into quotation marks as he said the word.

"We don't want Relliant casualties any more than you do," Bree snapped. "Especially against each other. Our goal is to leave this solar system and fight another day."

Captain Fravral nodded his head and the four soldiers who escorted them brandished their weapons towards Bree and Craig's entourage.

"The General is still young and needs time to come into his own."

Captain Fravral smirked as Craig's face flustered. When he looked over at Bree, his face faltered. Bree's expression was cold, like a blank slate. He seemed to remember that stare and knew it meant nothing good would come if Bree struck. Captain Fravral raised his hand and lowered it. The soldiers concealed their weapons and stepped away from the entourage.

"I was only joking. We will not fight against each other. Our enemies are always outside of the Command Fleet, not within. Tell Commander Gragor we will decide when the time comes. Not a moment before."

"That is all that we ask," Bree replied deadpan.

"Now that we have settled the matter, will you be doing an inspection of the ship?"

"Without question." Bree stepped closer to Captain Fravral. The two men stared each other down for a brief moment, making Craig nervous. "Lead the way."

President Lynmore went over the list of aliens from her predecessor's first interview session with them. The model, the basketball player, the actor and the reality star all had agreed to help with the upcoming war. She had yet to see what they were doing to fulfill those terms. No one had kept tabs on them over the decades and she blamed the cabinet for dropping the ball. They needed all the help they could get. The list had come to her over an hour ago and her brain couldn't concentrate on one more thing. It would have to wait until later. George sat on the loveseat across the room with his head resting on the back of it. His eyes were closed and his arms hung limp beside him.

The jackass is asleep!

She couldn't fault him for that. It had been a grueling forty eight hours with military meetings and intelligence briefings. Dark lines rimmed her eyelids and she felt drained. To her left was her Vice President nodding off while trying to read a report on his tablet. Taking a deep breath, she exhaled slowly, then slammed her fists down on the desk. The sound echoed, causing everyone to jump as things rolled off, crashing to the floor; making more noise.

George shot up from the loveseat ready for combat. His hands held an imaginary assault rifle as his eyes scanned the room. Finally, he realized where he was and turned to Lynmore.

"What's going on?"

"We," she said vehemently, "are all going to sleep, rest, whatever, for the next four hours. This is not up for debate. There will be no arguments. Understood?"

"Madam President," the Press Secretary began, "We need to…"

"Understood?" Lynmore yelled.

She watched them flinch at her command.

"Yes Ma'am," they all answered.

"Good." She stood and walked to the door. "Set you timers. I'm leaving. Goodnight."

George followed her out along with the secret service agents. He checked his wrist commlink then gave her a weary glance. It was one in the afternoon.

By six in the evening, the oval office was once again filled with an energized president and her closest associates. George lounged on the loveseat scrutinizing a report on his tablet while President Lynmore took a closer look at the list of allies from before.

"Do we know where to find these aliens, George?"

He looked up and frowned then switched off the tablet's screen.

"I'm sure it won't be hard. I can't see the previous administration letting them go on their merry way without some kind of surveillance."

"What about going to Regis? She knows them first hand."

"That old war dog knows too much, in my opinion."

Her Vice President, leaning over a desk flipping through a hard copy report, stood straight and turned to her.

"I would agree on that. But, we do need her. That list tells us nothing." He swung his gaze towards George. "My suggestion is to play nice and get her to offer her services to locate them."

George leaned forward, his long legs stretching out. The bags under his eyes had a tinge of grey yet his focus was clear. His thoughtful expression became one of determination.

"Fine. I'll go see the Secretary of Defense."

President Lynmore pursed her lips.

"You should be communicating with her regardless.

I know I said to keep things on our side but we are in a whole new ball game here." She sat back in her chair and shooed him away. "Send her my greetings as well."

"You want me to do this now?" He asked incredulously. Her eyes narrowed and he stood. "Alright, I'm leaving."

George left the room and headed down the dead end corridor. Two secret service agents followed behind him. On the side wall at the end, he slid a hidden panel down to reveal a keycard reader. He pressed his I.D against it and the wall opened to another hallway. The three men entered and the wall sealed up behind them. They walked in silence throughout the fifteen minute journey. All the while, George thought about Secretary Regis.

He had only met her a few times. The woman kept herself sealed off, making moves behind the scenes without checks. She had every right to do so, being one of the first to make contact with the aliens. George envied her. He couldn't imagine what it must have been like and wondered if he would act calm in that situation. The day humans realized they were not alone in the universe.

The men came to a dark section with a steel door guarded by two armed soldiers. George held up his keycard. There was a moment of hesitation from them before one of them tapped his earpiece.

"Homeland Security is at the back door," he said briskly. His face scrunched as he looked George up and down like a caught intruder. Then his head bobbed. "I understand. Yes ma'am." He gave George and his agents a look of disdain as he slapped his counterpart in the chest. "Open sesame for the gentlemen."

The other soldier grunted and pulled a card from his hip attached to a zip cord. He slid it through a reader, activating an eye scanner above it. While its beams swirled before his tight eye, an A.I came on.

"Please state your name and rank."

"Corporal John Martin, United States Army."

George forced himself not to make a face or comment. He knew damn well that was not the soldier's real name. More like a code name. The agents standing on either side of him couldn't hide their dubious stares.

"Voice recognition accepted. Releasing door locks."

A series of loud clanks emitted from the door. It popped out a few inches then slid to the left. On the other side was a bright white corridor in a separate wing of the White House. As they stepped into the hall, the door shut, leaving them to venture alone. Up ahead was a slew of agents guarding both ends of the Secretary of Defense's office. Some of them gave George dirty looks as he approached the door. It swung open and he nearly stopped at the threshold.

Secretary Regis stood center in a sea of activity. She wore her dress blues adorned with medals. A reminder that she wasn't merely another bureaucrat in the West Wing. Her office was more a command center with large vidscreens along the upper section of the walls. There were soldiers, office personnel and a few scientists roamed around doing tasks. Her head turned slightly towards the door and from that profile, he saw an ageless tyrant.

"What brings Homeland Security down this way? Have you finally come to the conclusion that you're doing this all wrong?"

George clenched his hands into fists. The Vice President's words echoed in his head to play nice. She was not going to make it easy.

"I wouldn't go that far. We may have made some mistakes…"

"Sending in the cavalry with a child murdering unit in tow. I say that was not ideal. And not knowing all the players was a detriment to all of us."

"If you knew all that, then why didn't you do anything to stop it," he snapped.

The room became hushed and he cursed himself for not remaining calm.

"Resume," she commanded the people in the room. To him, she said, "This way." When his agents moved to follow, she stopped. "Your pets stay here."

"That was uncalled for." He turned to his agents. "Please wait here. If I am not out of there within the hour, start the necessary protocol." They nodded in agreement.

Regis gestured to four women farthest in the room. Each one positioned themselves in a corner of the space. They seemed harmless in their pristine, tailored skirt suits. George knew better. He followed Regis into a smaller room that was actually an office. She sat in her chair and a subordinate shut the door. Alone with her, George took a deep breath and planted himself in the chair across from her.

"President Lynmore sends her regards," he stated.

"Is that so? Why has she sent you? You tend to steer clear of me for some reason."

"I feel you have more dire tasks to deal with. No need to disturb you."

She burst out laughing, throwing her head back.

"How disingenuous! Yet, here you are." She lowered her head to stare directly at him.

"We have the list of aliens from the first round up."

"Wasting no time, hmm? You want their locations."

"That would be ideal. We need all the help we can get now. Sounding like a broken record these days."

"True. But, the question is," she leaned forward. "Why should I?"

"Are you serious, right now?"

George felt his face get hot.

"What benefit would they have to our cause?"

"We won't know unless we ask, right?" George yelled, slamming his fist on the desk.

The door swung open and Regis raised a hand. It closed. Her lips formed a thin line and she leaned back.

"You're such a patriot," she said. "For a predator." George sucked air through gritted teeth. "Oh, yes. I know your kind all too well. Don't think for one moment I haven't been watching you over the years." She let out a sigh. "It will take some time. I have to contact the surveillance team involved."

George regained his composure and pulled down his jacket, straightening it out. He cleared his throat.

"How long?"

"Give me a week."

"You're going to do this personally?"

George gave her a quizzical look.

"Do you want anyone else involved?"

"Absolutely not."

"Then it's settled." They both stood. "Now, take your pet agents and go back to your president. I have work to do."

George left her office in a hurry, making sure his agents were close behind. They were in hostile territory and the quicker they got out, the better.

As the Director of Homeland Security left her office, Regis became agitated. She paced the room, pondering if she should go through with it or not. Only a handful of people knew where the aliens on that list were. They had blended in with society before hybrids became known. Now, with so many similar to their make up around the world, they could live freely.

She also knew the upcoming war would see the demise of humanity. Their offer to assist was not taken lightly and she was sure they had implemented their own plans. It never bothered her, not knowing what they were up to over the decades. Then she thought of Darnizva and frowned. A Captain he may be, but still a child with minimal battle skills.

Her mind made up, she hit the commlink button on her desk.

"Prepare my private transport. We leave in three hours."

"Yes ma'am."

Time to visit an old friend.

Secretary Regis' transport hovered over the enclosed clearing a few hundred feet from the sprawling log cabin. Beyond the tall trees was a laser perimeter fence surrounding the property. Regis stared down at the door, wondering if the owner would come out. The transport landed with barely a sound and she jumped out onto the grass. An agricultural feat given the climate and bad soil in the area.

"Wait here," she instructed the crew.

At the door, she placed a hand on her chest and took a few deep breaths before knocking. The door swung open. Former President Strickland, Pulham's successor, stood in the doorway wearing a fleece faux fur lined sweater and holding a tumbler of whiskey. She could smell its potency whiff through the air. As one of the youngest presidents in history, he now looked aged beyond his years. Tuffs of grey lined his temples and there were bags under his eyes.

"You better have a damn good reason for coming here, Regis. I can't take the stress."

He turned around and walked into the cabin. Regis shut the door and followed him into the den where a fire was already going to heat the room. He sat on the couch and took a sip of his drink. Regis sat in the big cushioned chair next to it.

Drink?" He asked, holding up his glass.

He moved to get up but Regis stopped him, getting up herself. She went to the bar set in the corner and poured herself the same. When she sat back down, she raised her glass.

"To humanity."

"Oh, fuck humanity." Strickland emptied his glass in one shot and got up to pour another. "We've shot ourselves in the foot and want to blame it on everyone else. The aliens should just leave us to our own destruction."

"Yes, well, I want to live. As do a lot of humans."

He plopped on the couch, drink refreshed.

"Why are you here?"

"President Lynmore has come across the list from our scouting days."

"What makes you think I…"

"Let's not play games," she chided. "I will not have my time wasted. We need to know the details. Tell me where to look." She took a large gulp of her whiskey, wincing at its ferocity.

Strickland leaned back against the couch and contemplated her words. He swirled his glass as he stared at her, unwavering. His first year in office, he was too green. Naïve to the tasks at hand. After a while, something inside him hardened. He began to resent being human and lost his love for his fellow man. Too much had happened to prove him right. At the first opportunity, he bailed, gladly giving Lynmore the reins.

His family was wealthy; old money. The cabin was built per his specifications in record time and here he stayed ever since. He kept out of politics, becoming a hermit.

"It doesn't matter if you find them. Earth has no more hope in the tank."

"Then so be it. But, I won't let us go down without a fight."

Strickland drained his glass and slammed it on the coffee table before him. He picked up the tablet sitting on its edge and unlocked it.

"I am going to send you an encrypted file from my guy. What you do after that is none of my concern."

Her eyes went wide and she leaned forward, teeth clenched.

"You sent one man to do the surveillance," she said angrily.

"Less mess, and no others to control."

"He could be anywhere!" She sat erect. "They could be anywhere!"

"Exactly." He tapped the send icon. "There you have it."

"Did we not become friends? What did I do to warrant such hostility?"

He smirked, tossing the tablet beside him on the couch.

"We're still friends, Regis. I just don't like visitors from the White House."

"I should have visited more." There was a sadness in her tone.

"No." He got up and went to the bar.

"You're drinking too much."

"What else am I supposed to do out here?" Without turning around, he said, "You should leave. I won't be any good in about twenty minutes."

Regis stood and headed for the door. As she opened it, she turned back to him.

"Thank you. I hope you change your mind about our race. You did the best you could."

The door closed and Strickland finally turned around. He went to the window, whiskey in hand, and watched the transport lift off with Regis looking away from the viewport.

The hell I did. He chastised himself. *I ran.*

MEETING OF THE MINDS

Professor Bartley leaned on the window ledge of his personal chamber watching over the nearly destroyed sectors of the facility. It had been infiltrated two years before by a guerilla group who somehow got into the transport system. The damage was extensive, setting his progress back after Professor Lancaster's brother had gone mad, and unleashing his hybrid species experiments on the other facilities along with the civilian research center he ran in the downtown metropolitan area of a city.

The chaos that ensued left a deep scar in the rift between Regulars and Bi-Genetics. A kind of truce had developed when the public realized the monster responsible was a Regular. Just a plain old psychotic human scientist, not a super genius Bi-Genetic. With this new assault, he had a good idea who was behind it.

More than twelve percent of Bartley's facility's population had been wiped out. The ages were across the board, from infants to seasoned talent users. The footage had been hacked into by Lancaster's technicians and then broadcast for all to see. For seven hours, the public around the world saw the slaughter of men, women, and children with nowhere to run.

Three of his seven children were also dead and his heart felt heavy.

With the impending war coming, Professor Bartley had to make a decision regarding the high level talent users still alive. He knew there was no way he could not send Janti and Tommy. Their power alone, combined, could wipe out a ten mile radius and the military needed that kind of destructive power.

Other possibilities were sealed in the lower region of the facility where very little damage occurred because those Bi-Genetics were a danger to even themselves, let alone anything else. He almost felt sorry for those experimental creatures who were dispatched until he surveyed the ruins of the housing sectors.

The commlink blinked and the vidscreen activated. One of his scientists, haggard from lack of sleep, appeared.

"Sorry to bother you sir."

"What is it?" He too was beyond exhausted.

"The transport system is back online. We can communicate with the other facilities and assess the overall damage."

He knew some of the scientists in the black wing had already found a secret passage. They could have at least shared their knowledge. Then he remembered how selfish and devious some of his people were and dismissed that notion.

"That's good to hear. Thank Terence in Ortega for getting it done so quickly."

"Of course." The screen went black as did the commlink.

It would take another two years to get the facility back up and fully operational. He was having second thoughts about rebuilding, as did the other facility holders. The main wings had been reconfigured out of necessity. General Perrara nor the public had seen the ruined sectors where cleaning technicians were still scrubbing blood from the walls. Maybe it was time to change tactics and make the facilities into something that could benefit the whole world before its demise.

$$\smile$$

The facilities chairman lounged in a seat closer to the overlook steps as he waited for the giant holoscreens positioned along the top of the conference room walls to connect. On his right sat Aleem, seemingly bored. In less than five minutes, every facility owner would appear on those screens and a new strategy begins. They had been independent for too long. Earth was not going to come out of the battle unscathed and they needed to be on the same page when it came to their charges.

A soft beep emitted from each screen and the live feed connected. Eight in all, four on each side of the room, the facility leaders looked down through their cameras at the two men. Professor Bartley appeared to have just awakened. The chairman knew he had been up most of the night due to the nature of the meeting.

"I hope you are all well," the chairman said.

The leader of the football facility snorted and wiped his nose with a handkerchief.

"How can you say that with a straight face? You know damn well, we aren't."

The leader of the Primer facility, Dr. Shriever, looked over at Doctor Lancaster's youngest son on the screen across from her. Her eyes narrowed as the young man met her gaze. Professor Bartley noticed and cleared his throat.

"We are not convened here to judge each other's past actions."

"That is correct," the chairman added. "The question at hand is whether to evacuate this planet or brave the onslaught. I would prefer a collective agreement on our decision."

"I wouldn't mind running from this tragedy," the leader of facility one said.

"And go where?" The leader of facility three asked. "We have no idea what is out there. And for all we know, the enemy could shoot down any vessel that tries to leave Earth."

"I have a proposal," Aleem interjected. They turned their eyes on him. "Each facility has the capability of sustaining life below the surface. I say, we lower them and wait out the war."

"That does us no good if the planet is razed to oblivion," Dr. Shriever said.

"I doubt their weapons will go that deep," Professor Bartley added.

"They can destroy planets!"

The owner of the football facility snapped.

"But they also want this one for themselves, if possible," the chairman said. "General Tartha may have boasted about annihilation but he wouldn't wipe out every natural resource."

Professor Bartley lowered his head and stared down at the two men.

"My facility is still not fully functional." He glanced over at Doctor Lancaster's son. Ezra. "It would take a few more years to repair the damage."

"All you have to do is ask," Ezra said. "I will gladly help."

"No one wants an abomination like you setting foot inside their facility!" Dr. Shriever yelled.

There was a hush as the young man's eyes glowed. A wide, flesh colored tail whipped behind him across the screen. It had become common knowledge that he was the product of Doctor Lancaster introducing his seed into one of his many experimental creatures. At first glance, he appeared to be a normal human man. There were attributes that he kept hidden, for good reason.

"No need for that!" The football facility leader spat. "You have no dog in this fight. What goes on in your facility is far worse."

"Are we done?" The chairman asked vehemently. He turned to Professor Bartley. "Do you accept his offer?"

"Of course. If he's still willing."

"Now that we have established that, let's continue with the subject at hand." A virtual keyboard appeared by his fingers on the table and he typed in a command. The main holoscreen lit up to show all the facilities blueprints. Each image turned slowly at different angles to give a three sixty view. "I believe if we can go deep enough, a pathway constructed that connects us would be ideal. This way, there is no need to come topside."

The other facility leaders seemed to squirm at the idea. For so long, they had kept themselves isolated from each other due to conflicting ideals about how to handle the Bi-Genetic population. Now, the planet was their new nemesis.

"To do that, we need to have a gauge on the surface to determine when it is safe to rise," the football facility leader said. "I can't see us hiding out down in the void for the rest of our days."

"Yes," Ezra added. "If that were the case, we should plan to get off this rock sooner than later."

The chairman turned towards Professor Bartley's screen.

"Your facility has the most advanced technology on par with Dr. Lancaster's son. What are your thoughts on execution?"

The others focused their attention on him as he lowered his head, thinking silently. His brow creased as if he had hit a snag then he looked up. Determination was present in his eyes.

"It can be done," he announced. "But only if we work as unit." That awkward silence emerged again. "And we tell no one." His gaze darkened.

That perked them all up. Even the chairman was taken aback by Professor Bartley's decree. It wasn't a ploy to be sneaky and cut out the rest of the planet. This was self preservation, pure and simple.

"When do we start? I have been commissioned by multiple governments to create new Primers for the war effort," Dr. Shriever stated.

Aleem sneered while the others made angry faces.

"Immediately," Professor Bartley replied. "And when you grow more Primers, make sure it is for our agenda, not theirs."

She nodded, contemplating her role. The chairman smirked, as if knowing what she was thinking. He tapped a virtual key and the blueprints disappeared.

"So, we are in agreement?" There were nods all around. "Good. Let's map out a timeline before we adjourn."

⌒

The military entourage was led out of their vehicle in the underground tunnel and corralled by four guards into a giant lift surrounded by bedrock. The guards positioned themselves in each corner. The military leaders recognized it as a show of dominance. They would have all done the same in similar situations.

As the lift ascended, the British general kept his facial expression neutral. He didn't dare let any of the others know he felt a sense of danger and animosity. The guard closest to him turned and gave him a knowing stare. If things went south, none of the military leaders would leave out alive, and the facility owner appeared to be comfortable with that.

After what felt like eternity, the lift finally stopped and its doors opened to a dimly lit corridor. All along the walkway were dark metal walls with a sporadic array of mesh windows. The group made their way down and the British general did a quick scan of what was behind every mesh opening. There was no divide from what he noticed. The rooms on either side flowed the length of the corridor.

Another door appeared at the end of the walkway and slid open. At first, the military leaders halted, not sure where the door came from. The two guards in the rear moved closer together, blocking any form of exit.

"This way," the two guards ahead of them ordered in unison.

Inside was a massive laboratory with ten foot tanks lining the far wall. Four rows spanned upwards nearly sixty feet. The viewports on each one had digital read-outs with vital signs and other information. The British general clamped his jaws tight making his lips into a straight line.

This is wrong.

A tall woman, easily six feet, in a white lab coat and black heels came walking briskly up to them. Her brown hair has undone, bouncing across her shoulders. The lab coat lay open to reveal she wore a white blouse and black pencil skirt. Her eyes conveyed her austere demeanor. She raised an arm out in anticipation of a hand shake before getting to them.

She wants this done quickly.

He barely got his hand up when she closed in and grabbed a firm hold. Her iron grip was painful and swift. His hand throbbed as she let go. The other generals were given the same treatment as she greeted them in a rush.

"Good morning, generals. I'm Doctor Lillian Shriever. Welcome to my facility." She turned away and walked over to the long curved console that sat below the wall of bullet shaped tanks. "This way, please. You can see the merchandise better up close."

The British general frowned at that term. Regardless of how they were born, the beings inside those tanks were derived from human DNA.

"I see you have already started," he said. He had been voted unanimously to be the spokesperson for the group. To show their support, the other generals stepped back a bit to give him good clearance. She seemed to notice, giving him a once over. He felt judged.

"These are blank canvases. Nothing has been indoctrinated into them yet."

"And what are you going to put in their," he paused. "I'm sorry, how do you do this?"

She twisted her body towards him while she leaned over the controls. Her eyes brimmed with excitement.

"Brainwaves. We plant objectives into their psyche per the client's request."

"That's horrifying," he said vehemently. The other generals' expressions mimicked his sentiment. "So, they don't have a mind of their own?"

"Of course they do," she snapped. Her stare darkened. "These are not automatons!"

"Are you sure about that?" He countered.

"Isn't that what you can here to order?" Her mouth twitched into a sinister smile. "I haven't met a world leader yet who didn't want well behaved sex slaves and soldiers for their own agendas."

A loud beeping interrupted their brief spat and Doctor Shriever rushed over to the far corner of the wall. One of the tanks in the third row up was glowing blue.

She pulled out a small fob and pushed its button. The tank detached from the wall and long mechanical arms attached to its back lowered it down to the floor level. It rested in a docking station and tilted back forty five degrees.

"You get to see one up close," she said.

The tank hissed as it opened, frost billowing out like smoke.

"Purge sequence initiated," a female AI's voice echoed.

Blue liquid spewed out from the bottomed of the tank and the frost cleared up. Inside the tank was a boy of teen years naked and slimy. His hair was covered in a sheen of goo that matted it together. Tiny electrodes extended from his pristine skin.

"Sending charge to awaken subject," the female AI announced.

"Charge?" The British general asked.

To his horror, he saw the electrodes light up and the boy's eyes flew open. He screamed as the electric current coursed through his body. They could see the blue light travel along beneath the skin. His body arched in painful defense. The tubes detached as he fell forward, hanging halfway out of the tank, his breathing labored.

Doctor Shriever knelt by him and lifted his chin so that he could see her.

"What is your prime directive?"

"For Christ's sake!" The British general moved towards them. The two guards stepped in front of him. "Give him a minute!"

She ignored him and continued to stare into the young boy's eyes. His body shook and clear liquid dripped from his mouth. He finally managed to speak.

"To obey and serve without question."

"And if there is a dilemma during your service?"

"Do no harm to my person or the client."

The British general's eyes went wide.

"Why?" He whispered. "Why would you put something like that in his head?"

Doctor Shriever let go of the boy's chin and his head flopped down. She stood and turned to face the general.

"We had an epidemic of Primers committing suicide when the going got too much for them. Some even killed their offspring and client family members before doing the deed. Of course, they never harm the client."

Her smile at that last bit of information was evil in the British general's mind.

"Now," she said, stepping closer to him as the two guards retreated. "How many do you want? What directive does the world military need them to have?"

Two men in lab coats came over and pulled the boy out of the tank. Another came with a floating stretcher and they laid him on it.

"Please, deliberate, if you must." She waved a hand at the military leaders.

The British general went over to his associates and the general from Asia leaned into the huddle.

"As horrifying as this may be, we need this."

"This is madness!" The French general seethed.

"There is no other way to jump ahead of our goal in such a short time," the Chinese general added.

"And that prime objective shit?" The British general asked angrily.

"Is pretty sound," the American general answered. They stared at him, mortified. He let out a long sigh. "We don't want them offing themselves, that's a given. Insubordination would cause too much hinderance."

"And if we get some asshole who goes mass murderer on us, they can't eliminate the threat because their leader is a client?" The French general asked heatedly.

They stood silent, assessing the probabilities.

"That will be a chance we have to take," the Chinese general said.

Moments went by without any of them saying a word. Then, they all nodded and gave the British general a look that gave him the answer. He turned back to the Doctor and got within a few feet of her.

"Fine. We have decided, the main directive is efficient. A first batch of one thousand to start off and if all goes well in the next couple of years, another batch, and so forth."

"Do you have the down payment?" She asked.

He reluctantly reached into his front pocket, pulled out the transfer stick, and handed it to her. She gladly plucked it from his fingers and went over to a different station in the center of the lab. The platform changed color when she set the transfer stick on it. A banking app popped up and he watched their combined military funds being moved from one account into the facility's. When it was complete, she handed the stick back.

"Thank you for your business."

"When is delivery?" He asked.

"Six months."

He stepped away from her. "That's a bit fast."

"I aim to please." She raised a hand and shooed them away. "We're done." To her guards she ordered, "Escort them out. If they resist in any way…" she didn't finish.

"If anything happens to us, it would cause a global incident," the Chinese general said.

"I care not," she replied, glancing back at them. "I will still deliver your precious merchandise. I don't need intermediaries to do that."

The guards forced the military leaders into a two line formation and were loaded back into the lift. The British general locked eyes with her, his disgust visible.

The lift doors closed.

Doctor Shriever frowned and walked over to the boy on the stretcher. She felt her chest tighten with anxiety as one of her scientists checked his eye movement with a light pen. Her assistant came up behind her.

"What are you thinking?" It was a casual question with no emotion.

Doctor Shriever crossed her arms and pulled on her bottom lip. She had heard the generals comment about mass murderers in their mist. There were plenty of them over the decades and most had killed more hybrids than regular humans. The term Biodes was thrown around constantly by those types.

No more.

She stroked the young boy's forehead.

"Put him back in and erase the directive."

The three scientists and her assistant looked up at her in shock. The first scientist cleared his throat before speaking.

"Is there a new directive for input?"

The way he asked, she knew he was expecting something nefarious. She gave him a lopsided smile.

"No."

Her assistant went to stand by her side. He gave her a strange sideways glance.

"Do you mean to not give them any directive?" He asked.

"Correct."

"They will end up having their own opinions and agendas," the first scientist cried.

"Which could be detrimental to the clients," the scientist next to him added.

"A Primer with no directive is ..." the third began.

"Like any other human," Doctor Shriever finished for him.

Her assistant nodded in approval and stared at the scientists.

"You heard her. Get him back in the tank. We have work to do."

"Yes," she said, walking away. "One thousand Primers with untainted minds will be unleashed. They don't make themselves, gentlemen." Her voice called out.

OUT OF THE SHADOWS

Shadow HQ sat uncomfortably quiet in the vast desert. Vehicles were stowed in the hangars and soldiers patrolled the perimeter without speaking. Inside, the atmosphere was much of the same. An eerie mood had taken hold of the place. Everyone seemed to be aware of humanity's eminent demise.

Hana sat in his dark office swaying side to side in the chair as he stared out into the empty hallway. He knew what was coming down the pipeline in regards to ramping up the number of soldiers to strengthen Earth's forces. It was a matter of logistics and time. The training grounds had stopped being used long ago, since Celestial Mother began letting her cohorts do it themselves.

Soft footsteps came from farther down the hall and Hana stopped the swinging motion of the chair. No one came near his office hardly ever. Only his husband on occasion, and he was out on a mission. Listening closer, he deciphered more than one set of footsteps. Alarms went off in his head. Had the soldiers gone slack in their duties? Was the base being infiltrated? A soldier appeared at the door.

"My apologies, sir," the soldier said while saluting. "He insisted on seeing you."

"Who?" Hana asked.

George, the Head of Homeland Security for the United States, came around the corner and entered the office. Hana reared back in his seat.

"We need to talk, Hana."

"How?" Hana cried out. "Who gave you these coordinates?"

The soldier looked confused as his hand went to his weapon. George gave him a side eyed glare. Hana stood.

"Everything is fine, soldier. You can go. Close the door when you leave."

"Are you sure, sir?" The soldier was leery, returning George's stare.

"Yes, I'm sure. Go."

The soldier obeyed, reluctantly, and closed the door as instructed.

"Can we at least turn on some light?" George asked. "I know this meeting is somewhat clandestine, but really." Hana switch on the desk lamp. "Can we sit too?"

Hana sat back in his chair and George in the one on the other side of the desk.

"You know, when I was a Senator, this place was just getting started. I had spies everywhere. People underestimated you constantly."

Hana frowned. He remembered all too well. Some still did.

"What can I do for the United States' Homeland Security?" Hana leaned back.

"Oh, your thoughts on our situation and how the Shadow Organization is going to help."

"You mean be coerced into helping?"

"Not at all." George wagged a finger. "Cooperation is key."

"I think we're going to lose no matter how much we grow our defense forces. Humans don't play nice with each other. Twenty percent is impossible and that is nowhere near enough to go head to head with such a large alien militia."

George rested an elbow on the edge of the desk.

"We still have to try. I want to get the president on board, but only if there's something to brag about."

"You didn't answer my first question." Hana's eyes narrowed as his head tilted downward. "I take pride in the tight security we have here."

George let out a tired sigh and leaning forward, locked eyes with him.

"You shouldn't be so trusting of everyone." He straightened his posture. "Those aliens are somewhat afraid of me." He smiled.

"What are you?" Hana demanded.

"Let's just say, I'm more of an omnivore these days. Strict diet of meat on this planet draws too much attention."

Hana kept his emotions in check so not to give any hint of fear. He had read the reports of the various alien races that appeared over the decades. Senigrahnkes were listed as man eaters. The revelation that one of them was in the upper echelon of the U.S. government disturbed him.

"What are you after?"

"This stronghold has the best training facility on the planet. We need to utilize it more."

"Celestial Mother…" Hana began.

"Has no dog in this fight. She, and her cohorts, couldn't care less about the human race."

"We already talked with the facilities. They are in the mix."

There was an exasperated expression on George's face. Hana grimaced. Even as he said it, they both understood what the outcome would be.

"She is going to go through with that stupid draft

idea," he said referring to Lynmore.

"You need to stop her. It will go badly," Hana suggested.

"I know this better than anyone." George smirked. "This new round of trainees will not be filtered through Celestial Mother. It's time the humans took care of this on their own."

Hana lowered his eyes in agreement. There were many regular humans willing to fight without undergoing DNA manipulation. They only needed a route for them to volunteer with an incentive worth dying for. That last part would have to be hashed out later.

"Fine," Hana said. "I was thinking of restructuring the intake process anyway."

George tilted his head to the side and stared at him. "Were you?"

Both men sat silently gazing at each other, knowing they had an understanding.

The Oval Office was busy as ever when George returned later in the week. Staff members ran errands with determined looks on their faces. He strolled over to the loveseat and plopped down on it. President Lynmore, standing with both hands flat on the desk, looked up from scrutinizing a hard copy document and focused on him.

"Decided to come to work?" Her voice was snappish.

"I had to tie up some loose ends. How have you fared?"

Her lips pursed as she stood straight.

"I'm having a hard time getting Congress to push for my draft."

"Can't blame them. No one wants to be forced into this thing."

"Humanity is on the brink of extinction!"

She slammed a fist down.

The sound echoed through the room, causing everyone to stop what they were doing. Her eyes glinted with rage and George could tell she was about to have a meltdown.

"Let's take a breather," he announced. "Everybody out."

The entire staff gladly complied, rushing out into the hall. When the last one was gone, he got up and shut the door. In the quiet space, he turned to her and waited until she calmed down. Lynmore tugged her suit jacket back into place and smoothed the sides of her hair.

"My apologies," she muttered. "I am under a lot of stress, you know."

"I do. You need a better strategy."

"I need able bodied soldiers. The countries who were in agreement with me are having the same obstacles."

"Maybe because not everyone wants to be subjected to being altered."

"That's to make them stronger. Why go against it?"

"Think about every human war and tell me why."

President Lynmore gave him a dirty look then averted her gaze to the ceiling as she thought about it. He could see her start to realize the answer.

Good. I'm steering her in the right direction.

"Pride?" She said condescendingly. "Stupid fucking pride?" This time she said it loudly.

"In a nutshell, yes. Most people want to defend this planet on their own strength."

"But, they need to go through training. One that is equivalent to what they may encounter when the battle starts."

"That is correct."

He waited for her to again, contemplate the answer.

She paced the room, one finger tapping her lips as

she walked. Then she stopped, her eyes wide. Lynmore pivoted and came up to him.

"I need you get a hold of that little shit, Hana. He runs that base in the desert."

"Yes. It's for soldiers recruited by the organization."

"Which means they can train regular humans just as well," she said. "It's what our military has been doing for centuries. We seemed to have lost sight of that with the dawn of an alien threat."

"What about the draft initiative?"

President Lynmore waved a hand as she went back to her desk.

"Scrap it. This will be the new plan. Set up a video meeting with Hana."

"Of course. I'll get right on I," George replied.

And, I win.

⁓

Facility three was the most famous and scrutinized. That didn't stop Professor Bartley from doing his job as its owner. One of his duties involved keeping track of the more dangerous talents that manifested in some of the Bi-Genetics in his care. They were housed in a separate wing overseen by Professor Vasence. He had heard a rumor about the chairman's telepath getting access and was none too happy.

He lounged on the bed inside his sealed chamber overlooking the entire east wing of the facility floor. The all white interior blended with the rest of the area, making him almost invisible. His eyes zeroed in on Professor Vasence and tracked him to the private doorway leading to the lower level where his lab resided. He waited until the Professor raised a hand for the scanner then hit the intercom on the bedside table.

"Professor Vasence."

The man's hand halted midway.

"I am coming to see you shortly."

He saw Vasence's face scrunch up as if in he was in searing pain. Some of the other scientists on the floor looked up and around with expressions of trepidation. He never understood why there was such a level of fear whenever he decided to leave his quarters. Professor Vasence touched the communication icon on the side panel.

"I look forward to seeing you, Professor Bartley."

He laid his hand on the scanner and the door opened. When he entered, the door sealing behind, Professor Bartley flung the covers off and got up. He wore white scrub pants secured by its drawstring. From the end of the bed, he grabbed a grey t-shirt. Donning that, he then found a white button down shirt and put it on, leaving it open.

Red strands of hair stuck out from under the covers on the other side of the bed. He leaned over and placed a hand on where his wife's head would be. Taking a deep breath, Professor Bartley swiped the tablet from the top of the dresser and headed to the inner chamber attached to his quarters. Sharp air whipped around him as he stepped in. When it subsided, the light indicator turned green and the outer door opened. He walked into the main corridor of the facility.

Professor Vasence was nervously moving about his lab when Professor Bartley arrived. His assistants moved out of his way while one of them went to Vasence and whispered in his ear. He stiffened, standing straight and turned to Bartley waiting patiently a few feet away.

"Professor Bartley!" He exclaimed. "To what do I owe the honor?"

"Don't play games with me. You know why I am here."

Vasence blanched at first then his face became flush.

"Then you know it was for the sake of mankind."

"It was for your own agenda," Bartley snapped. "Let's not sugar coat it."

"So, am I being reprimanded?" Vasence's eyes seemed to blaze with fervor.

"For now? No." Professor Bartley set his tablet down on the nearest counter and swiped a finger across its surface. A chart appeared. "The head facility does not get to be the only ones to utilize these specimens."

This time, Vasence's eyes went wide with shock.

"We can't trust the world leaders to act responsibly! They've wanted their dirty hands on them for decades, and now we're just going to ..." Vasence stopped short, angry.

Professor Bartley frowned, realizing a misunder-standing was about to occur.

"You don't think I am handing over those monsters in the sub level, do you?"

Professor Vasence blinked and stepped back.

"Well, I just assumed that's what you meant."

"That's not what you gave the telepath access to, is it?"

"Of course not! He was specific in his needs." Vasence's lips curled inward as he realized he had just confessed to breaking facility protocol. "I was only trying to assist in the cause."

"Now is your chance to do it correctly. I want you to categorize the talents from this list only and compile a document stating where they can be best used."

He tapped the send icon on the corner of the tablet's screen and the counter lit up. Professor Vasence went over and finding the blinking light on the edge of the counter, opened the file. He perused it briefly then nodded.

"I will get it done by the end of the week."

"Good. Once that's done. Only then will we open bids to the world leaders."

"You know, you could have sent this request via the link. There was no need for you to come out of your chamber."

Professor Bartley's stare darkened, causing Vasence and his assistants to back away from him. He could feel the mark on his spine heat up.

"Then I wouldn't be able to observe your research first hand."

He knew there were patients inside the lab being cut up and tested on with unsanctioned procedures. It was now a matter of how much Professor Vasence would let him see.

⌇

Intake lines at the Shadow Organization base were massive as cargo trucks dropped off new recruits by the dozens. Scott stood on the landing above the hangar bay and counted nearly twenty rows of people, each row with thirty count strips. Six hundred. And that was only the first round. Each month there would be at minimum this many until they met their quota. Of the six hundred he saw maybe half getting through the ramped up basic training. Instead of the usual three months of core indoctrination, they would get six weeks then off to combat maneuvers. The obstacle course had been reconfigured and dialed down to accommodate the skill level of non-enhanced soldiers.

His middle son, Shawn, came up next to him with a tablet and held it out. He took it from him and glanced at the screen.

"Mom says you need to go by these new regulations."

Scott's lips formed a thin line. Where the enhanced humans were treated like lab rats, regular humans had rights. There were laws against certain treatments.

"Where is she?"

Normally, Hana would have been here to see incoming.

"Hiding in her office. Something about the short-comings of humanity."

Yes, this was going to get ugly.

A lot of humans were about to be broken beyond repair. This would be a test of how much people truly want to defend Earth. He could see anxiety and defeat in many of the recruits already.

"Go down and help with grouping," he ordered him.

"Yes, sir!" Shawn went to attention and saluted him before pivoting to the right. He marched off to the lift that would take him down to the hangar level.

Scott shook his head and let out a grimace. His son was at times a disciplinary problem but when it came to getting a job done, he was all in. As a byproduct of an enhanced soldier and a Bi-Genetic, his children in the armed forces were an elite class of fighters.

There was a scuffle at the main doors and Scott leaned over to see better. A load of prisoners from jails around the world were being forced into the area. He looked down at his own tablet sitting atop Hana's and searched for the dossier. These prisoners were given a choice of rotting in prison or doing their civic duty. The fact they were struggling with the guards after making their decision was laughable.

"If they are not going to cooperate," his son yelled out. "Then pack them back up and have their deals revoked. This is not a democracy. There will be no deals made here."

The prisoners stopped moving and looked over at Shawn. Scott nearly leaned back too far as he saw the look on his son's face. It conveyed pure, unadulterated malice and contempt aimed at the unruly men.

Recruits already in line became agitated.
That's right, son. Rule with an iron fist.

Within the first week, fifty of the recruits were too far gone to continue, having failed the advanced basics. They had been told ahead of time to make sure they could do the entry requirements in their sleep because it would be ramped up at training. It was obvious that some hadn't take it seriously. Shawn debated on whether to wait for them to recover and try again or send them on their way. The world military needed as many soldiers as they could get, but not if too many of them were subpar. That served no one's benefit.

He went into the infirmary and took a good look at the failures. Soft cries and moans filtered the air and he half smirked. Scanning the room, he found some of the recruits looking frustrated. Those were the ones he decided to talk to first. A woman in her early twenties lay on the fourth cot down to his right and he made a bee-line straight to her. She looked up at him then averted her eyes in disgrace.

"Good afternoon, recruit. How are you feeling today?"

She didn't turn her attention back to him as she spoke.

"Recuperating, sir." Her voice was a whisper.

"Look at me when addressed," he demanded.

Everyone looked over at him, the cries and moans ceased. Her head snapped up and she seemed startled by the force of his voice.

"Recuperating, sir," she answered loudly.

"Good. How do you think you fared?"

"Poorly, sir."

"Did you give it everything you had?"

Her expression crumbled as she contemplated it.

"I don't think so, sir."

The acknowledgement pained her.

"Then, if I gave you a second chance to redeem your-self after you're healed, would you do so?" He watched her seem to struggle then ball her hands into fists.

"Yes, sir! I would very much like to redeem myself."

"Then heal up. Your reevaluation is in two weeks."

She nodded, in a much happier mood.

Shawn made his way down the line and through the entire infirmary. Out of the fifty, a mere twenty were willing to make another go at the training. The percent-age was not looking good.

Dark clouds rolled in over the isolated valley while the Relliant force that switched to Earth's defense trained. Hagen stared at the sky matching his mood. In all black battle gear, he stood on the platform high above the training grounds overseeing his soldiers' progress. Soft misty rain came down giving the soldiers a hazy shimmer. He frowned at the sky. Proper rain should drench everything. Disappointed, he turned from the edge and went into his headquarters a few hundred yards away.

As he entered his private chamber, a steady beep-ing assaulted him. Blue light emitted from the console against the wall. INCOMING MESSAGE, scrolled across the holoscreen above it. Hagen went over and tapped the message icon. The blue light disappeared and an image of General Perrara came up on the screen. He touched play and the message began.

"Commander Gragor, I hope things are going well. As you may know, six months ago we started recruitment of regular humans willing to undergo advanced training without having alien DNA injected. Half are being sent to the Karsilans and the other half to you. Expect incoming within the next few days. Let me know if you have any concerns."

The message ended, General Perrara's face frozen on screen.

Concerns? Plenty!

Hagen walked across the room to stand at the bay window overlooking the opposite side of the valley. There was no rain present, the system already moved on. Humans were too fragile, in his opinion. That said, he couldn't deny them the chance to save their own kind. A great roar of wind followed by rumbling made him turn towards his chamber's entrance. Craig and Bree stood in the doorway soaking wet. Water dripped off them onto the floor, forming a pool.

"Why have you stopped training?" Hagen demanded. "This bit of rain is nothing."

"I think you would beg to differ if you saw it," Craig answered.

The structure shook. Small items fell from the shelves and everything vibrated. Hagen frowned. Pushing them out of the way, he went to the main entrance and stopped short before stepping out. The training grounds were empty. In its place was a raging storm. Rain came down in sheets at a near forty five degree angle and the wind crashed against the valley. Lightning struck the surface in quick succession. He stood in awe of its raw intensity. Looking up, he saw the divide of climate. Sun rays on the other side struggled to penetrate the gloom.

Now, that's a proper rainstorm.

He headed back inside and found his two officers sitting on the sofa with drinks in their hands. Their battle suits were in a pile near the door. There they were in black bodysuits sans boots seemingly content with themselves.

"We have human recruits coming by the end of the week," he announced.

Bree halted his drink at his lips.

"You want us to train them?" His voice was hesitant.

Hagen turned to them both and squinted his eyes in exasperation.

"No," he snapped. "I need the two of you to find trainers who would fit the task."

"How many?" Craig asked after taking another sip of his drink. "I can relinquish one or two soldiers for a while."

"To start, four hundred. Another six should be in the wings."

Bree was deep in thought, his glass still hovering at his lips. He finally took a drink and set it down on the table.

"That is not enough," he said.

"Not by a long shot," Craig added loudly.

"In two years time, we should have trained ten thousand." Hagen sat at his desk and propped his legs up on the corner. "Which is better than nothing."

"Sacrificial lambs," Bree said.

"I don't think they see it that way. Would you say the same thing if Rellia was in this type of situation?"

Bree and Craig sat silent, knowing the answer. Of course, they would defend their home world against any enemy. Regardless if they could win or not.

Chapter Two: Preparation

INNOVATION

Dr. Quelly Riggs was going to be late for lab, again. This would be the third time in one semester and the professor was getting a little irate. She ran haphazardly down the hall, white lab coat held tight between one elbow while she tried to tie her thick black curly hair into a messy updo. very few yards she would try to get her right shoe on correctly. She could feel her sock bunching underneath the arch of her foot, making it uncomfortable to walk.

She found herself thinking back to her college days when she worked for the Shadowman Organization. The group went to extremes to get equality for Bi-Genetics. Although the project was a success, too many people had been murdered in its name. There were a few regrets but all the same, she would have done it again.

Her current residency would get her one step closer to becoming a professor and right now she felt her own self in the way. She was on to something big with the new secret project she was working on. It just needed another year or so of testing. Being in the science field had become cut throat since the alien crash landings. The applicants aspiring to be the next great scientist exploded within ten years and even more so after it was announced, in secret of course, that a way to evacuate

Earth was needed. All ideas were said to be on the table yet the extreme ones were tossed.

Bursting into the lab, she was confronted by everyone turning to the doors as the professor stopped talking and did the same. His eyes narrowed in anger and he said nothing. He only pointed to her seat and resumed his lecture. Quelly, standing like a rooted tree out of embarrassment, heard chuckling from both sides of the room. She walked hurriedly to her seat and got out her tablet. The person next to her made tsk sounds and he looked her up and down with disgust.

Now that was uncalled for. Getting her stylus, she started taking notes.

The great thing about being in the scientists' elite club was that you got a huge suite with a private lab attached on the back end. The military felt it a necessary amenity to keep the scientists in the zone of creativity. Many of the residents figured it was an excuse to keep them on a short leash. Quelly didn't mind one bit. Not having to commute to the facility labs meant she was able to work on her own without interference.

She walked over to the test specimen and took a reading from the monitors hooked up to it. The clear gelatinous substance was shimmying a bit. That meant it wasn't going to remain stable. Previous specimens had done the same except this time, it lasted three months. She was sure it would liquefy within the next few days.

"Damn it," she swore softly to herself, pacing the lab deep in thought. It was an improvement though still not there yet. She needed it to remain stable for years, not months, and so far she had not found the right combination of chemicals to produce those results.

"Come on, girl. Think. What is missing?"

She went over to the desk and caught a glimpse of herself in the mirror. All candidates had to have alien DNA introduced in their system to slow down aging and increase longevity. College came after four years in the U.S. Navy and she was a little rough around the edges in looks. Being around other young students helped her get that together and now at age thirty five, she didn't look a day past her twenties.

A timer beeped by the mini cryochamber she had acquired years ago. She went over and put on her gloves to remove the next specimen. With long black gloves that went up to her shoulders, she carefully grabbed it and placed it in a holding container next to the other one. The specimen resembled a block of dry ice. When the mist cleared, it was like a crystal. Quelly frowned as she shut the door and secured the latch.

Once stabilized, she could then work on a destabilizer for it. One step at a time. She had two more years before her residency was up. Even if her idea didn't save the human race, at least she'd know she accomplished something.

‿

So it's come to this.

The Joint President of the United States thought to himself, sitting down in the nearly empty conference room. All the world leaders had decided to do video face to face instead of in real life. No one wanted to leave their country unattended while they each pushed their scientific communities to find a solution for the evacuation problem. A meeting with the high officers of the League was scheduled for the day and he was informed an hour ago that only Commander Ammordia and Darnizva would be present. President Lynmore was in no mood for more bad news and instructed him to go in her steed.

With Earth headed towards annihilation, the United States had become the center of attention in a bad way. After the grid city debacle, a two president system was introduced to alleviate the pressure and duties of the position. He had been voted in unanimously and without his knowledge. The last thing he wanted was the responsibility of an entire nation on his shoulders.

"Sir." Secretary Regis, ageless from the days of the crash landing, slid in the seat next to him and set her tablet down. "We will find a way. If we don't…then it was meant to be. A lot of religious leaders are saying it's the rapture and the apocalypse all rolled into one."

"I am not going to lay down and give up!" He seethed. "Not yet! Not without a knock down drag out fight." The wall of video screens in front of them flickered on right as his Vice President strolled in. She took her place opposite the Joint President and they all waited for the world leaders to be present. "Humanity cannot come to a screeching halt. Not like this."

Two separate screens located on either side of the room came to life with Ammordia on one and Darnizva on the other. Seeing the Captain, the President felt a twinge of heartache. The young soldier looked exhausted, and not optimistic. Learning all the details a few years back gave him a clearer picture of what they were actually up against.

"Is everyone accounted for?" Ammordia asked. Heads bobbed in acknowledgement. "Good. Let's get started." An image of a solar system, clearly not theirs, replaced hers and she began to explain.

"During the research my technicians conducted, they came across a solar system not too far away and may be capable of sustaining human life. A rough analysis was prepared but you can't really know unless a human goes there." She turned to Darnizva's monitor.

"Given the data and location of the planets in that solar system, it is estimated to take about ten years to arrive there." Darnizva stated.

"In our spaceships?" The Russian President inquired.

"No. In one of ours. Your ships, though far more advanced than fifty years ago, is not capable of traveling at the speeds we can."

"Are we really so far behind in our technology?" The President of China protested.

"I'm afraid the answer is yes." Dour faces became prevalent across the screens. "It is not anything to be ashamed of. Every civilization has to go through an evolutionary stage."

"But, we are about to get wiped out before we can even realize our potential." The Joint President stated in defeat. He heard Regis squirm in her seat. "Now, with only a little under two decades left before the deadline, we can't afford to send someone out there and back to report their findings."

"The timeline just won't work," the Russian President added.

Darnizva was at a loss and he struggled to keep his composure. His hands were shaking and he couldn't understand why. He had been in countless battles and saw much bloodshed. This feeling of helplessness was something he did not like. He looked up at Ammordia, who was back onscreen.

"Mother." Ammordia's lips pursed. The President's, along with everyone else's, eyes went wide and they all focused on her image. "He won't help me, will he?"

"Your father is the General of the League. He has more pressing matters to deal with and returned to Karysilan to go over strategies for retaliation. The aftermath of the last battle was not for the weak of heart. Your brother..." Darnizva shook his head violently. "His wounds were too great. I should have told you before but you too had a lot to deal with." Ammordia's facial expression sagged and she looked ill. "We were able to use most of his tissue to regenerate a new body but we won't know if it was a success for a few years more."

Darnizva merely nodded and clamped his mouth shut painfully tight. He didn't regret saving his fleet, but the outcome ended up being a greater burden than he could have ever imagined. What happened after he jumped was a mystery to him and he felt guilty for not inquiring about the rest of the command ships he left to continue the fight.

"I understand," he finally responded. "Thank you, Commander Ammordia," he said in a formal tone.

"Darnizva…"

"I will take it from here."

He gave her a defiant look and they locked eyes before she nodded in agreement and terminated her feed. Knowing he was visibly shaken, he mustered all the energy he had and straightened his posture. He stared at the many human faces on vidscreens before him and made a decision.

"I have a ship that can exceed even our fighter's speed. I will send a reconnaissance troop to the solar system and do more research. They can make it back within fifteen years."

"That brings us right into the battle while we try to get everyone who wants to go, off Earth," the French President said in a panic.

"I understand. That is the best solution at this junction."

"Well you're going to have to better than that!"

The President of China snapped.

"I don't think we have the luxury of kicking a gift horse in the mouth here."

The Joint President stated his reply heatedly.

Everyone clammed up in hostile humiliation for they all knew it was true and better than anything they were capable of doing in the next twenty odd years. After that was said, many of the world leaders terminated their feeds out of frustration and clear embarrassment.

"Well, I guess that is all we need to know for today, isn't it?" The Joint President said leaning back in his chair. "I thank you all for your time." The rest of the vidscreens went black leaving Darnizva still sitting in a daze contemplating something. "What are you thinking, Captain?"

"That I should have been able to do more sooner."

"Oh, no you don't!" Regis snapped, causing him to jerk his head up in her direction. "This was an accident. Tragic, yes, but never the less, an accident. You can't rely on your parents to bail you out at every turn. This is war. Suck it up!"

Darnizva reared back in shock at her words which stung as they hit home. He was not a child anymore at the ripe age of one hundred and ninety four. Still far too young to have his own squadron yet seasoned enough to know when to draw the line in the sand. Swiping a hand down his face, he regained his composure.

"You are correct. I apologize for being childish just now. I will get on with my plan. Please coordinate with the Command Fleet leader on battle strategy. For humans twenty years may seem long but to us, in a battle, it's a blink of an eye."

"Will do, Captain. Good luck." The Vice President offered.

"You too." Darnizva terminated his feed.

"Well, Mr. President?" His Vice President inquired.

"Let's pray for a miracle."

～

Five years Later

"Oh, holy shit!" Quelly screamed at the block of ice sitting on the counter in her lab. "I fucking did it!" She slapped her hands to her cheeks and left them there as she slid to the floor with tears streaming down her eyes. Snot ran out her nose, dripping onto her lap and stained her lab coat. She sat like that for what seemed like an eternity until she decided to get up.

Wiping her face with the sleeve of her lab coat, she went over to the specimen and admired it for a few moments. There it sat, a crystal clear pristine block of ice that had not melted in nearly three years. Her residency ended up being extended due to the dire need and she was offered an indefinite position with unlimited resources.

"And it paid off," she whispered to herself. Realizing she was a mess and needed to change before doing any tests, she exited her lab and went to wash up. While in the bathroom, she hummed to herself and wiggled her butt from left to right. "Oh, you arrogant sons of bitches…here I come."

Arms filled with her materials, Quelly sprinted down the corridor towards the situation room inside the White House. She cursed herself for barely making it on time for her presentation. Of all the times to struggle with appearance and she still felt like a slob after all the fuss. At least her hair was not frizzy or tangled. It lay in neat waves and freshly trimmed to just below her shoulders. She was even emboldened enough to apply light makeup.

As she neared the double doors, she whipped out her access key card and displayed it for the two guards before being allowed to swipe it. The doors opened and her eyes ingested the vastness of the room. It was more like a command center with a platform off in the catty corner and a huge table right smack in the middle on the right side. Giant vidscreens loomed above on the far walls.

"Please, Professor Riggs, this way," A young woman in an impeccable suit came up to her and spread one arm towards the platform.

"Oh, yes. I'm sorry. Kind of awe struck," Quelly laughed nervously and felt even more awkward when the woman didn't acknowledge her reply. "Okay then."

"Madam President," the woman address another who stood with her back to the door and also wore a suit the best tailor on the planet would be proud of.

President Lynmore turned around and Quelly took a deep breath. She was face to face with the President of the United States and the weight of her research and all the work she had been doing hit her like a two ton heavy thing. This was real. This was a moment of truth.

"Professor Riggs," the President glanced at her, keeping one arm across her chest and the other holding her necklace up as she played with it. "It is an honor to meet you."

"The honor is all mine, Madam President." Quelly heard her voice cracking.

"Let's get to it." President Lynmore pivoted and walked over to the large elongated table that sat in front of the vidscreens. "Marsha, bring up the feeds."

The impeccably dressed woman went up to the platform and touched some icons on the console's virtual keypad. All the screens above came to life and every head scientist, world leader and military General appeared on them. Quelly gulped and started looking around for some water when a glass full magically came into view. The woman held it perfectly still until Quelly took it from her.

"Thank you."

"You're welcome. We must ensure this presentation goes smoothly. Their time is valuable so be prepared and professional." She walked off.

That was uncalled for.

Quelly felt insulted. Despite her demeanor, she was quite capable of delivering a presentation and speaking to high level personnel. *Bitch.* To her surprise, the woman stopped walking and glanced over at her with disdain. It was as if she had heard Quelly's inner thought because she was sure those words were not said out loud.

Oh, shit! A telepath. She saw the women smirk and walk away.

"Ladies, gentlemen. I give you Professor Riggs." The President announced.

Quelly choked on her water mid gulp and stared in shock at everyone in the room and on screen as their eyes diverted to her. Setting down the glass and wiping her mouth, she walked up to the platform where she found her specimen and all its data ready for display.

Give a girl some warning, why don't you? She was far from young despite her looks.

"Hello science community, world dignitaries and military elite," She started. "In regards to evacuating the human population and account for a long journey, I have discovered a better alternative to our deep cryo-sleep techniques. By utilizing alien biochemistry and the properties of ice, I have come to this."

Quelly pushed the cart holding the block of ice. She carefully turned it so all could see its translucent form. Her insides felt like they were flipping around she was so giddy from the rush of showing it off.

"It's just a block of ice?" One scientist retorted.

"Not just any block of ice," Quelly said calmly, fighting the urge to berate him.

"Please," she addressed the two aides waiting on the side.

One came up with an industrial flame thrower. Everyone in the room pulled out eye shields and donned them. The fire spewed out of the device, hitting the block squarely and the aide kept it there for a good minute before turning it off. Not a drop of moisture had formed on the block.

"Impossible!"

"We're being duped!"

"It's probably not even ice!"

"What kind of game are you playing at?"

President Lynmore went up to the block and touched it with her fingers and it stuck for a moment before she gently wiggled it off. Her eyes narrowed yet in them was a glint of hope mixed with fear. She turned her gaze to the vidscreens and touched her lips with the ice cold finger.

"I assure you, it is definitely ice."

The room was silent.

"Why do you look so apprehensive then?" A scientist asked.

"Because it gives me a bit of hope."

"Okay, it's a block of ice. How do we use it?"

Quelly stepped back onto the platform. "Everyone is injected with a pretreatment that allows them to sustain the freezing procedure. Instead of individual housing, the population can be frozen in layers and transported, just like this block of ice."

"Genius!" She heard a scientist whisper and she saw heads bobbing.

"How long does it stay frozen?" Another asked.

"As all the testing suggest, indefinitely." Murmurs echoed through the room. "So far nothing has been able to penetrate, damage or destroy it."

"Then how do we unfreeze our population when needed?"

"Thank you for asking." Quelly grabbed a large vial next to the block of ice and pulled out the dropper. "This block is twelve by twelve inches. All you need is three drops," she administered them, "and voila."

The ice block shimmied and started to deteriorate into a gelatinous state. As it oozed off the cart, making a loud plopping noise when it hit the platform, everyone followed its demise with their eyes. When it was over, they let out the breaths they had been holding.

"Any questions?" Quelly smiled.

"What's the productivity ratio?"

"How much is needed for each recipient?"

"How long will it take to mass produce?

"Are there transport avenues in place?"

Quelly stepped back from the backlash as if she were being physically hit. The President saved her from the assault.

"Please, be calm and stop asking questions she would know nothing about. What you want are logistics. She's just the scientist who created it." She put a hand on Quelly's shoulder. "Go get some rest." She motioned for two assistants to escort her out of the situation room.

Still in a daze from the onslaught of questions, Quelly let herself be led out of the conversation and essentially out of the loop for the time being. Even knowing that, she needed time to regroup. This was not the time to assert herself in front of powerful people who could easily take away everything.

Once Quelly was out of the room, the President turned her attention back up to the vidscreens and crossed her arms. She waited for the images to refocus their attention back to the situation room and cleared her throat.

"Now, to answer some of your questions. Professor Heines."

A tall East Indian man with short grey hair and caramel eyes stepped up to the platform and exchanged Quelly's data for his own on the display screen. His long fingers silently typed information into the database with the virtual keypad. Satisfied, he moved away from it and clasped his hands together in front of him.

"To answer the question regarding production. My calculations put us at ten years to replicate the substance in a quantity large enough to freeze entire city populations around the world. Then it will take another two to complete the project and get everyone transported."

"That's…"

"We're not going to make it in time."

"The time table is too close, just like the planet surveillance from the Karysilans."

"It will be cutting it close, yes." Professor Heines replied. "But, it is very doable. We need a strict contingency plan in order for this to go smoothly."

"What about the ones who are doing the round ups? How will they get off the planet?"

"The Karysilans on Earth will assist them after the task is complete. They will be briefed on how to use the system as well."

"Sounds like we have a plan, people." President Lynmore declared.

BEHIND CLOSED DOORS

On the side of the mountain facing the manmade forest, Telia, Celestial Mother stood at the large viewport. The sprawling living quarters could be seen behind her. Her mate, Attar, and the two Chombrazens were seated in the lounge area patiently waiting for her to join them. She scanned the surface below with her eyes, fascinated by the wildlife the humans introduced into the environment long ago.

Telia turned away from the scene and walked over to her overly large, plushy chair. She settled her tall frame into it and let out a loud sigh.

"I have a proposal, my compatriots."

Four tall glasses filled to the rim with ice cold tea sat sweating on a tray in the center of the table. She reached over and took one, sipping the contents daintily.

"I will assume it is one we all share," Karias said.

"Hmm." She drained half the glass and set it down. "We have been here longer than necessary. Many of the humans we trained are viable."

"Some having raised above our expectations higher than most of the other talented ones," Attar said. "Of course, it's only a handful."

"Precisely." She settled into her chair.

"They would not be missed."

The others were silent for a moment then they all took a drink off the tray. She waited until they set them back down. Lindo looked down at the floor as he spoke.

"You are making a wild assumption. From what we have seen so far, the human leaders are much more territorial than that."

Karias nodded in agreement before adding his opinion.

"We don't even know if they can survive on our home worlds. Even with their DNA manipulated, it hasn't been tested."

"I would rather they meet their demise elsewhere than throwing their lives away fighting for an ungrateful planet." Telia's head tilted back and her indignant gaze fell on them.

"The planet is fine. It's the inhabitants that needs cleansing," Attar said.

"You have a list." Karias stated.

"As do all of you." She smiled, lowering her head and taking another drink. "We want our favorite candidates, don't we?"

"And getting them off the planet?" Lindo asked.

Telia looked away and tapped a finger to her lips as she thought about it. The moment it became clear of their agenda, there would be backlash. She even predicted the silly humans fighting back to prevent the steal.

"We wait for the optimal time," she replied.

"And that is?" Attar seemed confused.

"In the midst of battle," Karias answered. His tone was one of triumph. "No one would stop fighting to address something so trivial as abduction."

"How sneaky." Lindo's expression approved the idea.

Telia's eyes narrowed as she crossed her long legs, exposing flawless tanned skin.

"These humans don't deserve to keep such evolved warriors."

The communications console flashed and AUDIO ONLY appeared on the screen.

"Excuse the interruption, Celestial Mother," a male voice began. "The Shadow trainers would like to have a meeting with you along with Hana."

"And, when is this meeting to occur?"

"Sometime today would be preferable. Hana seems to agree."

Hana.

She saw the knowing glares on the others' faces. After that short glimpse into the pretty man's memories, she had kept quiet about it. Instead, she fumed with silent rage against the world leaders and scientists. When the secret was too much to bear, she finally confided in the two Chombrazens and Attar. They too, became enraged.

"Very well. Set it for the afternoon."

"Of course, Celestial Mother." The screen went blank.

"What could they possibly need to discuss so late in this junction?" Lindo asked. He finished his drink and stood. "I am going to check on my charges in the infirmary."

"What indeed?" Karias leaned back on the sofa and closed his eyes.

⁓

The meeting was larger than Telia expected. Fourteen Shadow trainers were present, and they all seemed weary from anger. To her surprise, the head trainer who over-saw Grid City was seated next to Hana. A section set apart from the conference table was open for the aliens to sit, their size not compatible with joining the humans.

"Sweet Hana, to what do we owe this?" Telia asked, her tone like honey.

Some of the trainers frowned, not daring to meet her gaze. Formidable as they were, they knew to be afraid of Celestial Mother and the other alien trainers. Hana didn't flinch.

"We have a slight dilemma. It's about the Shadowmen we have in rotation so far."

"Oh?" Karias leaned forward. "How so?"

Neil swung his chair towards them.

"It seems the world leaders want to transition our operatives from missions to combat."

"That was the initial goal, if I am correct," Telia said.

"Yes, but on our terms, not theirs," one of the trainers replied.

"My trainers don't want to release control of our Shadowmen to the world leaders." Hana's brow scrunched up as he spoke. "We fight because we want to save Earth, not because we are being ordered to."

"As it should be," Attar added.

"They're not taking no for an answer." Neill tapped a finger on the table. "Since you have extensive documentation on each candidate, we would like a list of possibles we can send."

Telia leaned further back in her seat, shocked then angry. Her mate was none too happy either and the two Chombrazens looked about ready to come out of their seats.

"That is unacceptable," Telia seethed.

"That's what they want," Hana said heatedly.

Telia could see the frustration in Hana and didn't fault him for the brazen remark.

"How many are they seeking?" Lindo asked.

"All of them if they thought they could have them," another trainer replied.

"Maybe a few hundred to start with," Neill continued.

Karias' eyes darkened while Telia's glowed briefly. Every human in the room seemed to brace themselves for slaughter. The aliens' mood bordered on murderous. Then Telia smirked and the tension left the room.

"Fine. We will accommodate them for now. I want them all tracked, the ones we send."

"I was going to do that anyway," Neill stated.

"Rest easy, my pets," Telia said lovingly. "I will not let your world leaders dictate your fate." Her stare bore into them. "That's for me to decide."

Hana blinked at the declaration, trepidation on his face. Telia gave him a smile which made him flinch this time. She turned to her three comrades.

We are taking this is one.

They nodded in agreement, confusing the humans who had no idea why they did it.

A Step Forward

A twinkle of light appeared near the fifth planet and shot forth, straight towards the battle ship of Darnizva's fleet. He watched it get closer and decrease speed when it reached the hangar bay. The scout ship was worse for wear, its hull dingy and scraped from multiple voyages. Robotic arms grabbed the ship and clamped it down. Darnizva left his temporary quarters and headed out to greet the crew.

There were six in all. Two pilots, a maintenance tech, and three scouts. They too appeared to have some wear and tear. Darnizva approached them, waving off the salute they gave. He felt bad sending such young warriors on a scavenger hunt across the galaxy.

"Welcome back," he greeted them.

"Good to be back, Captain," the first pilot replied.

"Come. We have a meeting area set up with refreshments. You can rest after that."

They nodded in unison and followed him out of the hangar into the main part of the ship. Upon entering the meeting room, they all grazed through the spread of snacks, saving their drinks for last. They sat around the glowing table and took small sips.

"So, how far did you go, did you find anything, and if so what are the details?"

The first scout finished chewing and took a big gulp of his drink before answering.

"We went to the edge of the third solar system. Fairly close still."

The second scout chimed in.

"We were able to establish how habitable the planets could be through data collected. Four are good candidates."

"I think the evacuated humans can get to either of them in two jumps," the third scout added. "That would cut down their time in stasis."

"Let's see them."

The main pilot brought out the mini console from the ship and placed it on the table. A hologram of four planets rose up in 4D. Their positions were laid out on the map by proximity from Earth. Darnizva scrutinized each one and seeing nothing out of place, he decided on the closest planet.

"This one should do. Thank you for doing this. I know you all want to go home." The scouts merely nodded and finished their drinks. "Go. Get some rest. You've earned it."

"Yes, Captain!"

They all stood at the same time then saluted him before leaving the room.

Darnizva leaned back in his chair and rubbed his lower lip. Now he had to relay the good news to the world leaders. He touched the communication icon on the table.

"Prepare my ship for takeoff. I'm heading down to Earth."

"Yes, Captain," came the reply.

He touched on another icon that connected him to the mass messenger for the world leaders. It began recorded when he spoke.

"We have found a suitable planet for your evacuees. I am coming to the arena with the details. Arrival in six hours."

With that done, he got up and headed back to the hangar. He had to make a quick stop before the meeting.

When he arrived at the arena, most of the world leaders and dignitaries were already there. The landing area was littered with high speed transports. He recognized most of the logos on the hulls. The usual suspects had rushed to hear the news. Inside was packed. Everyone was already heading to their seats, the din of voices at a higher level than he cared for.

As he moved from the carpeted hallway into the auditorium, his boots struck the hard floor, causing the humans to turned towards him. The place went hush. He stopped for a moment, surprised at the echo then continued to the platform.

In his hand was a tablet he had transferred the data to. He set it on the dais and the three megascreens behind him lit up. Each one showed the same image of the four planets. They rotated three hundred and sixty degrees showing off every facet of their exterior surface.

"Are we ready? Shall we get started?" He asked. When there was no reply, he continued. "These are the planets we found that are able to sustain human life." He noticed some of the scientists and world leaders eyes gleam unnaturally. "Due to the time constraints, I have chosen the closest one. This cuts cryo time."

"How long does it take to get there?" A world leader asked.

"With two jumps, three years."

"So, by the time we get there, the war will be over and we won't know the outcome."

"That is a far-fetched assumption you have," Darnizva said, glaring at them all. "I have been in wars that last much longer than that. Even in your own history, that is extremely short."

"We're better off, either way," President Lynmore interjected. "If it only lasts a year, the planet will be ruined and not fit for humans. If it lasts longer, then we skirt disaster."

"What I am concluding from all of this is that we are running away with our tails between our legs," the world leader from France said.

"Only civilians and children are being evacuated," Lynmore snapped. "Everyone else will fight to the death."

"At least this way, mankind will survive," another world leader said.

"Isn't that the goal?" Darnizva asked. "To not let humanity go extinct."

"I liked it better when we thought we were alone in the universe," a dignitary muttered.

"But that is implausible," Darnizva stated. "There are billions of worlds. What made you think you were?"

While the world leaders and dignitaries squirmed in their seats, the scientists stared down at him knowingly. He never understood that kind of logic; or lack of.

The White House summons stayed up on Quelly's work station holoscreen as she read it for the tenth time. She had been given the reins of her project and was now required to report to the President for briefing. A promotion. A big one. She sighed with elation and pushed herself away from the counter.

Her hair was unruly and she had bags under her eyes. The tank top and drawstring pants had seen better days and should have been tossed with the rest of her clothes on laundry day. She stunk. Stripped of her invention, she was assigned to a new project that was mediocre at best.

The monotony of it had her fall into depression and she no longer cared about her health or appearance. Her lab associates complained daily.

Panic set in. She had to make herself presentable within the next three days. Quelly ran into the bathroom and took a good look in the mirror. She pulled down her lower eyelids one at a time and checked the whites of her eyes. Bloodshot. Her fingers stopped short as she tried to run them through her curly mane. There were knots all in it. Her skin had an unhealthy color and her muscles had deflated. She hadn't been to the gym in months.

"Okay woman, get your shit together."

She stripped naked, threw her clothes in the incinerator, and headed into the shower. On the way, she grabbed a pair of scissors. There was no time to try and comb the knots out. She would go to a salon tomorrow and have whatever butchery she committed fixed.

Time to up my game.

An official transport arrived at her complex entrance and she hauled ass down the stairs to the bottom floor instead of waiting for the elevator. There was a crowd of scientists rubber necking to see who was coming out of the vehicle. Quelly pushed her way through.

"Excuse me. Excuse me. Move! Damn it!"

She stumbled forward out onto the curb and took a moment to catch her breath. The hatch opened and a man in a black suit came out.

"Professor Riggs, please get in."

"Thank you. Sorry I made you wait."

She heard a few sucked in breaths and someone calling her a bitch. Okay, more than a few called her that as she climbed in. She used the viewport to check her hair and makeup. The stylist had shortened her hair to just below her shoulders and thinned it out to alleviate its weight. Her face was done in fresh neutral tones. Out of the corner of her eye, she saw one of her lab partners, the same jackass who gave her dirty looks during residency, give her the finger as the transport lifted off.

Then she remembered. None of the public nor any of the scientists she worked with knew of her invention. For all they knew, she was a subpar scientist who couldn't get to seminars on time and had a slew of failed projects. She giggled. Their fate was in her hands now. Then she frowned. That sobered her up from her ego.

Inside the White House, she was escorted down the hall to the Oval Office. It still fascinated her that all of this remained intact after centuries. The lead secret service agent knocked twice on the door.

"Come in," President Lynmore yelled.

The man opened the door wide.

"Professor Riggs, as requested, Madame President."

"Leave us." President Lynmore waved him away as she came from behind her desk.

Once the door was shut, Quelly stood nervous in the center of the room. President Lynmore walked around her, looking her up and down.

"You look like you've wasted away since we last spoke." Quelly felt her face flush. "I heard you were put on another project. Is it lucrative?"

"Not by a long shot," she laughed. She cringed at her lack of professionalism. "No, Madame President. It is not something to be rolled out yet."

The President burst out laughing, causing Quelly to become uneasy.

"Did you hear that, George? Oh, that was priceless."

Quelly turned and nearly jumped as she noticed the

man sitting on the loveseat mere inches from her.

"You can drop the formalities, young lady. This is crisis mode. We don't have time for diplomacy or kindness."

"Right." Quelly lowered her arms to her sides and relaxed. "Since my invention was taken from me, I figured I was no longer useful as a scientist."

President Lynmore frowned and turned to her.

"Taken from you? Who told you that?"

"I, well…" Quelly was confused.

"We needed to find a way to streamline first. Now that we've done that, you are in charge of finding a way to implement it. I hope you have some ideas."

Quelly's eyes went wide. She had been wallowing in self pity and anger for nothing all this time.

"Yes, Madame President. I have a few."

"Good. George, give her her pass and take her to her office."

"On it." He tossed Quelly a badge. "Let's go." Quelly attached the badge to her coat and followed him out. "You need to assemble a team and find resources. Make sure you fill out requisitions and maintain budget."

"Yes sir."

"Welcome to hell."

HUMILITY

Whenever there was a secret meeting to gather the former leaders, Hoskins always wondered how they could screw up being in disguise. It wasn't rocket science and many of the ones in hiding were the original scientists.

Get a goddamn clue!

He left his right hand man in the car at the docks and headed onto the giant yacht. It would set sail once everyone was onboard. From his left he caught sight of Professor Makoto looking weary and angry. Hoskins snorted, knowing why. The man had lost his pet project and his pet Biode. Three other generals were present along with two admirals. All the others were scientists shamed into exile for the horrors they committed over the decades.

On the main deck was a spread of food and drink with a bar option. Hoskins made his way to the bar. He needed something stronger than those premixed cocktails on the trays. The scenery began to move as the boat slipped away into the ocean. A timer on the wall ticked down to how much time they had left before the meeting started in the conference room below deck.

Let's get this shit done!

He tossed back a shot of whiskey and signaled the bartender to pour another.

As he moved away, some of the other guests arrived at the bar. The meeting got under way on schedule. More drinks were supplied in the room as everyone took to their seats. Some of the attendees already tipsy and pink in the face. One of the world leaders who hosted these things stood up and addressed the room.

"Good afternoon, ladies and gentlemen. I hope the world is treating you kindly despite being in hiding over the years."

"Hmph!" One of the scientists sniffed. "We had no choice, did we?"

"We were no longer useful. The younger generation has surpassed us tenfold." Another scientist replied.

"Same goes for the military," a Navy Admiral added.

"That's bullshit!" Hoskins said. "Nothing can replace experience."

"This from the man who almost got us annihilated with his dirty space bomb."

That was a sore subject. Hoskins glared at the man who grinned then averted his stare. Every now and again someone would bring it up and true to form, the moderator would shut it down.

"We are still here, aren't we?" the world leader said. "Constantly bringing it up is childish and petty. I would like to think we were above that considering the fate of the world."

"Well, this planet deserves what it gets after turning against us." One general stated. "We had the best intentions for advancements and were persecuted for it."

"Best intentions?" Hoskins cried out incredulously. "We had no such thing! I wanted elite soldiers. Plain and simple. We didn't even know about the enemy yet."

"Our research was pushing modern technology forward," a scientist snapped.

"Without our findings, medical science would be at

a standstill," Professor Morandi added. "Hell, none of us would still be alive."

"And maybe we shouldn't be," Hoskins said.

The room fell into silence and the tension built. He felt anger coming from them.

"We needed to continue our work! You selfish prick. The world needed us."

"For what? Your little nasty experiments?"

He countered, looking around the room.

"You got a lot of nerve," one of the scientists spat. "You hated both the hybrids and the aliens. What contribution was created from those Terrors?"

Hoskins stood up, letting his chair scrape across the wood flooring.

"You want to compare my Terrors?" He yelled. "The super soldiers your countries were dying to get their hands on? The hybrids that I took from your dens of rape, dissection, and God knows what else went on in them?" Faces covered in shame looked away from him. "I never hated the damn things! I just made them more useful than guinea pigs for science."

The world leader grimaced as the rest of the room became uncomfortable. As one of the other generals opened his mouth to speak, Hoskins glared at him.

"Tell me I'm wrong!"

The general clamped his mouth shut and the world leader gestured for Hoskins to be seated. He did so and made sure he got the attention of every person.

Look me in the eyes, you fucking monsters.

"On that note," the word leader said, breaking the silence. "Let's go around and exchange information we've collected so far."

Tablets came out of handbags and satchels and were laid on the table. It connected and all the info was displayed on the giant holoscreen on the far wall. Hoskins leaned back in his seat. He had already scrubbed most of the good bits from his files.

You fuckers aren't getting much from me.

⌒

At the entrance to the Shadow base, the senior General Perrara and Sgt. Scott Mitchum were in a stand-off surrounded by soldiers with weapons drawn. Five of them were behind General Perrara. The other twenty formed an arc behind Shawn.

"General, what brings you here after so long?" Shawn asked, narrowing his gaze.

"My son seems to think he is being pushed out of the loop," the General replied. "I came to remedy that thinking."

"On what grounds? We have no need for military scrutiny here."

"I founded this organization," the general started.

"Co founded," Shawn interjected.

"Which means I know more than you ever could. I am an asset," the general continued without skipping a beat.

"You know nothing. And your son, even less." Shawn cocked his head to the side and stared at him with disgust. "You and that professor created a haven of monsters. Now you want to come and pat yourself on the back and lay claim?"

"Where is Hana? I'm not going to stand here and argue with a child."

"My mother is busy," Shawn answered with malice. "If he moves, shoot him."

There was loud shuffling from above then a voice shouted.

"Belay that order!"

They all looked up. Hana stood leaning over the rails, her hands turning red from the pressure. Her eyes glowed with anger, causing her son and the general to stare at her wide eyed in fear. Hana was rarely in female form on the base and usually dressed in plain shirt and slacks. She appeared to have been rudely awakened from a terrible sleep. Her hair was in disarray and she wore a simple A-line dress made of fabric that slightly wrinkled.

"What are you doing?" She asked her son.

He frowned at her and pointed to the general.

"He came armed to the teeth demanding access. I'm doing my duty!"

Hana's lips pursed and she straightened her posture.

"Escort him to the conference room. I'll be there shortly." As she turned away, she added, "And stow those weapons!"

The soldiers on both sides obeyed and her son walked towards the lift. Without instruction, the general and his entourage followed. At the lift, Shawn gave the general a dirty look and tsked. On the conference room level, the general was let inside and left alone. His men were barred from entering by a barricade of ten soldiers, outnumbering them two to one. Hana arrived a few minutes later.

She sat at the opposite end of the table. Her arms were laid flat in front of her across the table while her stare conveyed irritation.

"Why have you come here?"

Her malice was evident and he realized how this would seem after the last time they talked. He remembered saying some unsavory things about her.

"I know we parted ways on bad terms. I apologize for that. But, we have more dire issues at hand with the upcoming war."

"I know that!" Her expression held insult.

"Of course. Then, I have to ask why there has been push back on getting Shadowmen into the combat units? A few thousand have trickled in over the years and that is unacceptable."

Something awful glimmered in her eyes as they narrowed further. General Perrara forced himself not to scoot back in his chair out of fear.

"This organization is no longer your responsibility. You and Professor Makoto forfeited that when you left it to fend for itself. I have kept it up and running. It is mine!"

The way she vehemently spat out the professor's name and declaring the base her own, made the general angry.

"I was right then. You really are an ungrateful little shit who thinks they're superior. You couldn't fight your way out of a paper bag, you twink."

Hands clasped around his throat and his eyes bulged as they focused on Hana, exchanging the same breath as him. He had not seen her move the twenty feet across the table. He was now able to see those glowing eyes up close. Silver, like white hot heat, they burned into his retinas. Her hands tightened, and his air supply was cut off. He struggled, grabbing hold of her wrists to pull them off, and was surprised at her monstrous strength. The blood vessels burst in his eyes and he felt his own strength fading. Her eyes stayed locked with his.

"Oh, dear Hana," a female voice cooed. "He is not worth killing." Celestial Mother stood over the two. "Let him go," she demanded.

At first, Hana stopped squeezing, contemplating the outcome. She again added pressure.

"Hana."

Celestial Mother did not yell but her tone was just as effective.

Hana released the general, letting him fall back onto the floor. She stood atop the table and walked back to her seat, stepping down into it. General Perrara managed to catch his breath and get one arm on the table's edge. He pulled himself up on his knees and laid his head on the table while gasping.

"General," Celestial Mother said. "We will not be complying further with your people's demands. You get what we have already given. This place no longer belongs to you."

"Get him out of here," Hana ordered the soldiers outside the doorway.

They let his own soldiers help him up then surrounded the group as they led them back to the lift. When it reached the hangar level, General Perrara had regained his composure and was able to walk on his own. At the entrance, Shawn waited for them with a new set of soldiers.

"General Perrara," Shawn yelled out as he approached. "Your access has been revoked." The General and his entourage walked past him without acknowledging his words. Shawn whispered to him as their heads crossed. "Don't ever come here again. I'll shoot you on sight."

General Perrara exited the base and followed his men to the transport waiting outside. As it lifted off, he cursed profanely.

"Goddamn it! That fucking whore! Fuck this shit!"

He took off his jacket and threw it on the floor. His hands grabbed hold of his hair, messing up the coifed slick back style. Then he yelled. Once that was out of his system, he smoothed his hair and sat straight in his seat. It finally dawned on him that this was not his son's fault. No, it was his and the professor's. They both saw the hybrids in the facilities as broken things to be manipulated, not taking into account their hatred towards their captors.

We underestimated them. And now, the world's salvation lay in the hands of an enemy.

George got out of the back seat of the government vehicle and stepped onto the manicured road that led to the gated community ahead. The sky was clear and he could smell various floral scents. Through the gate, all he could see was a winding road lined with foliage.

From the driver's side of the back seat, Secretary Regis emerged shielding her eyes from the sun before putting on her shades.

"So, they're in there?" She asked.

"According to Holmes, yes. He had a hard time finding them."

"Well, they are probably not going to be happy to see us."

"Oh, I guarantee that. Hopefully they won't shoot first and ask questions later."

Movement at the sides of the gate made George tense.

"That depends on your agenda," a man called out.

Four men fully armed, surrounded the vehicle. The driver reached for his weapon and Regis gave him a look that said otherwise. He eased his hands back down into his lap.

"That was smart."

George recognized the man as Felps.

"I guess Winters was too busy to greet me," George laughed.

"You'd be dead if he did. Get back in the car. We will guide you in."

"No blindfold?"

Felps gave him a dirty look.

Inside the car, Regis turned to him, whipping off her sunglasses.

"May I ask that you don't antagonize these people? We need them."

George gave her a side glance. He knew all too well how important they were.

They arrived at the cluster of cul de sacs and Regis' mouth gaped opened before closing into a thin line. Even George was impressed with the set up. He wondered who was supplying their resources. The former detective, Munston, came to the back passenger door and opened it.

"Hurry up. We have a lot to discuss."

"Did you refuse to go back to work?" George asked.

"And do what? Bust some murderers, drug dealers, pimps? Let 'em weed each other out. I have better things to do."

"That's not very optimistic," Regis said.

"Madame Secretary, nothing is very optimistic these days."

They were led to a house around the bend in the next section over and inside, George whistled as he looked around. The entire first floor was a communications room with a large conference area and giant holoscreens hovering near the ceiling. At one of the consoles was Winters, deep in his task. When George got close to the table in the center to sit down, Winters seemed to stiffen and turned towards the group. The two men locked eyes.

George halted midway down into the chair.

"Are we going to have a private chat or can we get down to business?" he asked.

Winters' cold grey eyes glinted with hate.

"Business always comes first."

He finished what he was doing and came to the table to join the rest of the group. Regis set her shades next to her on the table and pulled off her coat. George did the same once seated.

"We know why you're here," Emerson stated.

"Then let's get to it." Regis raised her arms onto the table and templed her fingers. "We need your expertise and manpower. This is about survival of the human race."

"We understand that," Felps said. "But, we also feel this is how it should be."

"So, you won't fight to stay alive?" George asked.

"No one said that," Emerson replied angrily.

"Then what's the difference? Why does it matter who you fight with?"

"Exactly." Winters leaned forward. "How we survive this war is of no concern to anyone except ourselves. No one needs to dictate or order us to do so."

"We need to be seen as a united front in the face of our enemy," Regis said.

"But, we're not."

Winters said it so bluntly, the rest of the room went silent. Even the workers further inside the house momentarily halted their duties. George wiggled his fingers to stop himself from balling his hands into fists. He was not human. If the war went south in favor of the Relliance, he would reap the spoils along with the Organics. The part that nagged at him was the fact that he liked humans and felt they should have a chance to redeem themselves in fair battle.

"But we can be," Regis countered with fervor. "We can be better."

"Not with this timeframe." Felps smirked.

"Say we do our own thing but let you state we are part of the main force." Emerson suggested. "That way both sides get what they want."

"You would need to be assigned a commanding officer. That's how it works," Regis said.

"Nope," Felps said.

"You want to assign a general, be my guest. Just know that we will not be answering to him and if he tries to pull that insubordinate crap, we'll slit his throat."

Emerson gave George and Regis a winning smile.

"That's quite unnecessary!" Regis cried out. "Is that all any of you know how to do? Murder people who you don't like?"

The atmosphere changed quickly and George moved to block access to Regis. He leaned close to her and whispered.

"Hey, hey. We were supposed to not antagonize them, right?"

Winters, Felps, and Emerson were on their feet as well, ready to attack. Winters' eyes seemed to glow silver then subsided to a dull grey. He sat back in his chair and the others followed.

"You need to tread carefully. No one will find your bodies out here." He extended a hand towards the table. "Sit. We're not done yet."

Regis looked over at George who nodded before returning to his set. She sat as well.

"Maybe we should post pone this for a minute. Take a breather?" George asked.

"Let's not, and make sure you stay in clear sight, you fucking man eater," Munston said from the doorway.

George tensed. Regis looked around amused. Winters and his men also froze, giving Munston a warning look.

"What is he talking about?" Regis asked. "Why would he call you that?"

Munston let out a heavy sigh.

"I was just talking out of my ass. He reminds me of one. It just came out."

Regis frowned.

"That is not something you should accused a person

of being. Those things shouldn't be on this planet and God help us if they decide to hunt us for food."

George rolled his eyes then changed his demeanor before Regis noticed. As the mood died down to an acceptable level, he noticed Regis staring at Munston differently.

Well, fuck me. She didn't buy it. George thought.

He knew he needed to be more careful about being found out but Munston was a bad liar.

NEW ALLIES?

"This just gets crazier and crazier," George turned and whispered to the Joint Vice President.

"I'm having a 'what now' moment," the Vice President answered back.

An emergency assembly had been called and all world leaders, military generals and head scientists were brought to the designated domed arena nestled in the city of Geneva. Its inner sanctum was upgraded slightly but remained as it had been decades ago. The reason being to keep it familiar. Each section was labeled according to title and the audience filed in silently.

The roar of fighter jets above signaled the arrival of their new visitors and the dome opened to let them in. On the giant vidscreen, the leader of the Organics watched eagerly. This was his doing. A ship larger than a 787 Airbus hovered above and made a slow descent to the landing pad on the edge of the field. Its engines cut off as it settled down, causing a whirlwind that spread outward forcing everyone to hold on to their belongings. The hatch opened, extending a ramp and five figures stood at the top of it.

In front of the approaching group was a male and a female. The male wore a black double breasted suit with a white shirt and black skinny tie. On his head sat a black fedora with white trim. A large weapon was held upright in one hand and rested on his shoulder. His head was down as he swaggered to the landing, his shiny black shoes clacking on the ramps surface.

"Holy shit!" A military general said softly. "That's a damn Tommy gun."

"A what?" Another general asked.

" If my history is correct, Circa 1920's or 30's. Can't quite remember specifically. That one's like a slight upgrade, but not by much."

"You're joking?"

The female made his era claim concrete as she walked upright with perfect stride, her hips swinging mildly. Her Marcel waves hair style was reminiscent of that era. She wore a full length form fitting black lace dress with capped sleeves and two slits high on each side. Under the lace was a hint of red and purple. Blood red heels comprised of laces went up her calves. Attached to one thigh under her dress was a garter belt housing a mid-length blade sharp on both sides.

In the middle walked a male of seemingly young age, maybe thirty at best, with one hand in his pants pocket. He wore an elegant pinstriped double breasted black suit with a purple handkerchief tucked in the breast pocket. A fedora of the same design sat atop his head. He too had a swagger in his steps.

Behind him were two other men. A blonde with slicked back hair in a ponytail wearing a black suit and white shirt opened two buttons down, the jacket resting on his shoulders along with a long rifle, sauntered down. The other man was shorter with brown hair also slicked back but his suit was only sans tie. Two bulges on his hips were a dead giveaway as handguns.

The man in the middle stopped on the field and looked up at the vidscreen.

His blue eyes glinted like jewels as the lights spanned across them.

"Brother. You look not so well."

A loud intake of air echoed through the dome. Secretary Regis clamped her mouth tight making her teeth clack together. She winced at the pain but kept her focus on the new arrivals. If they were siblings that meant the man in the awesome suit was also an Organic.

"I am as well as can be expected, in my state," Cresnia replied. A small smile touched his lips. He seemed a bit sad.

"You requested my presence on this planet yet you have not told me why."

Cresnia turned his attention to the audience.

"After observing your race's struggle for so long trying to advance your technology to match the enemy, I believe you would do better by tweaking your current level such as my brother's planet has done."

The man cocked his head to one side and made a quick glance around the arena. He could sense the desperation in the air. He looked back up at his brother and sighed as he removed his hand from his pants pocket. A pained expression crossed his face.

"I would rather help you than some random race I know nothing about."

"I know," Cresnia replied softly.

"I will do as you wish…for now."

Cresnia smiled fully and addressed the audience.

"Please, show him what you have accomplished so far. He has a great insight for these things."

Before he could sign off, the man said, "May I contact you soon?" Cresnia nodded, the sad look crept back on his face. "Good." When the vidscreen went black, he turned his gaze to the audience.

"Who will I work with here on this planet?"

Not one dignitary, scientist or military general in the stands spoke up. They all looked around at each other hoping for the other to step up to the plate. He had seen this display of shaky power on his own world before he corrected it through discipline and blood.

"We would be honored to work with you," Secretary Regis offered. "And you are?"

"Silas Monzetti. I am the leader of my world."

"Monzetti?" She queried.

"Is that unusual?"

"Umm, no. Quite the contrary. It is very… Italian." Silas raised an eyebrow. She went on to explain. "There are different regions on our planet that speak different languages. A place called Italy is one of them and they speak Italian. Their names are similar to yours."

"Ahh. Interesting."

"There is also a sort of stigma that they are all Mafia." As Silas was about to question her again, she continued. "Kind of like a large family structured organization that uses intimidation with guns and such in order to have compliance."

"Really? That is what we are."

His eyes glinted in amusement.

Secretary Regis, along with the audience took a closer look at their new allies and there was no mistaking that they appeared to be just that; a Mafia Don and his crew straight out of the history books. The Vice President sucked in his breath and started to shake his head 'no'.

"Just to be clear," Regis asked. "Are you also an organic?"

"That is correct. My father decided to evolve into this form and find a home."

"Oh, a place to rest and raise a family?"

"A planet to take control of and make his own which is now mine." He smiled. "And to create a family of course."

The Vice President visibly blanched. Silas gestured to the female of his crew.

"This is my assassin, and mate, Tios. To my right is Hector. Behind me is Yuri," he cast his hand towards the blonde, "and Micky." This time he pointed to the short man.

"Well," Regis licked her lips. "Now that the introductions are out of the way, shall we go for a tour of the facility that houses our weapons?"

"Of course. Lead the way."

They walked in tight formation towards the transport that awaited them.

Darnizva hurriedly pulled the Vice President aside as he entered the anteroom of the main cannon. He could barely contain his shock at seeing Cresnia's younger brother march in with his entourage. The two aliens made brief eye contact before he averted his gaze and focused on the Vice President.

"Are you out of your mind?" He hissed close to the man's ear. The Vice President's eyes went wide and he looked back at the group. "No matter what he appears to be, he is of the Organic race and should not be trusted."

"What do you expect us to do?" The Vice President snapped. "Their technology is closer to our own. We're struggling here, damn it!" He whispered back.

The Captain ran one hand across his face and caught a glimpse of the two Interfacers as they shuddered at the site of Silas. Darnizva felt like he had been stabbed in the back even though he knew the humans meant no harm. They were trying everything in their power and help from his race was shortcoming. He already felt bad about opening a pathway for every entity in the four solar systems to drop in and take a tour.

Silas Monzetti strolled slowly around the perimeter of the cannon's base, staring up at the cold and unmoving main mechanisms. His eyes held a look of amusement as he took in every part of the weapon. He stopped mid rotation of his second go around and locked eyes with Darnizva.

"Is this your doing?"

"No. They had already built it. We are just trying to make it function better with more output." Darnizva replied squinting in frustration because Silas would not severe his gaze.

"Well, it is impressive. But I wonder." Finally releasing Darnizva from the stare down, he turned his attention to the human scientists who had stopped their work to watch him. "Instead of applying an alien energy source you have no idea how to contain, would it not be better to utilize your own laser technology and continue enhancements on its precision targeting?"

You could hear a pin drop, the room becoming as quiet as the dawn. Eyes went wide and mouths opened in response to 'ah ha' moments. Even Darnizva's head involuntarily snapped back as the information struck him. The two Interfacers looked up sideways in unison, contemplating. Silas smiled, a little. Darnizva's skin crawled.

"Oh my God!" A scientist burst out loud. "How could we not have thought of that in all this time?"

The Vice President looked at Darnizva and raised his arms at Silas. "Well?"

"It would be more efficient," Sugil answered as the Captain was about to. "We don't really use that kind of weaponry because our goal is to completely wipe out the enemy in one fell swoop."

"Can the cannon be modified at this late stage?" Secretary Regis asked.

"Of course!" The two Interfacers exclaimed.

Silas walked away from the cannon and towards an unsuspecting Darnizva. When the Captain looked up from being lost in thought, the two were mere inches apart. Cinnamon red eyes locked with brilliant violet.

"Captain, I know you are having misgivings about my participation in this. Let me assure you." His eyes gleamed. "I do not have the same agenda as my brother. The last thing I want are humans in my midst on my world. Keeping this planet intact with them on it, suits me better."

"If I weren't so grateful, I would think you just insulted us," the vice president interjected.

"Believe me," Darnizva quipped, "He couldn't care less about your feelings."

"That is correct. Yuri!" Silas called to his bodyguard.

"Yeah, boss?" Yuri sauntered over, his jacket swaying as he walked with it still draped across his shoulders.

"Make sure you do your best for these humans and cooperate with the Interfacers."

"Sure thing, boss," Yuri replied with a side look of disgust at the Interfacers. "Are you sure you don't need me?"

"I have Tios. You know better than that, Yuri." The blonde muscle rolled his eyes. "Captain, walk with me." He headed for the door and stopped at the entrance to wait for Darnizva. "Don't worry, Tios keeps a good distance." Darnizva followed him out into the corridor and fell in step with him. Behind them, the cannon room became a flurry of activity.

Both aliens walked in silence, Tios trailing not far behind, until they reached a small empty conference room. Inside, Silas touched the sensor to shut the door while gesturing for Tios to wait outside. He put his hands in his pants pockets and sighed.

"Are you going to tell them?"

Darnizva sat down and put his head in his hands. Having been on Earth for some time he was starting to acquire certain human mannerisms like that. He knew what Silas was asking and couldn't bring himself to think about it. So much time and effort was put into preparing for the upcoming battle.

"I can't. Not until we have exhausted all avenues and there is no other answer."

"You're only delaying the inevitable. This race will lose."

"We have a plan to save most of them if it comes to that."

"It's not your fault, Darnizva."

Silas took his hands out his pockets and leaned on the table to meet his face. He waited for the captain to look up and they gazed at each other for a moment.

Silas stood up.

"You know," he began. "My father has been to this planet, even before you. It is how I acquired this style and manner of organization." He smiled mischievously at Darnizva's awe struck facial expression. "So, you were not the one who first opened the pathway."

"Why didn't you say anything?" Darnizva sighed in exhaustion and defeat.

"You are far too young to throw away a century of your life for a race who came into war accidently."

"I want to go home."

"Of course you do."

"I do have children that were raiesed on this planet."

" Are they still here?"

"No! I evauated them." Darnizva snapped.

"Then your bloodline is saved. Move on."

Darnizva ran his hands down his face and stopped so they covered his mouth.

He eyed the nearly ancient Organic.

"Why are you so cold?"

"Am I?" Silas chuckled. "I just have no use for trivial things." He leaned against the far wall of the room. "So, are you going to tell them?"

"No." Darnizva's eyes narrowed. "There's no need. It would cause unnecessary panic."

"Then what is the end game here?"

"They still have a chance, albeit slim. Will you help me?"

Silas glanced up at the ceiling, a slight smile on his face. When he looked back at Darnizva, his expression was serious. "If you can guarantee this race's survival, then yes."

"Cresnia is lying in wait for bodies."

"As he should. Our race always needs new soldiers." Silas push off the wall and went to the door. "Come. We have work to do." He swiped his hand across the sensor and the door opened. Darnizva reluctantly followed him out into the hall.

As they walked back to the control room, Silas glanced over at Darnizva. He remembered hearing about his father's first time on Earth and even though he enjoyed it, humans themselves left a bad impression on him. The quicker they could get off this planet the better.

Lab technicians were hustling about finishing their tasks as the head scientist relayed them. The oversized bunker buzzed with energy fueled by desperation. No one expected the middle of the room to suddenly turn into a liquid formation then warp inward like something was trying to suck the air out. Of all the things the scientists had seen over the last few decades, a mini vortex was not one of them.

Professor Heines turned to see the phenomenon as the pool of liquid became black as space. He saw stars beyond its edges. The entire room went still, everyone tensed up bracing for the unknown. He tried to remain calm but excitement ignited his very core. As an astrophysicist this was right up his alley. It was well known how the aliens reached Earth but none of the scientists had ever witnessed the unfolding from space.

Blinding white light shot forth from the gaping pool of stars sending a gust of super-heated air across the bunker. Some of the technicians' lab coats were singed along the sleeves as they dodged the assault. One did not make it time and was hit full force, his body pushed into the wall on the opposite side of the room. Professor Heines hurried towards him just in time to soften the impact by knocking him out of the beams direct path.

As the light died out, a tall figure emerged in a white robe that dragged on the ground. A light blue sleeveless one was draped over it and secured at the waist. Hair dark as pitch, cropped short just at the ears, sat atop the male's head in disarray. The vortex dissipated and the room's atmosphere returned to normal pressure, cooling down. Electric blue eyes peered at the inhabitants as he scanned the bunker.

A lab technician sat on the floor in fright not far from the being and locked eyes with him.

"Don't look into his eyes!"

Darnizva burst into the room shouting in distress.

Professor Heines found the young man's location and immediately felt Darnizva forcibly push his head down as the screaming started.

The being's eyes went from icy blue to white hot and burned into the young lab tech's. His body began to writhe in agony while he screamed and blood spewed from his mouth.

"STOP!" Darnizva yelled, barely holding back tears as he too kept his gaze averted.

The being tilted his head and smiled as his eyes returned to blue. The lab techs body finally lay still. Seeing the despair in Darnizva, he backed away a few feet from the young man. He raised a hand and the vortex reopened. As it widened, he grabbed the young tech's body by the legs and flung him in. It snapped shut the moment his body was fully engulfed.

"What just happened?" Professor Heines demanded, shouting loudly.

"His insides have been rearranged. He needs proper treatment to reverse it, which your race does not have the medical technology to do," the being explained, his full lips turned slightly upwards in a grin.

"Bryce!" Darnizva seethed through gritted teeth.

"Darnizva." Bryce stepped forward. "What a grand mess you have created."

 ⤴

Another emergency World Council meeting had been called based on Darnizva's urgent request. Even the Relliants helping in the upcoming battle were asked to attend. Lt. Sspark stood as far away from the platform as possible where Bryce awaited the start of the session. This time, every seat in the arena was filled. A hush fell over it when Darnizva held up a hand.

"I apologize for calling you all here on such short notice but something unprecedented has occurred." He gestured towards Bryce. "An historian has arrived. This is Bryce." He saw the eyes turn opaque. "Don't!" Bryce smirked as the blue returned.

Secretary Regis stood up and cleared her throat.

"What do you mean by historian?"

"Historians are beings who transfer their knowledge as they leave this plane. Each generation gains more as time progresses. Our galaxy's historian has over 300,000 years of knowledge from various parts of the universe."

A loud gasp resounded and Secretary Regis went pale. "That's," she took a deep breath and exhaled slowly. "Extraordinary."

"Is it?" Bryce responded. "I find it minimal at best. I am still considered quite young in knowledge."

"They can also tap into other historians if needed, going back millions of years." Darnizva continued, glancing back every now and then to make sure Bryce didn't target anyone. "Because of their vast knowledge, looking into their eyes is not recommended. Their stare can rearrange organs or turn an organism inside out."

Many eyes went wide with fear and some shielded their faces from Bryce's.

"Only if I wish it so." Bryce explained. "Seeing into so much does that and sometimes I feel one should see it," he stopped for a moment. "Before they die."

"He is a unique historian in that he is also a destroyer."

"A destroyer?" The military Generals sat up a bit straighter as the Secretary of Defense asked the question.

"There are two main forces in the universe, Creators and Destroyers. When a Creator forms a planet or an entire system and does not like the outcome, a Destroyer is summoned to annihilate it to nothing once more so the Creator can start over."

Bryce laid a hand on Darnizva's shoulder signaling him to stop.

"You have officially scared them to near death, Darnizva." He pointed outward to the people in the arena. Darnizva grimaced and his lips went thin, his brow creasing. Bryce smiled with full pity. "Let me continue," he suggested. Darnizva nodded.

"I am here for the worst-case scenario you are all preparing for. Evacuating the planet is a wise decision and would make our task much easier."

"And what task is that?" The Prime Minister of Russia retorted.

"If most of the population is removed before the entire planet floor is razed by the Relliant's fire power, then a Destroyer can finish the job and a Creator can rejuvenate it."

Bryce saw the looks of defiance on the human's faces and felt a twinge of exasperation. He could tolerate a bit of optimism, not misguided ignorance. They had no chance of winning against the Relliants, when even the League had trouble over the past few centuries. Nevertheless, he was here to serve a purpose should the situation arise.

"Say this scenario happens," Admiral Perrara began. "How long are we talking before Earth can sustain human life again?"

"We work very quickly. It would take approximately eighty years to complete."

"Earth was created in eight days, just so you know." A diplomat snorted.

"Where did you hear something like that? A planet, when done leisurely, takes up to a thousand years. Since this planet will just be resurfaced, it takes less than a century because the foundation is already established."

"Did he just tell a being with over 300,000 years

of knowledge how Earth was created?" The French President whispered to the diplomat sitting next to him. The other man shook his head in disbelief.

"So, you are here to assist the human race?" Secretary Regis asked tentatively.

Bryce smiled wide this time.

"I am intrigued by your race and would find it a shame to let it die out over the whims of a tyrant. So yes, and no. I am neither your friend nor the enemy."

Out of the corner of his eye he saw a man cock a firearm and raise it to him. His eyes went white and in an instant, the man was convulsing on the ground half screaming and gurgling on his own blood.

A few people near him dropped as well before they could look away as Darnizva yelled out, "Don't look!" He had also seen the rogue attendee a split second before Bryce. An entire arena of people were either hunkered down in their seats, eyes squeezed shut or their faces completely covered by jackets and tablets.

"There's always one, isn't there?" Bryce spoke, his eyes returning to pools of icy blue.

"Oh, my God," Regis whispered. Her head was still turned away, her body in the fetal position on the seat, as she peeked at the shooter's corpse.

On the ground, the man's body lay with half his organs slithering around. His heart, sitting atop his chest, beat a few more times before ceasing. Steam rose from the body due to the white hot heat from Bryce's stare. The others around him were immediately removed for medical attention. A silence filled the room, then came sounds of vomiting.

Bryce stepped down from the platform and strolled over to the dead man's corpse. He bent down and with one touch, the body began to decay, crumbling to dust and disappearing. All that remained was a dark smudge on the ground. A look over his shoulder found faces filled with horror. He sighed heavily, rising to his full height of seven feet two inches.

Such nonsense.

Darnizva turned to Sspark and Hagen. They shook their heads while taking a few more steps back away from the platform sending them up against the back drop. Historians were frightening enough. One that could also destroy was not something you messed around with. The fact that one showed up out of the blue at such a crucial time solidified the outcome in their minds. Of course, the humans were going to fight to the bitter end and there was no way to deter them from that path.

Hagen sought out Admiral Perrara. Finding him, the two exchanged a silent conversation, nodding in agreement. As many plans as it took to save humankind the better. He too had an affinity for the race.

⌇

Hagen chewed on his lower lip and stopped when he tasted blood from a cut made by one of his overly sharp canines. It wasn't due to nervousness, quite the opposite. The human soldiers he had acquired for training were doing better than he thought. Granted, their bodies were not nearly as strong, but their ability to learn was to be commended. Having them was a start.

When General Tartha learned that many of his troops on Earth were not on board with his plans, he declared treason and tried to strip him of command. His plan backfired because Hagen was the leader of the Command Fleet and his warriors would not concede to the General's demands. Seeing the Command Fleet as an enemy probably frightened him, Hagen concluded.

"Commander." He turned to see Bree strolling up in full battle gear. "We just received word that the humans have found a way to successfully evacuate the population if need be."

"Is that so?" Hagen felt a bit of relief. "What about the reconnaissance team Darnizva sent ten years ago?"

"They returned with five years to spare. Less than predicted."

"That was cutting it very close." Hagen frowned.

"Yes." Bree stood staring off into the distance.

"Are you worried about your children, or what the historian prophesied?"

"Maybe both. I will make sure they are put in deep freeze for transport. As for Craig."

Hagen watched a struggle going on in Bree's expression. He didn't know what it was like to have knowledge of your mate's death beforehand and felt he wouldn't want it.

"How is he taking it?"

"He feels what has to be will. We don't know when or how. It's not like he won't be reborn so it doesn't matter to him either way. "

That made Hagen angry. "He will not know you or his children when he is reborn! How cruel can he be? Why? Why do you love him when he does not return it?"

"I always have."

"Maybe you should think of finding someone who will actually cherish you."

"Perhaps." Bree turned away and went back down the stairs he came up.

The commlink embedded in the console attached to his platform beeped and made a gurgling sound before a male voice was audible.

"Commander Hagen, how goes it on your end?"

"Admiral Perrara, good to hear from you."

Son of the infamous General Perrara, the Admiral was just as tenacious and detail oriented as his father before the old man retired. Hagen met with him every quarter so they could touch base on what was needed. The Admiral had his father's looks and sometimes Hagen forgot he was talking to the son. Human lifespans were so short.

"Will General Tartha try to corner the Command Fleet and disable it? It seems to be the one thing he fears at the moment."

"You may be right. He would be stupid to try. I may not be on board the main ship but the crew will defend itself even against their own race if necessary."

"Oh, by the way," Admiral added. "The land to space cannons are ready to go."

"All ten of them?" Hagen asked incredulous.

"Yep. It's all thanks to Darnizva and Sspark's Interfacers. Those guys creep me out but they sure know their craft."

Hagen shivered a bit thinking of the Interfacers with their tendrils spewing out of their pores attaching to things.

"I'm glad."

"The soldiers?"

"Coming along beautifully."

"Can they hold their own against you?"

"Not even close," Hagen snorted. "Maybe in another fifty years."

"But will they survive this war?" Admiral Perrara sounded serious.

"Let's just say they have a fighting chance."

"Well, I guess that's all we can hope for isn't it?" There was a long pause. "I'll check back in on you in a few weeks. Got some small hiccups to clear."

The commlink went dark.

Hagen redirected his focus on the training grounds and rubbed his sore lower lip.

Too close.

He thought about the time table for the evacuation and the inevitable razing of the planet surface.

It's too close.

Quelly sat in her plushy leather chair spinning it from left to right as she contemplated her dilemma. She had been looking at the time table that was given to her by General Perrara plus the progress report from Janti. Her lower lip stung and she realized she had been pulling on it profusely.

Rubbing away the hurt, Quelly stood up and stretched. A sense of panic was trying to creep its way into her but she fought it. Saving an entire planet's population was no easy task and it would take years, up to the very throes of battle. Lives would be lost.

The goal was to get one hundred people to a cube for easier transport onto the vessels that would take them off the planet. Each inhabited area would have its own cube bays and so far the project's progress was at a dismal fourteen percent with under ten years to go. Janti's observation of the ground composition made it difficult. A new type of lining was in the works to combat the instability of the holes walls.

Out of the entire population not fighting, about five percent refuse to leave, especially the elderly. Still, she hoped there would be enough cubes for the ones who did want to get out of dodge. She had no choice in the matter since she was the one with the solution to dissolve the cubes. To give up her leverage was a different story.

Quelly reached over her desk and hit the intercom button.

"All personnel, please report to board room eleven."

Tapping it again to release, she grabbed her tablet and

exited her office. She needed help to nip this situation in the butt.

A creeping silence blanketed the observation room as everyone stared up at the vidscreens in a state of disbelief. It was really happening. There was no turning back. Images of three planets outside Earth's solar system loomed over them while Darnizna, along with Silas, explained the grim reality. He had wanted to hold off to see if other alternatives arose, but none surfaced.

"These three planets are not too far and can sustain human life for a short time." Darnizva paused. "Give or take twenty years. Transport should start soon for anyone who wants to leave Earth."

Silas stood, hands in his pants pockets, flanked by his crew. He had been the one to break the news to the humans first, seeing Darnizva not having the stomach for it. The stunned silence was amusing to him. How could they have not known? He asked himself. No matter how far their technology advanced, humans were still up against a race of warriors known to be a super power in the five galaxies.

He took a glance at the historian sitting in a chair off to the side with his legs crossed. A pair of dark sunglasses capable of blocking direct sunlight were resting on the bridge of his nose. Silas snorted. That was not going to stop him from killing anyone with those eyes of his. He had long ago decided not to engage historians under any circumstance. They were fickle and had a dangerous idea of what was funny.

"You're going to use the Litigator for the planet resurfacing." Silas directed this to Bryce.

"Of course. That's the only reason it would take so little time." Bryce replied.

"Now, wait a minute! Hold on!" A general snapped. "We haven't even begun to fight and you are just upping and calling it in the enemy's favor? Don't underestimate the conviction of mankind!"

A Hoskins follower. Darnizva thought in disgust. Silas had heard about the former General and nodded in agreement.

"I did say it was a worst case scenario," Bryce quipped.

He knew all about Hoskins too.

Silas turned to Tios. She raised an eyebrow, knowing exactly what he was thinking. If there was one human on the planet who could muck up their plans, it was Hoskins and this General may know where to find him. Followers like to keep in touch with their leaders.

"On that note, shall we continue?" He interjected waiting for the din of voices to cease. Having their attention, Silas began explaining the plan.

"The population will be moved off planet onto these three and once the battle is over, we will do a sweep to see if there are any survivors. Depending on the outcome, the Destroyer will eliminate anything unnecessary. Once that is complete, the litigator, joined by the Creator will resurface the planet to resume sustaining human life. In eighty years, when the ecosystem has been re-established, we will start to bring back the human race in stages, sector by sector. After that," Silas stopped.

"The human race must learn to strive on its own." Bryce completed.

"As it should be," Darnizva added.

Production had halted for the litigator's new show. Most of the equipment was still there, the crew not bothering to pack up beforehand. A sign on the outer door read DO NOT ENTER. That didn't stop him from going to the deserted set to ponder his next move. He understood why the crew abandoned ship with war looming so close. That being the case, he felt this was the perfect time to give humans something to escape with. He sat slumped in the wooden high chair with his name, Roland Barry, blazed on the back and stared at the stage still set up with prop furnishings.

A shimmer in the air by the stage entrance made him squint to see it better. Dark matter dyed it like spilled ink and a vortex appeared. The sofa and end tables were sucked in, taken by the void and Bryce stepped out. He waved a hand across the gaping phenom and it snapped shut.

"And what are you supposed to be?" Roland asked as he sat up in his chair.

Bryce smiled. His eyes began to glow. Roland raised a smoky blue shield before him, blocking the effects. Disappointed, Bryce's eyes returned to their electric blue.

"I heard a rumor that a Historian had shown up."

Bryce walked down the side stairs and stood near him.

"This planet is on an interesting course."

"Yes, it is," Roland sighed.

"How about we wait it out and fix this rock together?"

Roland snorted.

"There won't be much left. It would be a waste of my power."

"Ah ah," Bryce tsked. "Let's not give up hope just yet. I think they will come out of this fairly well."

"Changing the axis for each adjustment will only make it worse."

"You'll have me as a prepper."

"Hmmm?" Roland cocked his head. "Why would you do that? This race is unimportant. They can be re-evolved from scratch."

"After all the time you lived amongst them, there's nothing you wish to save?"

"You just got here, Historian. In no time at all, you will see as we do."

"We?"

"Every alien that's interacted with these humans."

Chapter Three: False Security

ANXIETY

All along the terrain on the outskirts of an abandoned city destroyed decades before, two groups of seven people stood in a semicircle looking over it. They were positioned nearly a mile apart from each other and for good reason. Each had very little time to complete their tasks.

Janti, the leader of the first group, knelt and grabbed a handful of corroded earth. It felt gritty yet gummy as he rubbed it around in his palm. From across the way, he noticed Tommy doing the same. They caught each other's attention and nodded. This was not going to be easy.

It had taken years to hone their talents to a stable, but deadly, level. Now, they had been commissioned by the lead scientists and the military to create giant, deep, box shaped holes in secluded areas. Large enough to hold hundreds of bodies each. The quality of the terrain was not what they had expected and Janti realized he should have sent scouts beforehand.

"It's too late for that." Tommy spoke telepathically.

"I know, Babe. Let's just see how it goes for now." He responded in kind.

"It will have to get plenty hot."

One of Janti's group members joined in the conversation.

"Is that the only way to get the sides to harden?"

"Got a better idea?" Janti asked.

The man shrugged, using a foot to test the ground.

"We would have to combine our powers then, cuz I know I don't have that much energy to super heat a hole that big and that deep."

Tommy frowned. *"He's right."*

Both groups looked around at each other silently asking, 'what now?' Janti pursed his lips in frustration. The whole saving mankind gig was starting to be not what it was all cracked up to be. He knew, as well as the others, that this could all be in vain. He also knew that humanity had to at least try.

"Okay," he decided. *"One hole at a time, two people make it and two super heat it. Tommy and I will map out each one in advance as we go along."*

"Cool." Was the unified response.

The first set of four came towards his location and positioned themselves in a square formation. The two hole makers stood diagnally across from each other and the heaters did the same. Janti visualized the required dimensions and projected it out onto the ground. As it expanded, the four moved outward until they were on the edges of the virtual square.

"Well, let's see what we can do, huh?"

Janti kept the hologram steady with his mind while he raised two fingers and signaled the two hole makers to begin.

Tremors ran along the terrain as the ground fell inward in a perfect square right on the lines of the projection. All the broken earth was then lifted out by one member as the other continued to push deeper into the ground. The two heaters immediately went to work when they saw the gummy dirt start to sag. Extreme heat made the air shimmer in waves and the group sweated profusely.

Janti let go of the projection and it faded away. Seeing the slow progress due to the nature of the ground's composition he stepped in to add more heat. Yep, it was way more work than what he originally thought.

"This is bullshit."

Quelly read the reports from the multiple block sites and felt a sense of discouragement. She had figured all that was needed were vessels to hold the ice and the containers could be shipped onto the transports. When there was no budget allocated for vessels she came up with the next best thing; or so she thought. She didn't take into consideration the quality of the ground from different regions around the world. The work around lining was still not ready.

Well, I guess I'm so smart, I'm just dumb.

The project was way behind schedule due to the extra work needed. There was also the fact that Janti and Tommy were doing such trivial work with their talents. Many of the military leaders balked at her suggestion. President Lynmore backed her up. Her reasoning was to get them away from being absorbed into the ranks.

Everyone was so filled with anticipation at seeing the hybrids and altered humans fight that they lost sight of the one thing that mattered. Those soldiers were not toys. They were people being forced to fight. Sure, there were volunteers amongst them. She had a real issue with the ones from the facilities. Children tossed away like garbage by their parents and subjected to an isolated life of tests. As a scientist she understood the fascination to create such places. As a human, she felt disdain for her race.

With a heavy sigh, she shook her head and stopped her train of thought. She focused on the issue at hand. Evacuation of an entire planet was more than anyone could handle. Her associates around the globe were having multiple logistics problems. The sight of giant holes resembling mass graves being dug out all over the place didn't help the aesthetic aspect. Technically, that's what the holes were; mass graves. At least until they were revived elsewhere.

Her next step was to try and get the electrical gauges to keep working within the ice once sealed. Each person needed to have a diagnostic system attached. Something small, streamlined and only taking up enough space the size of a narrow panel. The electrodes that connected to the body would have to be redesigned as well.

Another message came through from one of her lab technicians. A new module was being completed to regulate Biosystems. Her mind turned over an idea and a light bulb flashed in her head. She typed a reply. Combining the diagnostics with the regulator was the perfect solution.

I'm a genius after all.

On the lower level of the labs building, a group of medical engineers specializing in equipment huddled over four demonstration models for the readout panel. The lab was dimly lit with the only brightness coming from the glowing tabletop they surrounded. Quelly walked across the large room, eyeing the areas of tangled mess and discarded parts at the workstations.

The project manager raised her head as Quelly approached then stood to greet her.

"Professor Riggs," she shook her hand. "Doctor Mathis. I hope you'll give each variation serious consideration."

The others also stood and moved over to let Quelly peruse the offerings. Each one had what she wanted.

Organ functions, heart monitor, dosage regulator, brain wave detection, the works. All inside compact panels the size of a remote control from early in the century. There was a wide range in their designs. She was looking for ease of function and readability.

"Can this one have a larger font?" She asked, picking up the first one. "The display seems awfully small." It was heavier than the others.

One of the creators on the end leaned forward. He pointed to the device.

"We were trying to get as much information as possible on the limited screen space. Making the font any bigger, you would lose some data."

"This one has a large readout." She set down the first and lifted the third one. "I can see the numbers and words quite clear."

"Because it is only showing one thing," another creator piped in. "You'd have to flip through multiple screens to get all the data."

Quelly frowned at that. That was not a good option. Her technicians would need to be able to see everything at a glance when checking the blocks during transit. She was aware of it being a lot of data crammed into one console. Number two was clunky and the fourth was too narrow. The last one had the slimline look she wanted. She held it up.

"If we can get the readouts to look good on this one, we would have a winner." She saw signs of relief on their faces. "Which one of you made this one?"

"Actually," Doctor Mathis answered. "This one was a collaboration. As you can see, the others had things missing or not configured the way we wanted. This one we put all our heads together."

"It still needs works," Quelly admonished.

The creator at the end of the table leaned over with

both hands laid flat. His eyes appeared to twinkle with purpose as he responded.

"That's an easy fix. The body and components are sound. Finagling with the display features is minimal effort. We should have that figured out in the next month or so."

"Well then, I guess there's no real issue here."

"Lights!" Doctor Mathis yelled.

The overheads flickered on making the lighted table appeared a matted white. Quelly was about to walk off then stopped and turned back.

"What about the electrodes?"

She saw the first creator take hold of the chosen device and turned it over. With the touch of a finger, dozens of tiny tendrils slithered out, hitting the floor. Their tips glowed, pulsating red light.

"What the?" Quelly squealed in delight as she reached down and picked up a few in one swoop. "How? When?"

"One of the Interfacers let us do a bio scan. We modeled their technology and adapted it to our own. Pretty neat, huh?" Doctor Mathis said with a wink.

"Amazing." Quelly realized they were all getting a little too excited. She cleared her throat and raised her head higher. "Yes, well. Let's get this started then."

Doctor Mathis and her team also changed their demeanor to professional. "Absolutely. We will report to you as soon as it is completed."

"I look forward to it."

Quelly walked out of the lab. The moment she got into the empty corridor, she did a little jig while silently screaming. Then she remembered there were cameras everywhere. With a sheepish grin, she straightened her lab coat and continued to walk down the hall in dignity. In her head, she was still rejoicing.

Earth's Military Coalition leaders assembled at the cannon facility where scientists from all around the world were developing new weapons. Monzetti and his horde oversaw most of it, much to the chagrin of the leaders. The Interfacers had begun testing and everything appeared to be green. There were six large holoscreens hovering along the walls inside the massive lab, each showing a three sixty schematic of a weapon.

Two rifles, two smaller scale cannons, and two new energy sources with the capabilities equal to an H-bomb. The modifications were extensive. The military leaders approved. The double doors swung open and four lab technicians carted a roller table covered with black tarp in to the center of the room. They whipped off the cover to reveal the two rifles.

At nearly five feet in length, their girth was almost a foot wide. Multiple barrels that carried different ammunition were their defining features. Sleek and black, they were masterful pieces of work.

"Christ, those things are massive!" A General yelled.

"I don't know a soldier who could carry something like that and not be a target," another said. "How much do they weigh?

One of the inventors came into the room and stood by the cart. His face beamed with Pride.

"These are my beloved beasts. The first is modeled after the light weight model of the Gatling gun, its weigh just under nineteen kilos. It can fire off multiple rounds via the separate chambers you see here. The rotation ring has been modified to reduced rounds per minute to one hundred and a charging cartridge has been added."

"Christ almighty," another military leader whispered.

The designer stepped to the other side and splayed his arms open over the other one. It resembled a rifle right out of a science fiction movie.

"This one is also capable of multiple types of ammunition. Its for more close encounters but does have a sniper function if needed." He grabbed the weapon off the cart and slung the strap across his body. "Quite hefty. Our modified troops should be able to handle it with no problems. It's about ten kilos."

Monzetti's eyes appeared to gleam with something unholy. That frightened Darnizva.

"On screen," the designer said to the technician operating the main console.

The third one in showing one of the two smaller scale cannon images blinked out and a video feed took its place. An empty desolate field was enclosed in an energy barrier. Off in the distance was a large mobile unit like a tank. The camera zoomed in it to reveal it was three times the size of one.

"Our new ground to air cannons. Please, observe."

A piece of what looked like it came from a Relliant ship was position a kilometer away from the cannon and the soldiers placing it scrambled off. It was at least ten feet and equally as dense. The mouth of the weapon's middle cannon glowed to a hot blue intensity then fired a round. The target was struck and a gaping hole was left, the inner circumference dripping with molten material.

"That is just one of them. Imagine if all three on the other one were to be fired."

Not one person in that room couldn't imagine it. The destructive power was more than they could have wished for. A silent realization filled the room but no one spoke it.

"And those things?" President Lynmore pointed to the last two holoscreens that showed even bigger weapons. "Don't tell me those are also ground to air."

"More like, long range. Think Railgun. A round can reach the atmosphere but not space."

"Is there a demo for that too?" A world leader asked with disgust.

Generals Takayama and Perrara, exchanged looks that they were perplexed by the hostility. Humans were going up against an advance alien race. They needed all the fire power they could muster, in their opinion.

"Absolutely." The designer waved a hand at the technician. "Roll that beautiful footage."

The fourth screen changed to a similar field and zoomed in on the monstrosity that was indeed long. It was almost the size of a house, its nose protruding a good city block in length.

"These energy sources," one of the military leaders said. "Where did they come from?"

"Oh," the designer piped up. "As you recall, the main cannons were not getting sufficient output. Monzetti suggested a new way of harnessing the core's potential. These are the results."

Darnizva suddenly felt ill. He glanced over at Monzetti and went pale. The alien's head was raised far back and his eyes were lowered, staring at the weapons on the cart. His eyes were glowing bright purple, with elation.

Something is off.

He left the weapons demonstration in a hurry, ignoring President Lynmore calling out to him. He got to his transport and lifted off. From below he saw Monzetti come out of the compound and stare up at him.

"Fuck!"

He frowned at hearing himself evoke the human word that conveyed his mood. Earth really had gotten to him. Selecting the saved destinations menu, he tapped on the Shadow Organization's desert locale. In his mind, he knew he needed to have a talk with Celestial Mother and the other alien trainers.

Things were starting to go off the rails before the real fighting began.

As his transport approached the hangar on the opposite side of the canyon, soldiers guided him in. The moment he landed, he jumped out of the cockpit and went straight towards the lift. On the way up, he leveled his breathing. When it opened to the lounge area, he was taken aback by all four aliens turning to stare at him.

"We were expecting you, young Captain," Celestial Mother said sweetly.

"Why?" He moved hesitantly into the room and sat in an empty seat adjacent to the Chombrazens. "I didn't know I was coming myself until recently."

"Oh? Wasn't today when the humans rolled out their marking achievements in weapons technology? How was it?"

Darnizva's hands clenched.

Celestial Mother appeared before him and she clasped his hands in her own. He looked up and flinched at the excitement in her stare.

"It was," he struggled with the word.

"Terrifying, wasn't it?" She let him go and stood tall. "It will be their demise."

"Not if we take it from them," Darnizva blurted out.

All four stared at him incredulous.

"And how we would do such a thing?" Celestial Mother asked.

"I don't know!" Darnizva snapped. "I just feel like," he breathed out through his nose. "They aren't ready.

"I will agree with you on that. But in the end," she smiled. "They must decide their own fate. Unless, they want to be conquered."

Darnizva let his head fall into his hands as he leaned over in defeat. Celestial Mother charged back at him and grabbing him by the hair, lifted his head.

Their eyes met. Hers full of rage, his submissive.

"You don't get to wallow in pity, Darnizva," she seethed. "Get off this planet."

She let him go, knocking his head back as she did. Darnizva looked up at the ceiling and for the first time, contemplated running; again.

SAFETY FIRST

Every open field around the world now resembled a mass grave site for giants as the containment molds were completed. A lottery was put in place to minimize a flood of people trying to get off the planet. Each empty block could hold one hundred people layered in rows of ten by ten in the unmeltable ice.

The Prime Minister of Russia personally oversaw every filling procedure to ensure his countrymen and women were safely encased. Once the block was done, a crane with a large suction cup came and lifted it out of the ground. They were then loaded onto an industrial transport that could accommodate four of the blocks. Another group of civilians waited behind the barrier for their turn.

He could see some of the children were frightened, their parents not knowing what to say to comfort them. A tanker pulled up to an empty block and opened the valve. Silver water gushed out creating the bottom layer. The hardening solution came after that. It took nearly an hour for the set up. He walked over the barrier.

"My comrades. Please rest assured, this is a safe process. There is no pain involved. When you wake, you will be on a different planet safe from harm. And when this war is over, we can all return home."

He knelt before a little boy pressed against his mother's thighs while clinging to a stuffed monkey. "You'll be fine. Your mother will be right by your side." He ruffled the boy's hair.

"We're ready for the first layer," the logistics manager called out.

The first ten people were let through the barrier and escorted to the empty block. They descended via a portable lift and medical technicians stood waiting. Ten rectangles were evenly spaced across the hardened ice. Next to each one was a digital readout and tubes splayed outward. The civilians laid in the rectangles and were immediately given a sedative.

Within five minutes, they were all asleep and the technicians went to work attaching the tubes. They checked the digital readouts to make sure vital signs were being recorded. When their heartbeats slowed to a crawl, the manager gave the tanker a thumbs up. All the operatives and medical technicians boarded the lift. Another layer of the silver ice water washed over the sleeping beauties, sealing them in, then more hardening solution to prepare for the next group.

Have mercy on us all, the Prime Minister thought to himself.

⌒

President Lynmore watched the freezing procedure on the vidscreen in her office. Standing next to her were Quelly and George. She had heard what the operation entailed and seeing it done was eye opening. She turned away from the screen after the third layer was done.

"It looks like everything is going smoothly."

"So far, so good," Quelly said.

"How long would it take to evacuate an entire planet, you think?"

"Years," George answered.

"Well, we don't have that kind of time."

"We would be cutting it close, but everyone who wants to leave will be off this planet before the real shit hits the fan," Quelly added.

Lynmore stopped and let one of her arms unfold then drop.

"Well, I'll be. You do have some brass ones, don't you?" Quelly blushed. "Hear that George? She's sassy." President Lynmore started laughing.

"Finally got tired of that prim and proper façade you kept up?" George asked.

"Something like that," Quelly muttered.

"Where's your partner in crime, George?" Lynmore asked.

"Who would that be?"

"Mrs. Thunder draws, Regis."

"Now who's being sassy?" George commented. "That's downright crude, and disrespectful."

"Like I care. She's done us no favors over the past few decades. If she had done her job, we wouldn't be in this mess."

Lynmore turned to head back to her desk and ran square into George. He looked down on her with disgust, his eyes glinting with an unnatural sheen. Frightened, she stepped back.

"And what would you have had her do, Madame President?" The secret service agent moved, ready to defend the President. George averted his gaze to the agent. "You pull your weapon and I will fucking eat you." George's eyes glowed blue and the agent backed away until he slammed into the wall. Sheer terror was on his face.

George turned his attention back to Lynmore.

"We may be in the throes of tossing away diplomacy

and kindness, but a bit of decorum and respect is still required."

"Of course," President Lynmore stuttered.

George went and sat on the loveseat. He let out a long sigh and stretched his body until his head fell back. He closed his eyes.

"Don't even think about trying to get rid of me," he said.

"Never crossed my mind." President Lynmore sat at her desk and eyed Quelly standing awkwardly. "Have a seat, Professor. This is going to be a long haul." When Quelly's stare went to George, Lynmore let out a small laugh. "Don't worry about us. We tend to have a good row every now and again."

"Sure. Okay."

Quelly sat in one of the straight back chairs.

Lynmore stared at George. His eyes opened, and without turning his head looked over at her. Quelly knew that look. She had seen it from many of the Shadowmen assassins. Caution.

As if nothing happened, Lynmore continued about the evacuation.

"I see we have completed small towns. Is that our first target?"

"Those were dry runs," George replied. "We are going to do an official push in the major cities. That gives them a year to decide if they want to go or not."

"Dry runs?" Quelly asked. They both looked over at her. "You didn't trust my invention even after it was tested?"

"We are doing something unprecedented. Of course we wouldn't trust it."

"But all those people! If something did go wrong."

She stopped as their expressions went slack.

"Then there's be minimal damage to the population."

Lynmore answered nonchalant.

"We can cover up a few thousand across the country," George added.

"Is this what the other world leaders are implementing?" Quelly asked angrily.

"What do you think?" President Lynmore replied hotly.

Quelly clenched her fists tight as she bit one side of her lower lip. She didn't like this at all. This isn't how she imagined it.

⸺

Darkness enveloped the inside of the lift as it ascended. Flashes of light streaked along the outside, lighting up Terence's face when they occurred. He glowered at the top of the doors with his head slightly down. Hands clasped behind his back, he stood at ease and waited to reach his destination. The lift finally stopped and opened to the main hub of Metropolis.

Every worker on the floor was hustling to prepare the city for descent. He had sent the notice to his second in command, confident the man would only relay it as needed. The view ports took up three quarter the height of the level and was broken up into four spanning the front half. He could see every territory above land. The farming community was on the far left, the Southern Lands on the opposite side far right. Oretega City was shown in the middle left. The fourth, Neo City, usually displayed on the middle right was in the waters below. That screen was dark.

"How are we on time?" He asked.

His second in command came out from one of the meeting rooms.

"Preparations will be complete in ten minutes." The man glared at him. "Your timing is impeccable as ever."

Terence smirked and went over to the console raised out of the floor in front of the viewports. The inhabitants of Metropolis went about their everyday lives unaware that they were about to be saved. A communication came through on the middle left viewport, obstructing the scene. He frowned at the multiple sender details.

"You should probably take it before we are cut off," his second suggested.

Using the console, he took control of the screens and tapped the open channel.

Four separate feeds popped up. Hana was the first followed by President Lynmore then General Takayama. They all seemed furious. On the fourth was the facilities chairman calm and collected.

"Why have you contacted me together this way?"

"What do you think you're doing?" President Lynmore yelled.

"This is not how to handle this," General Takayama shouted.

"What about all the people in the territories," Hana cried out.

"I hope you know what you're doing," the facility chairman said vehemently.

Terence didn't like being gang up on. His eyes glowed a hostile purple. They all appeared to rear back in fear.

"I will not tolerate your tone," he said through gritted teeth. "You will respect my authority, or I will disconnect this feed."

"No one is usurping your authority," the chairman said.

"The hell we aren't!" President Lynmore stated. "Every able bodied person on this planet is a potential soldier. What you're doing is a crime against humanity!"

Terence burst out laughing. He laughed so hard his torso tightened painfully and tears squeezed out the corners of his eyes. The four on screen looked uncomfortable. He finally regained his composure and glared up at them.

"You and humanity can go fuck themselves. I answer to no one."

"Did you ask them?" Hana asked. His face expressed pain. Terence tsked. "Did you?"

"They are my responsibility. I determine what is best for them."

"Don't do this, Terence," the General cautioned. "You will regret it, I promise."

"Then that is the price I will pay. I will not let my charges be used as lambs to the slaughter for a planet of degenerates." Terence smiled.

"We will hunt you down and make you comply," President Lynmore said.

"Goodluck with that. See you on the other side." He grinned. "If you survive."

He disconnected the feeds one by one, watching them try to continue the conversation by raising their hands towards the screen. As he went to the chairman, the man gave him a look that made him halt over the icon.

"Once the sequence is complete, I will establish a passageway for emergency only."

The chairman merely nodded and sat back in his seat. Terence returned the gesture and hit the icon to disconnect the feed.

"Initiate descension!" He shouted.

The main hub workers scrambled to their stations. His second came to stand next to him.

"You can be angry with me all you want," he said. "I figure they needed to know why they wouldn't be able to contact you all of a sudden."

Terence glanced over at him in disgust.

Off the coast in the distant horizon of the ocean, the mega city shimmered. A clear barrier enclosed the land in multiple layers, forming an island, and the entire thing moved out farther into the deep waters. The separation made the rest of the coast rock with small earthquakes. When it reached a certain distance, it stopped and began to slowly sink, causing huge ripples that hit the coast as giant waves.

Inside, Terence's attention was glued to the viewport screens as the main power shut down and the emergency lights kicked on. The screens went dark as the water levels reached depth, sunlight now blocked. The audio had been muted but he could see the inhabitants screaming as they ran around in confusion from the shaking and darkness.

Forgive me, he whispered silently to the people.

In his personal chamber, Darnizva watched multiple holoscreens with feeds from around the world. Wearing only his two-toned body suit, the top white and the bottom black, he felt more relaxed. Until now. He stood rooted in anguish watching the first round of evacuations occur. It was too soon to start and he concluded it was a test. Guinea pigs. That was one thing he despised about humans. Their capacity to harm each other with no sense of shame. All around the globe, he saw small communities being fed half truths and led to their possible deaths.

He was sure the scientist who created the ice had all the good intentions they could muster. They miscalculated one thing; the grand scale of it. A few hundred bodies was doable. An entire planet population? Even with other races he had encountered, this was nearly impossible. There would be casualties, and many left behind from access being cut off during the fight.

Invasion was worse.

His door slid open and Nellan came in. The young soldier was still in his battle suit with the cloak open and not secured at the waist. He stood by Darnizva and also watched it all unfold.

"To think they would do such a thing," he said softly.

"Are you surprised?" Darnizva turned to him, brows raised.

The Interfacer frowned.

"Not really. I figured, after all this time, they would have learned."

Another feed appeared and Monzetti's face filled the screen.

"That is beautiful naivete," he said.

Nellan ducked, looking around while Darnizva stayed still, letting his gaze scan the room.

"How did you manage to hear our conversation?"

Monzetti smiled and cocked his head.

"We listen to everything."

Dranizva's skin felt like tiny creatures were crawling around. He didn't like having the organic being in such close proximity.

"You are paying attention to the wrong thing."

"What do you mean?"

One of the feeds moved to the front and enlarged. Nellan's eyes went wide. Dranizva cursed inwardly. Monzetti had control of something in his ship.

"Don't fret, Captain. I will release it momentarily. First, observe."

Darnizva focused on the feed of Metropolis separating from the mainland and descending into the deep depths of the ocean, causing havoc in its wake.

"Goddamn it!" Darnizva yelled.

Monzetti gave him a quizzical stare.

"What a very human reaction."

Letting his arms drop to his sides in defeat, Darnizva

hung his head. Terence was an angry, misguided hybrid who had seen and experienced too much. That Cresnia influenced him to adopt Organic technology was disheartening.

"My brother is not usually one to think too independently. I am sure he regrets giving it to the half human." Cresnia shrugged after that. Darnizva was about to say something. "Theirs is nothing you can do now."

Nellan crossed his arms, while continuing to watch the feeds.

"At least they would be safer than most."

"Until a Relliant ship fires into that part of the ocean," Darnizva chided.

Monzetti let out a loud guffaw. Realizing it was only amusing to him, he cleared his throat and addressed Darnizva.

"Stop wallowing in pity, Captain. You're too young for that."

Monzetti's feed disappeared. The others rearranged themselves back the way Darnizva had them. He felt drained. And disappointed in humanity.

TREASON

Seeing the way things were going on Earth so far, Hagen decided it was time to set his own agenda into motion. He had been briefed by Bree and Craig regarding Commander Fravral from the Command Fleet and wasn't too happy with the news. The fact that the Commander was being ambiguous about whose side he was on disturbed him. There was also the issue of the new Cyboks.

Who in their right mind would order such a thing?

First on the docket was a meeting with General Tartha. The communication feed had been established and would connect automatically when the time came. Hagen sat at his desk in the training facility's office in full combat gear and the cloak bearing the Command Fleet insignia. The vidscreen displayed its manufacturer's logo that spun intermittently counterclockwise.

Without warning, the screen lit up and General Tartha's face filled it. Hagen immediately sat straight and salute. General Tartha's eyes narrowed.

"Were you not expecting me, Commander?"

"Of course, General. I was waiting for the correct time." Hagen saw the connection was three minutes early. "My apologies."

"How are the forces coming along?"

"Training is still ongoing." He paused.

"We should be at full strength when ready."

"Is it because that planet has made our warriors weak?" Tartha spat. "They should never have to bring themselves up to par. We are always ready for war."

"That may be the case," Hagen replied hesitantly. "In order to blend in, we had to forgo our regimen and act human."

General Tartha's expression turned sinister.

"The Command Fleet is not in range. Why is that?"

Hagen made sure not to show any hints of his plans.

"I don't believe it is needed for something trivial as this war. Are you considering wiping out this race?"

"Not at all. I prefer not to get my hands covered in human filth. It can occupied and stripped of resources without me."

Hagen forced himself to keep calm. A shallow exhale escaped through his nose and General Tartha seemed to sense his unease.

"Stripping it of resources would not benefit us if we occupy this planet," Hagen managed to say. "We would be comingling with humans."

"Whatever you're thinking, it should be dismissed," General Tartha interrupted him. "I want the Command Fleet on hand. Do you understand me, Commander?"

"As you command, General."

Right when he saluted, the connection was severed. Hagen sagged back in the seat and letting his head flop backwards, let out a loud sigh. He stayed like that for a while then sat up. The cloak was whipped off and tossed cross the room onto the sofa. His battle gear was removed until he wore only the black body suit. Movement near the door made him turn towards it. Bree and Craig stood in the doorway with looks of trepidation.

"Is it okay to come in?" Craig asked, looking around the room. "Or are you going to throw more things?"

"How long have you been there?" Hagen demanded, shouting.

Bree blinked, leaning back.

"Since the video meeting with the General."

Hagen seethed, his eyes glowing slightly. He slammed a fist on the desk. After a moment, he raised his head and stared at them.

"Get in here! We have to figure this out."

They walked in and sat in the chairs across from him. Bree reached over and placed a hand over his fist. Startled, Hagen wrenched it away, unfolding his fingers. Craig let out a laugh.

"You gave yourself away in that last interaction with the General."

"What do you mean?" Hagen shook his hand to get the feeling back in his fingers.

"Even I saw the wheels turning in your head," Craig replied. "He's always been paranoid about his reign. You came off leaving him suspicious. Not good."

Bree got up, went to the bar and came back with a bottle of Tequila and three glasses. He poured some in each then handed them out.

"I think we all need this first."

"Brilliant," Craig exclaimed. He raised his glass. "To treason!" Both Hagen and Bree gave him a nasty look. "Okay. To a successful coup."

They finally raised theirs along with him and clinked them together.

"This shit is going to go south," Hagen muttered.

The trip to the Command Fleet took three months each way. Hagen didn't want to be away from his ground forces that long but it was necessary. He needed to speak to Commander Fravral directly. Bree and Craig were ordered to stay behind. He felt a twinge of shame knowing even the General saw his forces as inadequate. They had to keep up the training regiments. In their steed, four capable soldiers from his upper echelon accompanied him. They were sympathizers yet still loyal to the Relliance.

On approach to the main ship, he took an intake of breath. His ship. Now sitting in space with some jackass he had not sanctioned for promotion. Only the General was above him to do that. He wondered if he could reclaim it before the fighting started. His title had not been stripped, he was merely on a different mission planetside. The main ship's guidance system locked on to his transport and it coasted into the open hangar.

Safely docked, the pilot opened the transport's hatch for Hagen and his entourage to exit. At the bottom of the ramp stood Commander Fravral along with two of the deadly Cyboks and six soldiers. The smile on his face was one of being pleased with himself.

"What is the meaning of this?"

Hagen asked, gesturing towards to greeting party.

"I was prepared in case you needed to be contained for treason."

The other soldiers working the docks stopped what they were doing and gaped at Commander Fravral. Everything went still.

"I feel you have misunderstood something very important, Commander."

"And what is that?"

Hagen was on him in a flash, one hand wrapped around his neck and slamming him down into the floor. The Cyboks turned to move. His four soldiers blocked their way to the commander. Hagen's gaze seared into his eyes, his face contorted in rage.

"I am your superior! This is my Command Fleet. You are only here to oversee it in my absence."

The tension in the air thickened.

"Do you understand now?"

Commander Fravral managed to blink as an acknowledgement.

"Yes, Commander. I apologize for my arrogance."

Hagen released his grip and stood over him.

"Get up. We have much to discuss." He turned and came within inches of the two Cyboks. "Call them off."

Commander Fravral gave them a hand signal Hagen had not seen before and the Cyboks retreated. Knowing there were two more lurking on the ship, Hagen took a good look at them. He began to walk towards the doors that led into the main corridor. His soldiers followed with Commander Fravral and his group in tow. Commander Fravral moved up to walk side by side with Hagen.

"General Tartha has now decided to occupy the planet. He also wants to strip it of its resources."

"That makes no sense. It would also put us in a bind living on the surface," Fravral replied.

"Correct. I am not sure who is advising him of this situation."

"No one is advising him!" Commander Fravral snapped. "That is the problem. He believes his ideas are sound without asking for guidance."

"You know this yet scoff at my plans to remedy it?"

"But, your plan is not a remedy. It pits us against each other."

"Not if the Command Fleet does not engage."

Commander Fravral stopped. Hagen did the same.

"You don't want the Command Fleet involved? General Tartha has officially requested we wait on standby for his orders."

"I understand that. The fact remains, the Command Fleet is a separate faction of the Relliance. We do not take orders unless it suits our needs."

Hagen gave him a side glance.

"Or, have you forgotten that?"

"Thank you for the reminder," Fravral said with clenched fists.

They resumed walking and reached the main bridge. The crew saluted and continued with their business.

"One ship will be sent to show good faith. That ship will be used for extraction once this is over. It is to not engage in any fighting unless fired upon."

"Who would fire upon it if you have already relayed the plan and it's merely sitting there?" Commander Fravral frowned. Hagen could see he had already figured out the answer. "General Tartha wouldn't be that reckless. The Command Fleet can annihilate his own."

"As you have said, he is not being guided properly."

"The extraction procedure?"

Hagen took a breath and exhaled slowly. He was giddy from being on his ship and needed to keep his composure. This was no time for nostalgia.

"If remote transport fails or is interrupted, you can send ships down to retrieve as many as you can."

"And you?"

"I will take command of the ship and get a safe distance from Earth."

"I am not bringing it back?"

"You will not be on it. If things go wrong, I need you to defend the Command Fleet."

"You are going to trust me, after today?" Fravral asked, shocked.

Hagen turned to him and smiled.

"I like your conviction. You would do well with your own ship."

They both stared out at the vast space through the viewport. Hagen missed journeying the galaxy. He did not miss home. Not many of them did due to their home world being overcrowded and lacking resources because of it. He had a nagging feeling that Earth may become his new home.

⌐⌐

Lines of cargo trucks went in and out of the makeshift base on the outskirts of an abandoned town. Soldiers were stationed around the entire perimeter. The guards kept watch while fully armed and the dock personnel directed traffic, checking identification cards. Chad Hoskins sat in a vehicle parked on the ridge a few kilometers out from it. Due to the treatments that altered his DNA, he didn't look a day over forty.

From his vantage point he could look through his surveillance goggles and zoom in on the areas he wanted.

In the vehicle with him were two guerilla soldiers and a new terror. This one was older than the last and happy to kill for him when required. He felt kind of bad for leaving his forces in the jungle along with the terror's body decades ago. He had gotten reports from the soldiers who fled and met him at the rendezvous point about his death.

Fucking Shadow pricks!

He zoomed in on a spot near the warehouse where a crate was being unloaded. The shiny new rifles were pulled out one by one and attached to a standing gun rack designed special for them. It was no secret how much he despised the new technology based off the aliens. His father didn't do his job properly. What should have happened was a demand to get those beings off their planet and there would be no need for all this.

We'll remedy that starting with this shipment.

He got out of the vehicle and went around to the back. "Alright men, get the cavalry. We're going in to have a little fun and do some damage."

"Yes sir!"

The first soldier tapped the commlink in his ear.

"We are a go. Get into position."

Chad could see his group of fifty soldiers appear out of their hiding places from all sides of the base. He turned to his new terror bodyguard.

"You got my six."

"As you wish. I am ready."

Chad looked up at the partly cloudy sky and grinned. Hitting the base in broad daylight felt kind of dirty.

"They won't know what hit them." He waved a hand towards the base. "Let's do it!"

The first wave of Hoskins' soldiers jumped down from the hillside along the base and fired on the guards at the checkpoint. By the time the other guards realized they were under attack, the second and third wave came crashing through the base. A small group got to the warehouse and ambushed the workers inside.

"Find the cartridges!" The leader of the group ordered.

They shot every soldier in sight and went to task cracking open crates until the ones with the prize was found. One of the men tossed the others some non metal hammers. They began destroying the cartridges by cracking open the casing then mutilating the inside components. Since they weren't attached to a unit the energy source was inert.

The loud click of a pump action rifle made them halt. Out from a back room in the corner was a soldier holding one of the modified light weight mini guns. He held it below waist level with two hands and the top barrels glowed.

"Oh shit!" Was all the leader could get out.

The soldier fired the weapon.

Huge holes appeared along the walls along with blood splatter that sizzled as it hit the ground. The enemy had been pulverized. He spotted four of Hoskins men fleeing towards the main gates. He didn't dare fire the gun for fear of killing his own people in the vicinity. Looking down at the gun, he set it on the ground and stepped away from it.

George was in his office for the first time in three months getting some much needed quiet time away from Lynmore when an aide knocked on his door.

"Excuse me, sir. I know you don't want to be bothered, but this is urgent."

He sighed heavily and swinging his legs off his desk sat straight in his chair.

"Bring it in."

The aide opened the door and stepped inside.

"Sir, the gun shipment at Delta base was hit this afternoon."

George's eyes went wide and he leaned forward.

"Say what now? When?"

"Thirty minutes ago. Fighting is still live."

He shot up from his chair and walked around his desk to stand before the aide.

"Get my transport ready. I'm heading out." He grabbed his jacket from the rack by the door and pulled it on.

"Yes sir." The aide turned and left with George not far behind him.

Who the hell would be that bold?

Hoskins Jr. cursed as he and his soldiers were forced to retreat in defense mode when the tables suddenly turned. There were two warehouses on either side of the base and his group had hit them both at the same time. He was merrily destroying cartridges on the west side when he heard the sound of rapid booms like a bunch of rocket launchers firing in succession. Then chaos broke out. A fresh unit of soldiers flooded the warehouse and he had to let the terror protect him as they forced their way towards the exit.

Once out in the open he saw a few of his men coming around the corner from the East side. They were covered in debris and blood and their eyes had a wild abandon. Whatever they had seen scared them shitless. Hoskins took a peek behind them while heading through the checkpoint and saw the damage done to the warehouse and surrounding area.

"Holy Jesus!"

That's when he realized the few soldiers running away were all that was left of the unit. He frowned in anger at having lost so many. The plan called for a few wounded, not casualties. Not like this. He had witnessed his share of gruesome combat deaths. What was in that warehouse defied reason.

His forces on the ridge and hillside returned cover fire as they got out of range of the base and back to their rendezvous points. Hoskins noticed the base soldiers didn't bring out another of those new guns to mow them down. He wondered why. Scrambling to the vehicle, he finally took a deep breath and slumped into the back passenger seat. The terror got in beside him and his two personal guerilla fighters hopped in front, weapons still in hand.

The driver hit the start button and drove backwards a ways, keeping his eyes forward as a barrage of gunfire came at them. His companion leaned out the passenger window and fired back. When they were far enough from the base and in the clear, the driver whipped the car around and sped off. Hoskins had to hold on to the handle bar above his window.

He looked back and let himself smile a little. The entire shipment may not have been destroyed but his men had put a significant dent in their supply. He could only imagine how much it cost to manufacture those things. There were at least a hundred count in each crate and they had gone through ten of them on his side. He hoped the dead soldiers got at least that many before their cruel deaths.

George arrived two hours after the fighting had ended and immediately went to assess the damage. He had seen some of the carnage from above as his transport approached the base. From what he could see, it looked like the East warehouse had been hit with giant loads of shrapnel. Huge sections were obliterated. There were soldiers down all over the place. The West warehouse appeared to be intact.

He stepped out of the transport a few yards from the checkpoint ready to see it all up close. The reinforcement team that followed him there switched to support and helped their fellow soldiers either to medical or back on their feet. Four guards accompanied him along with the two he had brought to the East warehouse. He stopped cold at what would have been the entrance. One of the other guards retched, covering his mouth and moved away to the side.

Holy mother of God, he said to himself.

In the far corner a soldier sat on one of the unopened crates. A few feet in front of him was one of the new guns. George knew right away the soldier was shell shocked. He carefully maneuvered around the carnage of enemy soldiers torn apart, their remains showing signs of the wounds being cauterized by intense heat. Standing in front of the soldier he let out a soft sigh and set a steady hand on the man's shoulder.

The soldier flinched then jumped up from the crate, backing up to reach for his hand gun stowed against his thigh.

"Easy soldier," George said calmly. "It's all over. Everything's alright."

The soldier raised his hands to cover his face and a high pitched squeak came out of him.

"No," he said, shaking his head. "It's not alright, sir. I can't. Those weapons. I can't use that thing."

"I understand, soldier. But, you have to realize one thing." The soldier shook his head and cried, angering George. He yanked the man's hands from his face and pulled him close by the front of shirt. "These weapons are for the enemy. What kind of weapons do you think they have? I guarantee, it will be much worse than this shit!"

The soldier's eyes went wide with fear then comprehension. George let him go, pushing him away. He walked over and picked up the gun. Against his massive frame, the gun seemed almost normal sized. Hefting it up a few times, he nodded in approval and set it back down.

"This one is yours now. Take good care of it."

Then he saw the torn up crates. He had come to this warehouse first since it had the most damage. Now he saw what the culprits were up to. Hundreds of cartridges lay destroyed all around him.

"Son of a bitch!" He turned to one of the base guards. "I need to know how many were hit in the West warehouse."

"Yes sir, I'm on it." He left to hear his commlink better as he contacted the warehouse.

George walked out of the warehouse and his group headed towards the communications room on the top deck. He climbed the stairs two at a time, not wanting to wait for the lift. A soldier saluted him at the door then hit the call button on the side panel. The door buzzed open and they were let through. Inside, the crew was hard at work going through footage.

"I want to see the visuals of the enemy," he said to the officer in charge.

"Got it right here. I was going to send it to you ahead of time but figured you ant to see it when you arrived instead."

"You would be correct."

He stood behind the officer as he queued up the footage with the attackers retreating. Something about the man ahead of the other twice his size made him stare a bit harder.

"Back up a second and freeze it." The officer did as instructed. "Now zoom in and enhanced the resolution." When it was done George leaned back, slackjawed.

You have got to be kidding?

He walked away from the screen, wiping his face in a downward motion. The others in the room followed him with anticipating stares as he slowly paced.

"Did anyone take pursuit?"

"No sir. We chased them as far as the ridge. There were more up there and on the hillside. We prioritized the base."

George merely nodded. In his mind, he waas struggling between sending out a search party or tapping an assassin to take out the former General.

"Is there an office I can use?" He asked.

"Absolutely." The officer turned to one of the guards. "Escort him to the admin space."

"Yes sir!"

The soldier saluted then turned to George.

"This way."

George followed him out and remained silent the whole way. Lynmore, hell the world leaders, were not going to like this even if it was only the United States shipment that was hit. He was sure Hoskins was planning to hit the others around the world.

You miserable bastard.

BLINDSIDED

All the Karysilan ships on Earth were preparing for lift off in the next few years. Each one would position themselves strategically around the world as a secondary defense. Captain Darnizva pulled up a trajectory chart covering the entire solar system. A few years was in a blink of an eye to his kind which meant they didn't have much time left.

His fleet was nowhere near enough to defend Earth. With Sspark's ship gone, he was one less battle cruiser. Then again, Sspark would not have engaged in the fight anyway. Darnizva snorted as he imagined the Lieutenant's response.

"Weapons check," he called out.

His artillery chief's voice came over the ship's commlink.

"Nearly sixty percent. If we keep up the steady rate of energy flow, we should be at full capacity by the time Relliants come crashing down."

"Good to hear." We're cutting it close. "I want them online preferably ahead of schedule."

"Incoming message, Captain," his communications officer announced.

"On screen."

His mother, Ammordia's face appeared and she seemed tense.

"Commander Ammordia," Darnizva greeted her.

Her face contorted in anguish at his use of her title. He knew she was about to give him unsettling news therefore he had no reason to address her informally.

"Darnizva," she began. He held up a hand to stop her. She relented and her shoulders sagged. "I, we, pleaded you case with the elders and your father, the General, one last time."

Darnizva felt his heart beat a little faster. He braced himself for the outcome.

"Despite your previous campaign successes, your last action has put us in a bind. Your fleet is only a spec of our forces as a whole and deemed an acceptable loss."

Some of his crew hug their heads while others stared up at her in shocked anger. She lowered her eyes, not wanting to see their faces.

"So, we are being abandoned," Darnizva whispered.

"I am sorry, my son. You know I tried everything."

"I don't know." He lifted his head and met her eyes. "Are we being recorded as deceased? Will there be a memorial for us?"

Ammordia became incensed. She leaned closer to the screen, her eyes glowing.

"Don't you dare! I am your mother and would never allow it! You finish this and get back to Karysilan where you belong!"

Darnizva kept himself calm even though inside he felt hurt and shame.

"That was the goal from the start. Goodbye," he paused, lowering his stare. "Mother."

"Darnizva!"

He gestured his officer to cut the feed. The screen went black.

"Captain?"

His second in command turned to him.

He suddenly felt drained of energy. Like he had been beaten nearly to death and no longer had the will to fight.

"Carry on with preparations. I will have a list of resources to fill the commons by the end of the year."

"Of course, Captain. I look forward to it." His second went back to his task. "You need to lie down and rest, Captain."

"Yes, that's a good idea."

Darnizva barely made it down the winding hallways to his chamber. He fell onto the cushions and closed his eyes. A heavy sleep engulfed him.

Awake after ten hours of sleep, Darnizva felt awful. His whole body ached from shifting into an awkward position during his slumber. His eyes were scratchy and dry, causing his vision to blur. He sat up and nausea hit him. Lying back down, he took a few deep breaths to make it go away. The conversation with his mother replayed in his mind.

With only his ships, plan B was going into effect. Instead of trying to go head to head with a full Relliant fleet, his ships would defend from space a good distance away. He was sure, General Tartha would try and stop them so he needed to get hem in position earlier than scheduled.

We've been abandoned.

Those words weighed heavy on him. This was his punishment alone, not his fleet. They didn't deserve such a fate. Finally calm, and feeling a little better, he got up and went to the viewport of his chamber. He could see beyond the vast forest to the cities and towns on the other side. All that lay before him would be decimated in a few years' time.

"I'm sorry."

He stripped off his body suit and tossed it into the sanitizer. The timer counted down to when it would be complete. While it did its task, he went into the cleansing compartment. It activated as soon as the doors slid shut and he felt the cleansing agents mist his whole body. It swirled around engulfing him a cloud of white, reaching every crevice. Sharp air blew into the compartment dispersing the cloud and leaving through the exhausts positioned on all sides.

Darnizva would have preferred a shower, having gotten used to them. He loved the feel of water drenching him. It was not the same as swimming. Completely dry and clean, he pushed the icon for release and stepped out the moment the doors opened. The sanitizer icon blinked off. He retrieved his body suit and put it back on. The fabric closed in to hug his frame.

The entrance intercom activated and he heard Sugil's voice.

"Excuse, Captain. May I come in?"

Darnizva frowned at the door then saw the privacy setting had been turned on. He didn't remember doing that. Then again, he was in a mind fog at the time. He went over and turned it off. The door slid open.

Sugil walked into the chamber and waited for Darnizva to say something.

"Sit down," Darnizva ordered.

"Sorry." He sat on a seat in the lounge area. "I was wondering how you were doing? It must have been a shock to hear that." He lowered his head. "We were all shocked, really."

"I'm fine. A bit angry, but still on track."

Sugil seemed to slump in relief.

"Then I have a proposal."

Darnizva raised a hand to stop him. The red head stared at him confused.

"Before that, I need to tell you the change in plans."

"Are we going to coordinate with the human forces?"

"Absolutely not."

Sugil stared at him. Darnizva walked back to the viewport. He had decided. The less the humans knew about his agenda, the better off they would be. First on his list; getting Monzetti and his crew off Earth.

⮾

A dagger lay against his neck as Darnizva entered the Monzetti ship's perimeter. The slender fingers holding it were unyielding and steady. From the height of where he felt a head close to his back, he concluded it to be Monzetti's pet assassin. From the top of the open hangar, one of his henchmen stood sentry glaring down at him. The two Interfacers' demeanor changed and Darnizva glanced back to give them a warning. They relaxed a bit but kept their eyes focused on the female assassin. The henchman let out a huff and went inside. Within moments, Monzetti came out.

"That's no way to greet our guests, sweetheart," he practically purred Tios. At Darnizva, he smiled. "Come. Join me. Let's have a drink." His eyes glowed playfully yet narrowed in disdain. "We can discuss why you came here."

The dagger left his neck and Tios stepped back until she was behind the Interfacers. She took an offensive stance.

"Proceed," she ordered.

The three Karysilans marched up the ramp and followed Monzetti into the dark interior. Darnizva felt the hair on his body stand on end as he got farther in.

He had never been on a ship quite like it. The whole thing seemed to be aware, sending tiny tendrils of thought floating into the air. Monzetti looked back at him knowingly.

"I would be careful how you react on my ship, Captain. She likes to take it upon herself to defend me if she senses hostility."

"I am not here to cause a fight," Darnizva said.

"Are you certain?"

Monzetti stopped at a door that slid open automatically. A parlor area straight out of an old movie sprawled out before them.

"Please, make yourselves comfortable." He gestured towards the seats.

At first glance, the scale of the furniture seemed off. When he sat down, he understood why and laughed inwardly. Both alien races were taller than most and the original tiny loveseats could never accommodate them. The seating and tables were twice the normal size. Darnizva indeed felt comfortable. Something about the vibe in the air made him look up to see Monzetti eyeing the Interfacers with such intrigue, it bordered on lust.

"They are not for you to touch," he stated bluntly.

Monzetti frowned then sat in a chair front and center before his guests.

"So," he held out a hand and Tios brought over a drink, placing it there. "What can I do for you, Captain?"

Tios moved quietly from one person to the next, handing out heavy whiskey glasses half full of liquor. When she was done, she perched herself on a seat close to Monzetti. Darnizva took a sip before speaking.

"I'm wondering why you're still on Earth. There is nothing more to be done. I feel you should leave."

Monzetti sipped his drink slowly and lowered it just as slow.

He set his glass down on the side table and leaned back in his seat.

"After all the time and effort we put in to assist this planet? We are going to watch the fruits of our labor and see how the humans fare." Monzetti's smile seemed off kilter.

"Or you are merely stalling, and like your brother, waiting for the spoils of war."

The tension was thick in the parlor. Monzetti reached over and closed his hand over the top of glass, his gaze never leaving Darnizva. He swiveled it around to uncover the mouth and took another swig.

"What makes you think I require such a thing?"

Darnizva thought about what he had seen so far. Monzetti had come without an army and his personal entourage were not a mish mash of body parts. Something about it nagged him. Monzetti seemed to recognize the look on his face and smirked.

"I don't," Darnizva replied. "I think you would do anything to help Cresnia."

The glass halted inches from Monzetti's lips. There was a pause as everyone turned their attention to him. He regained his demeanor and continued drinking. As he set the glass back down, his shifted in color, glowing a bright yellow. He didn't reply.

Both alien leaders sat locked in a silent contest of will. Darnizva didn't need him to answer. He already knew he was right. Monzetti would leave the planet, but not the solar system.

A small victory.

Stationed on the outskirts of the solar system, the Command Fleet posed no immediate threat. Its entire force was on standby until further notice. There was a sense of unease and mixed feelings about the upcoming battle. Command Fravral half smirked.

If that's what you want to call it.

He had observed the humans through random feeds over the decades and deemed them no match for the Relliance's might. The fifty year window was not an opportunity to become equal. It was a farce, like dangling a prize before their eyes with no intention of ever letting them have it. His fleet had conquered more advanced civilizations than that.

As a subordinate of Commander Gragor, he was inclined to obey his orders. That all depended on what the General wanted. He would not disobey him, rather get somewhere in the middle of compliance and rebellion. He also understood that Gragor's request was not stemmed solely on his affinity for mankind. It was his pride in the Command Fleet to not allow it to be used for trivial fights. A waste of resources and fire power.

While the main battle fleets were engaged full on in an unknown system nearly a century ago, the Command Fleet sat on the outskirts, waiting for any opportunity to leave. Their fire power was not needed at the time. Seeing an entire fleet crippled with damage flee the scene in a hasty unstable jump, Commander Gragor became curious and followed.

He remembered asking what they were going to do when they caught up to the Karysilans. Commander Gragor smiled and said simply, "Destroy them, of course." After that horrendous crash landing on Earth, a new strategy was made. Attacking their enemy on a planet that lacked advanced technology was not appealing.

He chose to stay on the ship and move the Command

Fleet farther out. As the acting Commander, he completed a mission. A short run of conquests in a nearby solar system. In truth, he was bored, waiting for Gragor to come back.

Commander Fravral sat in the main chair on the bridge deep in thought when a priority communication came through on the screen. The communications officer panicked, trying to figure out how to stop it. His console was lit up in every color.

"What's going on?"

"My controls have been taken over, sir."

Right as he leaned forward to get up, General Tartha's face filled the viewport screen. He stumbled down to his knees having no time to correct his motion and stand.

"Hmm? We're bowing now?"

"My apologies, General. I was caught off guard." Commander Fravral stood and saluted along with the rest of the crew on the bridge. "To what do we owe this privilege?"

General Tartha's eyes narrowed.

"I am wondering why the Command Fleet is not within striking distance of our new foes." He leaned back and Commander Fravral saw the General was on the bridge of his own ship. "Did Commander Gragor not brief you with my instructions?"

"Yes, he did. We are prepared to launch when the battle begins to assist if necessary."

"I deem it necessary," General Tartha sneered. "Move your ships."

"If I may."

Commander Fravral raised a finger. The General frowned.

"Would it not signal a renege on your promise if the humans saw our fleet arrive ahead of schedule?"

The General's expression got worse as he seemed to struggle with a thought. He was definitely going to break the deal since it had been delayed a few years.

"And you propose what?" The General's stare bore into him.

"That we wait until the humans are confident in their readiness. It only takes one short jump to reach Earth's space."

"I don't care about how prepared they are! You will move your fleet and stand ready to annihilate those pests in the way of our ongoing battle." Blue lines formed along the sides of his face and brow as his rage became visible. "Obey my order!"

Commander Fravral gave salute.

"Of course, General. As you command." He glanced up at the screen as it went back to a view of the solar system before them.

Thought he was going to blow a few blood vessels, he said to himself.

"What are your orders, Commander," one of the crewmen asked.

He sat back in his seat and crossed one leg over the other while letting his head rest. So many scenarios went through his head. Coming to a decision, he raised his head straight and stared out at the crew.

"We will move the ship close enough so that the General knows we are indeed within striking distance. But," he stood and walked to the edge of his landing. "The fleet will be hidden behind one of the planets."

"Hiding?" Another asked, frowning.

The Command Fleet hid from no one. Commander Fravral knew how they felt and didn't want to do it either. This served a deeper purpose.

"We want the General to be able to ping us at a shorter distance, giving him the appearance that we have complied. By hiding, we ensure Commander Gragor doesn't know."

There was a feeling of anxiety that filled the air. They would be disobeying the commanding officer of the fleet in exchange for the General's, yet not entirely. As if sensing their dilemma, he smiled.

"We will not engage as commanded by Gragor. This is merely a show." Relief replaced the anxiety and Commander Fravral let out a sigh. "We leave within the next few months."

"We're not jumping?" The navigator asked.

Commander Fravral had turned away to sit back down and stopped midway.

"The General didn't specify how we got there. We'll take out time."

"Of course, Commander." The navigator focused his attention back to his station.

Well, Commander Gragor. It looks like we're caught in the middle of a powerplay.

Back in his seat, he looked down at the display panel on the left arm rest. By the navigator's calculations, they would reach their destination in three years. Plenty of time to come up with a new plan before the chaos.

A LONE PATH

It had been a long time since Hana set foot in a facility. His anxiety revved up a notch as he was escorted through the all white maze that led to a meeting room. The glass doors sild open and he walked in, keeping his eyes focused ahead. Professor Bartley sat at the far end of the large conference table, his bare feet planted on the chair so that his chin rested on his knees. In one hand was a coffee mug he sipped from gingerly. One of the escorts ushered Hana to the second seat down from him.

"No need to be afraid, Hana. It's not like you haven't been here before."

Professor Bartley leaned over and set down his mug while Hana settled in the chair.

"It's still a facility." Hana's face darkened.

"But not the one you were raised in. I assure you, this facility was not run like that."

Professor Bartley's expression turned hateful.

"I would never have allowed it."

Hana was taken aback by his level of animosity. He knew that to be true and didn't equate Bartley with the other facility owners. He only wished they all had the same sentiment as him. Sensing the mood change, Hana pushed his hair behind his ears.

"I came here," he began.

"I know why you came, Hana."

"Then why won't you help?" Hana could hear the anger in his own voice.

"For the same reasons why any of us won't. Tell me, Hana. Do you wish to fight this war for the sake of humanity? Or do you merely want to survive?"

Hana sat back in his chair as if he had been struck. The questions took him off guard and he couldn't answer immediately. For the sake of humanity? His mind tumbled that thought around and came to a conclusion. No. That's not why. To only survive? Maybe. More than that, he wanted to prove something. As if reading his mind, Professor Bartley smiled.

"You want the human race to acknowledge that they need us more than we need them. That our alien DNA does not negate our designation as humans."

Hana felt weight lift from him. He leaned forward, feeling elation.

"Yes! That's why!" He clenched his hands into fists. "We were not asked to be born. But we are here in force and no longer willing to play victim."

"Then you know my answer." Professor Bartley dropped his legs down and he seemed to straddle the chair as he moved it closer to the table. He set his hands on the ledge. "It's not that I don't understand, Hana."

"We shouldn't have to be wiped out to be taught a lesson."

"I beg to differ. Humans need to see the brink of extinction. Only then will they come around and change."

"And what if you're wrong? What if it only makes things worse. Coming together as one race is a step in evolution. We see it in the alien races among us."

"And yet, war is looming and we are where?"

Professor Bartley took another sip from his mug. His eyes narrowed over the brim and seemed to gleam.

Hana felt himself deflate inwardly. There was no use sugar coating the reality of the situation. They were out of time. He looked into Professor Bartley's eyes, pleading.

"Not even to assist? You won't even," Hana said before choking back a cry. "So this meeting was a farce?" Hana became angry. "Just to waste my time for your enjoyment?"

The mug slammed down on the table, creating a pinging echo. Professor Bartley's eyes glowed silver and dark brown, leathery wings sprung from his back. They spanned out nearly two feet on both sides of him as he stood, staring down at Hana with rage. He leapt onto the table and bent over him.

"My time is never wasted," he spoke in a guttural tone. "My reasons are not yours."

"I'm sorry, I'm sorry," Hana whimpered as he slid down in his seat to get some distance between them. "I didn't…"

Time seemed to suddenly stop. When it resumed, Professor Bartley's expression softened. He caressed Hana's cheek then stood straight and stepped off the table. His wings retracted. Sitting back in his chair, he craned his neck.

"No, I'm sorry, Hana. I shouldn't have frightened you."

Hana cautiously sat upright, never taking his gaze from Bartley.

"What are you?" Hana asked in a whisper.

Professor Bartley grabbed his mug, looked inside and took a sip as he shrugged.

"I have no idea."

Hana slumped, dumbfounded.

With the knowledge of the aliens, he was sure they could steer Professor Bartley towards the answer. Then it dawned on him. The Professor didn't seem to care. And that was okay. It didn't matter. He saw himself as another human except with extra talent. Hana envied him.

◠

Something about the way the Relliant General's ship repositioned itself made Darnizva nervous. He checked the date which gave him no comfort. On the holoscreen in his chamber was a map of Earth with a glowing triangle where each of his downed ships sat idle. The energy cells had been replenished decades ago when his parents arrived. All that was left to do was lift off and take a stand in space. He wondered if General Tartha would dare to fire on them, signaling the start of war.

Only one way to find out.

Staying planet side was no longer an option. Getting hit while grounded would be catastrophic, stranding them for who knew how long. He was hunched over the console resting his folded arms on the ledge as he thought of the logistics. Only a third of the fight cruisers were necessary for combat. The main ships had the capability to hit targets from space. Darnizva hit the all-com that linked the ships.

"Deploy the fighters as previously instructed and prepare for launch. We will take formation around the planet."

A communication from the bridge blinked. He tapped the icon.

"Where are we staging the fighters, Captain?" His second asked.

"Move them five miles outside the ship's perimeter. That should be enough room for a buffer."

"As you command. Stand by for lift off." There was a pause. "Are you staying on the ship or should I ready your fighter?"

"I'm going to fight with the humans."

"Of course. You fighter should be in the green.

"Thank you." His tone was apologetic. He knew his second understood. "I'll be down in the hangar shortly."

Darnizva sent all the data he needed to his fighter's system and stood. His hair fell back in place, brushing against the top of his cloak. In full battle gear along with his usual uniform, he was ready for whatever the General had in store. He took one last look around his chamber then headed out.

The maintenance crew was busy doing last minute system checks on each fighter when he arrived. They stopped for a split second to acknowledge him then resumed their tasks. He approached his ship and the workers moved away.

"Your fighter is fully powered and ready for combat, Captain."

"Thank you. Stay safe up there," he said.

"Oh, many of us will be in the new maintenance hub ship on the surface. I will be one of the technicians staying."

Darnizva halted halfway into the cockpit, one leg over the other side. He looked down at the group of workers staring at him proudly. His second in command had done something else without his approval. The time now being too late to denounce it, he let out a sigh and settled into the cockpit. As the hatch closed, the seat moved back to lock into the main control hub. Lights lit up the darkness and the console displayed read outs.

From his viewscreen he watched the first wave take off and head to the staging area. His group was the last to leave with the maintenance crew positioned in the center. When they landed at the area still deep in the forest, he hit the communication icon.

"We will talk later, second in command."

"About what, Captain?"

He's actually going to dodge it.

"You will know when this is over."

"If you say so, Captain."

"Launch the ship."

He disconnected the link.

Thirty minutes later, the ship's engines fired and it raised further from its hovering position. Surrounding trees bent away, some snapping in half. The steady hum turned to a loud boom. Birds flew off into the horizon, scared by the sounds. It was above the forest, rotating so that the bridge faced towards the sky when his console flashed with an emergency communication. He knew from the signature that it was President Lynmore. With reluctance, he connected the feed.

"What is going on, Captain? Why is you ship, scratch that, all of your ships, taking off?"

"President Lynmore, how are you?"

"Cut the shit!" Her voice nearly screeched. "You have a lot of nerve to cut and run with the deadline close." She paused, sneering. "But, then again, that's what you did before and got us involved in your mess."

Darnizva stared at the console, his eyes glowing red with rage.

"Be very careful what you say to me next, Madame President."

"Are you…" She was cut off by another on the feed

"That was uncalled for and foolish!" A man's voice interrupted.

He realized it was a multiple call with the world leaders who had one of his ships in their country. He heard Lynmore sputter. That didn't satiate his temper. To throw that in his face at this junction, he concluded she must be feeling mighty confident.

"I am curious, as are the others, as to why you are

leaving, Captain," the man continued.

"We are not leaving. Only the surface. My ships would better serve this battle in space in a defensive formation. There will be fighters left for ground to air combat."

"Oh. Well, that makes sense then."

"You could have told us your plans, Captain," another leader said. "Unlike President Lynmore, we would have at the very least heard you out."

"And not toss around baseless accusations," the first leader added.

"This is a bold decision. It weighed heavily on me. There's no guarantee that General Tartha won't try to stop us from positioning ourselves as such."

"And that's why you should have consulted with us first," Lynmore snapped.

If she were in front of him at that moment he was sure his hands would have wrapped around her neck to throttle her.

"We will trust your judgement. Good luck, Captain. If the battle starts, then so be it."

The feed was disconnected from their end and Darnizva sat in silence. A second communication came through. He exhaled slowly and connected.

"Pay no mind to Lynmore," he heard Regis say. "We are activating one of the cannons closest to the Relliance mother ship. We have your back."

All the rage deflated inside him and he slumped in his seat.

"You have my gratitude."

"We just ask that you give us a wide enough window."

"Understood."

The connection died and he stood straight, readjusting his hands on the controls. He wasn't getting out of his fighter until he was sure his ships were safely in place.

General Tartha glanced over at the viewscreen to his left as he sat in the command chair contemplating strategies. At first, he thought maybe he was seeing things, then the Karysilan ship came into full view. There were others rising from the planet's atmosphere. He leaned forward, shocked at the scene.

"Oh, no you don't!" He turned to his weapons technician. "Ready the bays. I want that fleet shot down."

"Which one do you want targeted first?"

The technician asked tentively.

He scanned the ships one by one and found Darnizva's with his insignia larger than the others displayed on the front hull.

"That one." He used the armrest controls to zoom in on it and pointed. "Destroy it."

"As you command."

Regis saw the Relliance ship's weapons bay open and light up like an angry fire. She watched the counter for the cannon's charging percentage. Sixty percent. Almost there.

Darnizva watched the incident unfold from his fighter's console and sucked air in through his gritted teeth. His worst case scenario was coming to a head. The other ships were moving into formation as planned. A barrage of cannon fire left the Relliant ship.

Regis saw the cannon's counter read eighty five percent. Good enough. She only hoped it would make it in time before the Darnizva's was struck.

"Prepare to fire," she ordered the cannon operator.

On the outskirts of the moon, Monzetti sat back in the command chair on his ship's bridge and narrowed his eyes at General Tartha's action. From the Earth's surface he recognized the heat signature of the cannon. He tapped his console and zoomed in on it. It was not at one hundred percent.

"Hector!"

"Yeah, boss?"

"Target Tartha's little display. Protect the other ships if necessary."

"Got it, boss."

Monzetti crossed one leg over the other and leaned to the side, two fingers on his right temple. A second volley left General Tartha's ship.

"You don't get to play just yet," he chided the General.

General Tartha gaped in anger as he saw a shot fired from the other side of the moon strike the first volley headed towards Darnizva ship. Before he could fathom how that happened, another came after the second targeting another Karysilan ship close by. His attacks thwarted, he let out a bellow, slamming his fists on the armrests.

"Communication coming through, General," his comm officer called out.

"On screen," he hissed.

Monzetti' face appeared and Tartha reared back in his seat. The Organic was visibly hostile yet there was a half smile on his face.

"You will wait, Tartha. Or, have you forgotten my brother's stipulation?"

"They are trying to flee this battle!" Tartha yelled.

"Oh, I think not. Look closer."

General Tartha watched as the ships moved farther apart until they were in a pattern around the planet. They covered every quadrant.

"Are you denying them the right to construct a defensive perimeter?" Monzetti asked.

"I guess," General Tarth replied through closed teeth. "I was mistaken."

"I'm glad you recognized this. Play fair, General."

The vidscreen blanked out, returning to the scene outside.

Regis breathed a sigh of relief as she watched the ships being saved by Monzetti. She tapped her screen and brought up the forest via satellite. Zooming in, she saw the Karysilans exiting the fighters. At the front stood Darnizva with a pained expression. She knew why. Like Cresnia who interfered, Monzetti may have something up his sleeve. Darnizva didn't want to be indebted to the alien.

At least, we get more time to prepare ourselves, she thought.

Chapter Four: Combat

DEADLINE

One of Quelly's old lab mates came barging down the hall where her office was located, making her stop in her tracks on the way in. He wore a lab coat and a fierce expression. The tablet in his hand would probably scream from his grip if it could.

"What the hell?" She managed to get out before he nearly knocked her down. "Hey!"

"Out of the way!" He snapped, not missing a stride.

Two of the secret service men blocked his path.

"That behavior will not be tolerated. You need to apologize to the Professor."

He gritted his teeth and turned to her.

"Sorry." He turned back to the two agents. "I'm in a hurry, so if you please."

"What are you doing here?" Quelly asked tersely.

She distinctly remembered seeing him give her the finger as she boarded the transport in front of the housing complex. To see him in the same halls was not pleasant.

His eyes grew wide as he stared at her incredulously.

"I could ask you the same, you hack. At least I have something to contribute to humanity."

He gave her a malicious smile.

That's right, Quelly said to herself.

None of the scientists in the area knew what projects the others were doing and didn't have much contact with each other. The fact that he was also working on an innovation made her skin crawl though. He was an arrogant ass who still, in this day and age, revered men over women in the science field. She was about to say something nasty when George came up behind them.

"Follow me," he ordered.

He passed between them and the two agents moved out of his way. Quelly and the other scientist did as instructed, keeping pace behind him. They went through a secret door posing as a wall with a plant set atop a small table. Inside they walked for what seemed like eternity until they came upon the two armed guards at the vaulted security doors. Neither scientist said a word as their credentials were checked and the seals released. Another small trek and they were at Secretary Regis' office door. The secret service agent standing to the side of it, reached over and opened the door.

"Good, you've brought them," Regis said as she got up from her seat behind her desk.

"It seemed feasible to do so now. They were having a spat in the hallway."

"Oh? About what exactly?" She eyed them both.

Quelly felt embarrassed. Much to her surprise, her counterpart spoke.

"I was wondering what an inferior mind like hers could possibly be working on to require access here."

Right out of his ass, she thought.

Regis leaned against the edge of her desk and gave him a stern look. Even George shook his head in amazement.

"Inferior how? By your assessment that means the same could be said about you."

He balked at that, clearly indignant.

"I have the accolades to prove my worth."

"Accolades do not make a scientific genius." She glared at him. "Know your place."

His mouth snapped shut and Quelly could tell how angry he was.

Serves you right!

"Now, we need a briefing on both projects."

"I am not allowed to tell anyone outside my team what my project entails."

George rolled his eyes in exasperation and Regis just stared at him in awe. Then she got angry and grabbed him by the front of his shirt. She was equal in height and pulled him close so they were eye to eye.

"You will obey me, young man or there won't anything for you after today."

The sheer terror in his eyes made Quelly quiver with amusement. She held in her impulse to laugh. He gave her a side glance. She could tell, he was humiliated. Regis let him go and went back to lean on her desk.

"Professor Riggs, how is the ice transport coming along?"

Before she could answer, the male scientist turned to her wild eyed.

"You?" He cried out. "You are the creator of that?"

George came over and placed a hand on his shoulder. He seemed to stiffen then relent.

"Slow going, I'm afraid." Quelly pushed her unruly hair out of her face. "We are still burrowing into the ground to make the containment blocks."

"And you, Professor Dunlop?" Her attention turned to her male colleague. "Is it done?"

He became proud like and puffed up his chest, making his button down shirt tighten against well toned abs. She pursed her lips in disgust.

"The new shield system is on track."

He a Quelly a quick glance.

"We should be able to go live within the year."

"Good, good. We need them to cover the containment areas sooner than later." Regis paced the room. "If we get caught off guard, the casualties would be catastrophic. All those people in suspended animation murdered."

"We can't have that," George added. "You two need to work together now and figure out how to protect them until we can get them off planet."

"Work with her?" He pointed at Quelly. When both Regis and George turned to him with intentions of harm, he backed down. "If I must," he muttered.

"I feel the same way, you ass hat," Quelly said out loud instead of to herself. She clamped a hand over her mouth. "My apologies, Madame Secretary. I'm usually more composed than this."

Regis burst into laughter and George followed. The male scientist didn't seem to find it funny in the slightest. She wiped her eyes as her chuckling subsided.

"Yes, I agree on that assessment. Sit down," she waved a hand at the chairs in the room. "We have much to discuss."

After the meeting, the two were escorted without George by secret service agents all the way back to hallway of their offices. Quelly quickly walked past him and got to her secured door. As she got ready to swipe her keycard, he made a sound like a snort.

"Excuse you. You could have some courtesy." He said.

"You're kidding?" She wondered if he forgot how he nearly knocked her down earlier. "Ladies first."

"My ass. Who told you, you were a lady?"

"You're such an asshole." She swiped her card pushed open the door.

"What's got your panties in a bunch? Not getting laid enough?" His expression became comical. "I could lower my standards again and do you a solid."

There she stood, slack jawed, wondering how she ever let herself be screwed by such a jerk during her practical exam term over a decade ago. Nothing about him now was appealing.

"Go to hell."

She let the heavy door slam shut as she walked over to her desk. No way was working with him going to be easy. She might have to get rid of him discreetly.

Later in the week she was escorted to his work lab which turned out to be a mini environment created on the outskirts of a small town. Its size and scope made her feel jilted by the budget department. The area was running like a well oiled machine and she tried not to seem impressed by the man's work. He was indeed a genius. His personality stunk. At the center hub, she found him giving orders to his workers in that aggressive tone he used to show superiority.

"And make sure the output is stable. I want a full report at each four hour interval," he told a group of lab technicians surrounding him.

He glanced over at her standing there waiting patiently. His expression changed to something hateful then settled on haughty.

"Let's get this done, people!" He clapped his hands together twice as he said it.

The enthusiastic command appeared to throw them all off as they hesitated, staring at him in confusion. She understood then that he was not usually that nice. Sensing the mood, he frowned and straightened his posture.

"Get moving!" His tone was harsh.

The workers hurried off to their tasks. He turned to her while checking his multi media wristband.

"You're late."

"I have been here. Loved the showmanship for my sake," she joked.

"I didn't do anything for you. This is an everyday occurrence." She saw one of the workers looked from his desk at that, a frown on his face. He continued. "I don't have to prove anything to you."

"But, you do," she chided him. "If your shields aren't effective, I will look elsewhere to keep the people in cryo safe."

There was an awkward pause in the area and she looked around, perplexed. He stepped closer to her.

"You don't get to come in here and insult my team's work," he said loudly.

She stiffened, realizing everyone had turned to stare at her.

"My apologies. I didn't mean to do that. That's not what I meant," she pleaded.

Work resumed and he stepped back from her.

"You want to see it or not?" He snapped.

Startled by his venomous tone, she was still rooted where she stood while he walked off to another part of the environment. He glanced back at her and she rushed to catch up. She got a rear view of his long gait and firm buttocks defined by his tighter fit slacks. He surely wore them that way on purpose.

"And stop staring at my ass, Professor. I deserve more respect than that."

Her eyes went wide as she came up beside him.

"The only reason anyone would be looking at your ass is to see which part of it to kick."

He stopped.

"This is my lab, Professor." He emphasized her title.

"In here, you abide by my rules. Get in," he commanded while gesturing towards the entrance to a containment room the size of a building.

"I demand respect as well, Doctor," she sneered back, emphasizing the lesser title.

Inside the room, she slowed her pace. There was nothing on all sides, just white walls.

"Activate the shield system," he said. His earbud commlink blinked.

"Activating shield zero zero eight one." A male voice came over the intercom.

She gave him a side glance.

"That many versions, huh?" She smirked.

He in turned glared at her.

"Really? How many versions of your project do you have?"

She bit her lower lip in defeat. Bad move on her part, calling him out.

The room seemed to vibrate and the floor shimmered in prismatic colors. A buzzing traveled from her feet to her head as the walls also took on the wave like aesthetic.

"Shield percentage," he yelled.

"Forty percent. ETA to full power, three minutes," was the reply.

He walked away from her and paced the area.

"It would take ten times as long for a large scale containment during battle."

"That's too long," she said.

"I know that!" He sounded exasperated.

And for good reason. She chastised herself for trying to antagonize him when the situation was dire. This was all to save mankind. He was working just as hard.

"Opening enclosure," the male voice said.

She looked up, surprised as the roof opened up to the afternoon sky.

"Shields at eighty percent."

"Cannon status?" He asked.

What? She screamed in her head.

"All green."

"Fire when ready."

"What's going on?" She asked through gritted teeth.

He merely turned and smiled at her viciously.

In answer to her question, she saw the sky light up. And within moments found herself staring at a beam of light coming straight at them.

"Oh my God!" She screamed, falling hard on her butt as it made impact.

The containment rocked and the shield flickered. Inside, the two of them were unfazed. There was no motion but the temperature rose a few degrees.

"You bastard!" She yelled as she got to her feet. "You should have warned me!"

"Huh?" His face scrunched up. "I work on a shield system. You should have known what to expect."

"Not a live cannon demo," she shrieked.

"How else are we supposed to know if it works?" He asked matter of fact.

He had point. She brushed herself off.

"Shields at full power. Second round incoming," the male voice announced.

Quelly looked up in shock as the volley hit. The intensity was less than the first but the place still shook. The heat was evenly dispersed and she could feel it. The sheer awesomeness of the demonstration sent shivers through her body.

"Impressed yet?" He asked with his winning smile.

She unwittingly nodded then stopped herself, regaining her composure.

"Are we supposed to feel the heat? The shaking is nominal as long as it doesn't effect the environment as a whole. Did the shield not hold entirely at eighty percent when hit?"

"You just can't be satisfied, can you?"

"I want to make sure we all live!"

"As do I!"

"Cooling system engaged. Please stand by."

Both professors looked up at as the air above changed color.

"Shield system deactivating when temperature reaches normal levels."

"I think I need a drink," Quelly whispered.

Her hands were shaking and she stared at them. When she looked up, he also had a strange look on his face. Was it anger, disappointment, caution? He turned to her.

"I think so too."

Shit! I drank too much!

She shouted in her head as he slammed her against the wall inside his personal lab. Their lips were locked in a heated kiss, his tongue deep inside her mouth. When he disengaged, their mingled saliva dripped down between them. One hand reached between her thighs and his fingers expertly dug in, fervently massaging her walls. She gasped in shock and ecstasy, her fighting with not wanting it from him. His fingers came out and wrapped around her panties. She felt the fabric rip apart and heard his pants hit the floor.

Oh no! Too late.

He rammed his hard cock inside and her whole body went numb for a split second before a buzzing, tingly feeling filled her. With each thrust, her hands gripped tighter on his shoulders, her eyes and mouth open in sheer panic and awe. She let out a loud moan.

"Ahh!"

He planted one hand on the wall behind her and leaned closer to her neck.

"You like that, huh?" He breathed.

His mouth closed on her neck and she felt his tongue circle around on her flesh. The combination made her walls squeeze him. She was on the verge of climaxing. He positioned himself so that she dropped down further onto him and her legs naturally wrapped around his hips.

"Uh uh, not yet."

He kissed her again, his hot tongue sending her into state of euphoria.

I hate you! I hate you, so much! She cried in her head.

They came together letting loose mutual sounds of elation and stayed tangled against the wall. She held on, mentally telling her body to stop shivering. Eventually, they both slid to the floor, cradling each other.

The one person in the whole world who could make her feel this way was the one man she despised. Because, deep down, she envied his intelligence. And that was sexy as hell.

⌒

Images from around the world filled the main holo-screen in Telia's personal chamber. Each one represented a Shadowman recruited under her reign. She stood leaned over the counter, her arms supporting her on its ledge as she swiped through them via the virtual remote glowing under her fingertips. Her hair was down, splayed a across her shoulders, cascading down her back. The white plunge necked shroud hugged at her waist and the split from the top of her thigh down showed off her golden skin.

Finding the image of Damon, she zoomed in on him working a case with his new partner. The previous one had become his mate and per regulations, they could not work together. She found that ridiculous. If warrior clans implanted something like that it would mean defeat in battle. Trust was a key part of it and who better to trust than your soulmate.

She saw the deadpan look on Damon's face and knew what it meant. He was in pain and trying to mask it. The stick of gum laced with a customized drug came out of his pocket. He unwrapped it and shoved the candy in his mouth. No one near him seemed to notice the slight glow in his eyes as the drug took effect.

When the shadow agents with hybrid DNA began to transition away from their human traits, the world leaders panicked and created a new doctrine that forced them to keep the ratio at fifty percent. Still human yet something more. She detested that rule. They essentially halting the evolution of species.

Attar came out of the bathroom, naked and drying himself off with a standard sized towel that appeared small against him. He tossed it back into the bathroom and reached for his robe. Slipping it on over his head he walked over to her and rested his shin on her shoulder. His damp, dark wavy hair brushed against it.

"Damon, huh?"

She glanced over at him then back to the screen.

"I won't leave him here. He'll die."

He straightened up and leaned on the counter with one hand.

"He is the one agent I am sure they won't want to let go of. He's as powerful as they come minus the Snowman."

"Hmm." She froze all the images and faced him. Her fingers played in his damp hair. "You smell delicious. I want to devour you."

He smirked, caressing her sides.

"I could say the same about you."

She kissed him softly then swatted his backside.

"Get dressed, we have work to do. We will continue this afterwards." She walked to the kitchen area and felt his gaze follow her. "Don't disobey me. Hurry."

He gave her a forlorn look before doing as told. She smiled as he stood naked yet again. Such a young, strong body. And, it was hers to do as she pleased.

⌇

The counter on General Tartha's personal schedule dropped to display mere months before the deadline he proposed to the humans. Reports from his spies relayed their hopes of a fair fight. Some of the new weapons rumored to be in play were quite terrifying. He expected no less from a primitive civilization. In all the time he gave, not one warship capable of space combat was built. Yet, there were plenty of fight cruisers manufactured.

He sat up in his bed and pulled his lounging robe from the other side. The two females he had ravaged earlier stirred from their near comatose state. Ugly, dark bruises had already formed on their bodies where he had grabbed hold and held them down for his pleasure. Without a care for their well being, he slipped the robe on and exited the bed. His movement pushed one off onto the floor and disturbed the other awake in pain.

"Get them out of my chamber," he ordered the guard outside the door as he passed.

"Yes, General."

The guard disappeared into the room.

General Tartha strolled down the corridor and headed to the bridge. Some of the soldiers he passed quickly glanced at his attire in amazement then moved on just as fast. He didn't care how it looked at the moment. He had one thing on his mind. War.

Well, at least a battle to kill the time. The Karysilans always put up a good fight and having to defend a helpless planet my kick it up a notch.

On deck, the crew saluted and returned to business. Ahead of him through the viewport Earth loomed close before them. He admired the blue and white swirls mixed with green and brown from the land mass. Compared to Rellia, it was overly bright. It hurt his eyes.

"Zoom in," he said to the console operator.

"Anywhere?"

He thought for a moment, calling up some of the regions from the reports.

"The United States. That's where that damnable bomb came from long ago." The viewport changed scenery and he saw most of the country. The lens panned over it and he found one isolated section that stood out from the other states. "There. Show me that." He pointed to a giant black monolith looming over an entire city. "What have we here?"

The way it stood majestic, casting shadow over the region, irked him. As the lens zoomed in more, he saw beautiful structures and perfect landscapes spanned throughout. Rellia, on the hand, was overpopulated and couldn't have sectors like that. They lived atop one other in dark high-rises that spiraled up into the clouds.

Envy consumed him.

"Ready weapons. Target that city."

There was a strange silence that followed. He went to the weapons officer standing at his console and got very close to him. The officer turned to him.

"General, sir. It is not the deadline. Cresnia may be near and thwart our attempt."

General Tartha's stare darkened.

"Do as I command. Cresnia will not interfere." He smiled then. "He has found other fodder to toy with."

"As you command." He tapped his commlink. "Ready weapons in bays five through nine. Confirm full charge when complete." He looked back to General Tartha. "How many rounds?"

"Just one," he replied coyly. "It's a warning shot."

Hagen felt the change in the air and knew what was coming even before he looked to the sky and saw the first streak of searing red beams burn away the clouds. General Tartha had begun his assault on planet Earth with no warning and ahead of schedule. Hagen watched the beams make contact with their target. A mushroom cloud blossomed up into the air. He knew an entire city had just been wiped out. His only hope was that the population of that sector had already been frozen and transported out.

Next to him stood Bree and Craig looking put out by the scene. They were ready. The humans, not so much. If this didn't make them get with the program, humans were doomed.

SCRAMBLE

Hana watched from a live feed the Grid City nearly obliterated in an instant. Infrastructures crumbled to dust along with the trees. When a clearing opened in the thick smog, only scorched black Earth remained. The base was enclosed in the latest version of the shield system. He doubted it could handle something that powerful.

We underestimated.

To be safe, everyone was relocated underground. Scott was trying to figure out how to deploy the combat units stealthily. At this conjunction, Hana saw no point in that. Many of the residents from Grid City had been evacuated. The few souls that were left either died on impact or safe in the bunkers constructed at the last moment a year ago. Hana hoped for the latter.

The second vidscreen on the wall lit up and President Lynmore's face came up. The other vidscreens came on in succession until all the world leaders were staring down at him.

"He attacked ahead of schedule! That dirty son of a bitch!" Lynmore screeched.

Hana leaned back, eyes widened, at that verbal onslaught. He blinked a few times.

"I figured as much. He seemed the impatient type."

"We're not yet fully evacuated and the weapons." The French president trailed off.

"There's no choice in the matter now." Hana sighed heavily. "What is it you need from me? We are on lockdown for the moment."

The European President's gaze darkened.

"We need you to deploy the troops in your care to our srtonghold locations. Especially the cannons. They must be protected at all costs. I'm sure they can reach the rendezvous points within the week."

Hana became enraged. His face went flush and he was about to unleash a barrage of insults when Scott came up behind him.

"That is not an option at the moment. Deployment will start when we know specific target areas. The Relliants did not become a super power without strategy. Once they show their cards, we move."

"This is not up for debate!" The Russian president scoffed. "Preemptive placement is key here." He got nods from the others and gave a victorious smile.

"Unlike all of you who see Bi-Genetic and enhanced soldiers as expendable commodities, we will not send our people out to be slaughtered without solid intel."

All the world leaders' expressions changed, ranging from shame to anger. Hana clenched his hands into fists and lowered them under his desk.

"Celestial Mother is nearly finished with her assessments of units. Once completed, we can assemble them and do as you ask."

"Those aliens don't give a damn about our fight!" Another world leader snapped.

"Yet, we needed them in order to accomplish our goals," the Asian ambassador chided.

"We'll keep you up to date," Scott said as he leaned over Hana and disconnected the feeds despite the world leaders faces indicating they weren't finished.

"That was rude," Hana laughed. "They must be livid."

"Don't care." Scott stood.

Hana turned his head and got a good look at his husband. Scott had dark circles under tired eyes and his skin was pale. Alarmed by his appearance after not seeing him for days, he jumped from his chair and grabbed the sides of his head. To his surprise, Scott reached up and removed them.

"Don't. You can't worry about me right now."

"The hell I can't!" Hana forcibly pushed him against the wall. "Don't you ever say that to me again!"

Scott relented to Hana's will ad wrapped his arms around him.

"I'm sorry," he whispered.

Celestial Mother had tapped into the world leaders feed. If she could reach through the holoscreen and wipe them all off the face of the planet, she was inclined to do it then. On a separate screen she indulged her guilty pleasure of watching Hana in his office. When Scott disconnected the feed, she applauded his nerve. She too saw how beaten down the soldier was from his nonstop duties. That angered her further. His condition greatly affected Hana.

Behind her, Karias replayed the warning shot from General Tartha's main ship. His expression was one of cruelty. She could only imagine what was going on in the warrior's mind. The element of surprise was not a new tactic. The problem was a broken promise on the battlefield. General Tartha apparently had no fighter's code.

"What say you?" She asked him.

He lifted his head up from the screen and stared ahead into the kitchen area.

"We see how far this debauchery goes and then make our own move."

"I agree. This war is a farce. I'll not play a hand in it."

They both shut down their holoscreens and exited the lounge. Time to check on the elite soldiers they handpicked to fight.

With the shields erected over the evacuation sites and strongholds around the world, Earth forces readied themselves for defense. Since the Relliants fired the first shot, they had every right to retaliate. The cannons were powered up, aimed at the enemy ships coming forward. This was the true test of the cannons capability.

The first shot hit one of the ships as it breached the clouds and blew a hole through its hull. That didn't bring it down. Its weapons bays opened and unleashed a hail storm of fire power that pummeled the surface. Everything in the vicinity was turned to ash.

"Hit it again," George ordered through the commlink for the cannon operators.

The secured bunker was equipped with everything needed to keep track of the battle. Inside, the lights were dimmed to see the multiple screens better. He waited anxiously, watching the second shot go forth until it made impact. This time the target was hit head on and the cannon shot went through the entire length of the enemy ship.

"Yes!" He slammed his hands down on the table. Before he could rejoice further, a swarm of fighters spilled from the crippled ship. "Son of a," he whispered softly.

The troops on the ground were sitting ducks. He could only watch helplessly in the confines of his bunker as a third of their forces were wiped out.

From the commlinks around the world he could hear orders of retreat to regroup. For a split second he regretted not evolving into a litigator. Then he thought about the lost causes dying in the dirt, bleeding to death, and his mouth salivated.

Remembering where he was, he straightened his posture and wiped his face with both hands. Lowering them, he caught a glimpse of two officers at the communications console staring at him in confusion and fear. He figured they must have seen the look of hunger in his eyes. They slowly focused their attention back to the console.

If you knew what I was, you would know to be very afraid, he snickered to himself.

⁓

"This is a slaughter," one of the technicians exclaimed while frantically connecting a civilian to the block of ice.

On the other side of the shield was a dark smoky sky lit up with the occasion explosion. The shield was still being erected when the enemy attacked. Technicians and civilians were hit, the casualties minimal. Still, Quelly felt heartbroken. Evacuation had fell so far behind that it seemed like she would never catch up. She had never been in a war of this magnitude. The helplessness was unbearable.

Her hair was a tangled mess, her face and lab coat smudged with debris from the initial blast that sent her flying. She was certain some of her ribs were broken. There was no time for that. Fighting through the pain, she directed the workers to keep the people calm and speed up the process.

The icon on her wrist for the transport beacon was flashing. It was nearby and ready for intake. Slumped on the ground unconscious was Dunlop. He had been hit full on. The only other person capable of shutting down the shield for the transport was busy helping her.

Not yet.

Quelly winced as she moved one of the roller diagnostic monitors out of a technician's way. She was determined to get every human in the ice blocks before dropping the shields. Dunlop's assistant came into view on her left and she called out to him.

"Hey! I need you to get ready. How many left?"

He looked up from watching a block fill up with the solution.

"Less than a hundred. We should be done in the next hour."

Quelly looked up at the sky and saw the transport hover over the landing pad. She frowned at its timing. The shields flickered. She whirled around and saw the man at the station. The screen showed the animated shield lowering.

"What the hell are you doing?" She yelled, running over to him, holding her side.

"We need the transport inside the shield."

He nodded upwards.

The shield stopped halfway down and the transport lowered itself in. Two enemy fighters took notice and swoop in for the kill. The shields rose back and closed right as the fighters' weapons hit. The entire area shook, knocking some of the equipment down.

"Damn it!" Quelly cried out. She coughed up blood and wiped her mouth with fingers.

The transport operator came out and started barking orders to his crew.

"Start loading! If the block is on the last fill, help with the curing and get it on!"

The man gave Quelly a nod before going back into the transport. She bowed her head in defeat. The shield operator was correct in his actions. She was too tired and numb to think straight. Seeing as there was nothing else she could do, she slid down next to her counterpart and closed her eyes.

The shield operator stood over Professor Riggs and his boss. His sad expression conveyed what the others felt. Those technicians who were not in the blocks were to handle the monitoring and then go into a cryo state on the ship during the journey. They would be awakened before landing to prepare the blocks for a second transfer on a new planet. The humans would remain in the blocks until it was safe to return to Earth.

"Get them in the last block." He said to the nearest technician.

"But, they're the supervisors," the man sputtered.

"Does it look like they're in any condition to supervise?" He snapped.

The transport pilot came back out and walked over to them.

"I agree. Get them prepped. You." He pointed to the shield operator. "Grab the remote access for the shield and get onboard. The moment that last block is secured, you hit it and we're off."

"How are we going to get past all that?" He pointed to the sky that was a battlefield.

"Oh, we have a defense unit on the ready."

The transport operator replied slyly.

"And what?" The shield operator shrugged. "We possibly get shot down in the fray?"

The transport operator looked at him, puzzled.

"Did the good doctor not tell you?"

The shield operator's eyes narrowed in confusion.

The transporter sighed.

"The remote access also lets you transfer the shield

system to the transport. How else did you think we got out of the hot zones?"

"Sheet luck," the shield operator replied.

"No luck here. This is solid planning."

A group of technicians came and took the two unconscious scientists to the block.

"Be careful with them," the shield operator chastised them. "You did good," he said to the Professors. "We'll take from here."

Newly manufactured smaller scale cannons were rolled out far behind schedule as the factories continued to build them in the midst of battle. Exact replicas of the monstrosities positioned in the mountains except half the power. Which only meant they were just as deadly on the ground. Hoskins Sr. was in charge of overseeing their departure to the battlefields. He made sure security was beefed up in case his crazed son decided to show. Shame had become a frequent emotion regarding him over the last two decades. When he heard about the destroyed cartridges, he volunteered to take the blame and make it right.

Since the start of the war a few weeks back, humans became sorely aware of how far behind in technology they truly were. A few of the weapons created with alien input made up for the gaps. Hoskins shook his head. Regular humans couldn't keep the pace. The hybrids and genetically altered soldiers were barely holding on.

The first group of cannons were being transported via a massive cargo rig with a shield enabler. Two of the cannons would escort the rig: one in front, the other in the rear. The enemy had cut off many routes and human forces didn't dare try to fly with deliveries.

A soldier carrying a tablet walked up to him on the upper level where he could see the entire hangar.

"Excuse me, sir." The soldier leaned forward and used the stylus to point at a section on the screen, "We seem to be short on a couple of orders."

"By how much?" Hoskins did a quick scan of the work order. "Not seeing the discrepancy, yet."

The soldier tapped the section and it zoomed in to reveal a second layer of data.

"Here, sir. Three from this order and two from the other in red."

"Five, huh?" Hoskins sniffed, thumbing his nose. *That's all?* He was sure they could make do without them. "Well, son, it's too late to fill it. We go in hard and fast and hope we got enough fire power to survive this shit storm."

"True. I'll let the recipients know."

The soldier walked back down to the hangar's main level. Hoskins snorted. The 'recipients' were not going to be happy. Logistics had already been established based on number of weapons and troops. This would put a monkey wrench in their plans.

Nothing is guaranteed in war, except death.

His earbud commlink beeped and he tapped to answer it.

"I sure hope you have good news for me, Hoskins," he heard Regis say.

"Wouldn't let you down," he replied. "Rolling them out as we speak.

"Let's see if it does any good. We're getting our asses handed to us."

"See? I was trying to stop this whole thing decades ago."

There was a pause.

"You almost got us annihilated with your foolishness.

Don't pride yourself on that."

Hoskins rolled his eyes. Everyone involved seemed to always throw that incident in his face. He had already apologized. What more did they want?

"Yeah, yeah. Tell your president she's getting her cannons within the next ten days."

"We can hold for that long." Another long pause. "Thank you for doing this."

Before he could answer back, the commlink was disconnected. He leaned over the railing and watched the workers secure the cargo.

Shit! I owed at least this much.

In the deep desert where the Shadow Facility once stood, a flat metal surface miles wide in square footage lay in its place. It peeked up from the sand a few hundred feet. Enough to make a clear path for the weapons lined around inside it to fire on hostiles when they got too close. Balls of fire and explosions went off in every direction. The top had been struck multiple times and held up to the assault with thanks from the shield system. It was down to seventy percent.

"We can thank our lucky stars, none of the main ships have targeted this place." Shawn mused while he ran up the metal stairs to the observation deck. Two soldiers were close behind him. "I say we show their ground troops a little more action."

"I think you have jinxed us, sir," the soldier directly behind him said.

"We need to take possession of the weapon first," the other added.

"Oh, no need to worry about that."

Arriving at their destination, Shawn walked up to the window and stared down at the terrain. A few kilometers out was a convoy with a cargo truck right smack in the center.

"There's our cannon," he said gleefully.

The convoy was taking heavy fire. One of the escort vehicles lay smoldering some distance behind it. The soldiers who survived were taking cover against it, the blasts keeping them pinned down. He turned to the weapons operator.

"Target any ships by that vehicle." He addressed one of the ground technicians. "I want a transport sent to retrieve our guys. Take the one with the mini gun mounted."

"Yes sir! I'm on it." The soldier did a quick salute and ran out the room.

"What do you think, boys?" He asked his two companions.

"We're getting clobbered," the first replied.

"How do you figure?" Shawn gave him a quizzical stare.

"I think he means humanity as whole. We are holding our own." The second said.

"That won't last. The only way we don't get annihilated is if we go full under and wait this thing out." The first added.

"You mean liked what Metropolis did?" Shawn asked. His tone was vicious.

The soldiers on deck all seemed to frown at that. It was no secret how the governments and the military felt about what Terence did. They would have understood if the purpose was to run from the fight out of fear. No. The reason was way worse in their eyes.

"Not at all. I'm saying, it should be a last resort. There's no need in us all dying and no one left to defend."

"I'll agree on that," the second said.

Shawn watched a transport launch from below with

two fighter jets flanking it. They made a beeline to the downed vehicle, never veering off course amidst enemy fire. The mini gun did its job as did the fighters.

The transport landed, a few holes showing, right near the soldiers. They clambered in through the half opened hatch, dragging the dead and wounded along with them. All three crafts turned in unison towards the base and duplicated the precious run to head back.

By the time they reached the hangar, the transport had lost most of its landing gear and skidded across the tarmack, sparks flying. The maintenance crew came running with the hose and doused it with foam.

Shawn turned his attention back to the main view port and saw three of the enemy fighter carriers in a straight formation across. Their speed was steady and headed towards the base. Others around them appeared to be protecting the group. When the carriers suddenly dropped altitude and sped up, Shawn hissed in anger. The ships were now in the direct line of sight of the exposed levels.

"Shoot them down! Now!" He ordered.

The base cannons in the center rotated to target them. One of the carriers accelerated and smashed right into the them. The second did the same, aiming for the hangar. From the convoy, he saw soldiers scramble out of the support vehicles and unclamp the cargo. The shell fell away and the cannon was revealed, its nose already glowing hot. It moved down, centering on the third enemy carrier and fired.

Oh shit! Scott yelled internally.

"Incoming!"

The blast engulfed the enemy fighter, obliterating it and kept going. It struck the base at the same time as the second fighter hit the hangar. Amid the smoke and flames, the fighter carriers broke open and enemy soldiers swarmed into the base. Shawn smirked. While the emergency crews went to task, he pivoted towards the soldiers on the deck.

"Well, ladies and gentlemen. Looks like we get to show our skills in hand to hand combat. Defend this base at all costs. Once the convoy is secure," he took a deep breath. "Descend."

There were no arguments or signs of resentment. The entire personnel stood, saluted, then went to fulfill their duties. He looked at his two men.

"Are you ready?"

Their eyes glowed and a smile crept on their faces.

"We don't need to hold back now," the first answered.

"Yes. Let's hope we get to show off." The second said playfully.

"Why wouldn't we?" The first frowned as he asked.

"Maybe the shadowmen lying in wait will save us some toys to play with."

"Let's get going." Shawn commanded. "Just in case."

Scott's son snorted. Yes. There was always the chance of the base being infiltrated. A slew of shadowmen trainers were on standby with a small group of their pupils. If the human forces failed and the enemy somehow got into the mountain level, they would wish for death. That is where the four aliens were, and he was sure Celestial Mother was itching for a fight.

INTERCEPTION

From her personal feed in the commons lounge, Celestial Mother watched soldiers, advanced humans, and shadowmen go head to head with Relliant fighters inside the compound. The Chombrazens sat on the sofa and Attar in the plush chair observing the scenes as she flicked through each sector. The walls shook with multiple blasts hitting the structure outside. She stood legs shoulder width apart, wearing a white battle suit, her fur drape dangling.

"This is nonsense," she exclaimed.

The Chombrazens stood. They too were dressed in battle gear, ready for war.

"I say we get our pets loaded and leave this place," the second one suggested.

"Yes. It's a good thing we had trackers and an extraction sequence imbedded in them."

"They will probably despise us for taking them out of the fight."

"I don't care," she snapped.

"Who do we get to first?" Attar asked.

"We split up and meet back in the launch bay. The cryochambers are prepped."

Karias smiled as he went to the screen and located his targets.

"Time for a bit of fun."

"Oh?" Celestial Mother smirked. "You hate Rellia as much as we do?"

"At least your planet wasn't decimated like ours."

Karias stepped back from the holoscreen and tapped on his wrist band. It synced with the information on the screen then he winked out of sight with a thin vertical flash. Lindo did the same, leaving Celestial Mother and her mate in the room. She turned to him.

"Go get our boy," she ordered.

He got up and synced his wristband to the coordinates she already had up on the screen.

When he disappeared, she turned to the private elevator. Another blast shook the foundations. She was going out into the fray to get the ones she wanted. No need for teleportation. Along the way, she would kill a few Relliants.

$\sim$

Thick ash rained down into the crumbled half of the mafia mansion's main hall. Eldan held a sword in each hand, both dripping with darker than normal blood. A slew of dead Relliant soldiers lay at his feet, surrounding him. Only a few feet away, Vic Marzonetti stood in a defensive stance, one of the special swords he had snatched from the training facility long ago poised to strike. Blood streaked his clothes. Eldan glanced down at himself and found he was also covered. Some of it was his own. He didn't win the last round unscathed.

Everyone had been evacuated except for them and a handful of crewmen. The first ones they kicked out were the children. Young and old. Vic's oldest son protested, claiming his fighting skills were just as good as theirs. His father proved him wrong by knocking him unconscious with one blow. That silenced the others, enabling the evac technicians to sedate and transport them away.

Rumbling from the sky made the two look up. A carrier cruised by, dropping nearly a hundred Relliant soldiers on the front lawn. Eldan's eyes glowed silver and he adjusted his grip on the swords. Vic turned to him.

"I will always love you. Until the end of eternity."

"I know that."

They were about to die. Neither had the strength left to take down another round of enemy soldiers of that number. Even so, they would fight to the end. Eldan fought back tears of heartache and rage. The first wave breached the threshold. They rushed to meet them halfway.

A blink of light, bright as a star spanned across the room dividing the horde of soldiers to one side and Eldan with Vic on the other. Karias appeared in a flash, slamming both fists down into the marbled floor as he let out a primal yell. The floor cracked then caved in, sending all the soldiers from the entrance and beyond down into the abyss.

Eldan and Vic skidded to a halt, landing on their butts a few feet from the alien. He stood, gesturing the rest of the soldiers to come forward to their doom. When they seemed ready to obliged, scaling the walls to avoid the gaping hole, the Chombrazen laughed. He turned to Eldan and Vic.

"You come with me now," his voice boomed.

He tapped his wrist band and all three disappeared.

The enemy soldiers stopped their advance in confusion.

Eldan looked up to a familiar ceiling and knew he was inside the training compound. Vic got on his knees to stand and was struck down by Karias. A group of technicians came and dragged him off. Eldan crouched further to the ground, staring up at the alien, ready to fight.

"You will not be a part of this farce. We are taking you from this place."

"What?" Eldan raised his head. "Why? This is what we were trained for. To fight the enemy and defend Earth." He saw Karias glance up at something behind him. "Was all this for nothing then?" He yelled.

Before he could move, a needle pushed into the back of his neck. He heard the trigger and felt the liquid being injected. He instinctively slapped a hand over the area when it was withdrawn. His vision blurred.

"Don't fight it," a technician said. "This is for the best."

With both targets secured, Karias scrolled through the data on his wristband and located the next one.

⁓

Erica jumped sideways, firing her guns as she sailed in the air before landing behind the giant chunk of a downed enemy ship. She ejected the spent clip from one of her guns and reloaded. It had taken days to exhaust the charging cartridge and she thanked the Gods for the new technology. On the other side to her left was her husband and oldest daughter hunkered down under another piece of wreckage. She had tried so hard to convince her daughter to evacuate to no avail. The woman was just as stubborn as she was.

Her husband held the deadly sword made only for shadowmen. He had already bloodied the thing ten times over and sustained some critical wounds. She was faring no better. Their training conditioned them to withstand those kinds of wounds and the pain associated with them. Make no mistake, the moment they stopped fighting, their bodies would give in. She dreaded that outcome.

The swarm of enemy soldiers got closer and she raised her guns over the side edge and shot down the first row of fifteen. She ducked back down as a hail storm of laser fire came at her. The rounds hit the metal, searing holes in it all the way through. She lay flat on the ground to avoid getting hit. The firing stopped and she peeked out.

Dozens of enemy soldiers were being tossed into the air by an invisible force. Squinting, she deciphered the large figure coming down the middle of the horde. Karias had an expression of elation and malice rolled in one as blood sprayed on him from his prey. There was no enemy air support in that sector so the ground forces were on their own. They were no match for the Chombrazen.

A few managed to break free and advanced to the side of where her husband and daughter were. She sucked air through her teeth and debated if she should move. Her husband stood right as the soldiers got within striking distance and slashed his sword across their numbers. Her daughter opened fire on the ones behind them then her mouth gaped open.

The first group of soldiers seemed to falter. Like a domino effect, the top half of their bodies slid to the right and fell to the ground. Distracted, her daughter was hit in the shoulder. The shot spun her around and she hit the ground too. Erica took out the three enemy soldiers along with the culprit and started to get up.

A foot slammed into her back, holding her down. From her side view, she as able to make out the hem of the Chombrazen's robe.

"We don't need your help!" She cried. "We can beat them on our own."

"No," the alien said. "You can't. And you won't find out either."

He looked over at her daughter bleeding. He messed with the band on his wrist, frowning at whatever was on it. With one hand, he picked her up as he took his foot off and carried her over to the where her husband and daughter were. She cringed, ready for the onslaught of laser fire and when none came, she glanced out at the horizon. All the enemy soldiers were down.

The Chombrazen dropped her next to her daughter. Her husband stared at the alien with disinterest.

"You don't want us to fight in this war."

"Correct."

"I'm tired," he said. "I want to rest."

Erica let out an anguished cry knowing he as about to give up. His wounds were bad. He may not wake up if he succumbed to them. As if reading her mind, the alien caught him before his body hit and answered.

"We will fix you while you do that." He grabbed her daughter by her good arm. "We're leaving." He hit the icon on his wristband and they all blipped away.

&seffect;

The evacuation queue of the north district was longer than anticipated. Inside the dome, technicians scrambled to get the blocks filled and ready for transport. Enemy forces had already converged on the area. Damon stood sword in hand as the first line of defense. He, along with a few others, vowed to hold the line until every person was frozen.

From his position, he could make out his wife clutching their two youngest children tight. One was barely four, the other almost two. The older ones had already been evacuated. He cursed himself for not forcing her to evacuate sooner. But she wouldn't budge without him.

Out of the corner of his eye, he saw a group of enemy fighters come at him from the left. He pivoted towards them, raising his sword. When they were ten feet within his personal space, he swung at a forty five degree angle, slicing clean through them. Their bodies separated seconds after with them not realizing they were already dead.

He was tired. A third of the blood covering his trench coat and shirt was his own. There was no time to acknowledge how badly he was hurt. The other four were behind him holding the line closer to the dome. They too appeared exhausted and were bloodied. A second wave was charging towards them. Damon stepped back and regained his stance.

A blast hit the dome and the shield flickered. Technicians rushed to the controls to try and stabilize it. The lines had shortened considerably. Most of the people were already inside the blocks. Damon figured they would be done soon. Reinforcements were on their way to escort the transport.

Dark swirls appeared midair inside the dome, forming a black hole. Its diameter expanded until it was the size of a small room and Attar stepped out directly in front of Damon's wife. He looked down at her huddled on the ground with the two infants. He grabbed her by the front of her shirt and lifting her inches above his head, smiled. Damon abandoned his post and ran towards the dome.

"You first," Attar hissed.

He tossed her into the vortex screaming, reaching for her children. They began to bawl uncontrollably.

Attar stared at them with disinterest.

Damon stopped a few feet from the dome as he encountered the shield. Its energized static sent ripples through his body.

He clenched the sword, contemplating if he should strike.

"Drop the shield," Attar ordered.

"We can't!" A technician cried out. "Dropping the shield would mean all of us getting killed."

Attar cocked his head and his eyes glowed a vibrant yellow.

"Do as I say, human."

The technician at the main controls hit the deactivation icon on the holoscreen. Damon rushed into the dome the moment it cleared at his feet. The other fighters followed. Once the last person was inside, the technician reactivated the shield. A barrage of laser fire got through. Everyone hunkered down, arms wrapped across their heads. Attar raised one hand and another vortex appeared, spanning the entire upper section of the dome, and swallowed the assault. It then shrunk to nothingness.

Damon continued his advance to Attar. When he was within reach, Attar turned and was on him instantly. To his surprise, Attar easily grappled him to the ground despite being ready for a fight.

"Now you," Attar whispered in his ear.

Damon was able to get out of his grip and roll over to his side. Attar kicked him in the abdomen, then again. The third sent him flying into the vortex. Damon felt the air leave his lungs.

He came tumbling out of the vortex and into the cryochamber bay he knew so well. Getting to his feet, he scanned the room and noticed his wife already in one of the pods, sleeping peacefully. Technicians and doctors went around in a flurry doing tasks.

"What is this?" He demanded. Attar came out of the vortex with a child under each arm. Damon turned to him, seething. "Put down my kids."

His voice was low and sinister.

"You will not stay here. Being with humans is not in your best interest."

"What? You're going to just take us off this planet?" Damon yelled.

"Absolutely."

Attar gestured behind him. Damon raised his sword to strike and was instead hit hard in the side of the head. He felt his head ringing and staggered in a zig zag. He tried again to raise his sword. This time Attar struck him point blank with an open palm. Damon fell to the floor.

"We will not let you or your family come to harm. It's better this way." He nodded to the technicians. "Take care of him. And these two." He handed the infants to them.

Damon's eyes fluttered as he was being dragged off to the nearest cryochamber. Attar saw the rage in them.

I understand.

$\backsim$

The base shook with fury from the constant onslaught of attacks. Any of the Shadowmen who had stayed behind were already deep in the fight. The soldiers were acting as support units for them, making sure the movement of the enemy forces that had infiltrated were halted. Hana half ran towards the center of the base where the non combat staff was located. They knew how to use weapons to defend themselves but were by no means trained. Trailing behind her was a combat unit to assist.

He had crossed the intersection of the corridor and found himself flying into the railings. A fireball came whooshing down the hall bringing a wave of heated wind. His eyes went wide as it came closer. Then he was hit hard and lifted off the ground away from it. He watched the fire engulf the area where he once was and melt the metal railing. On the other side of the corridor was the combat unit hunkered down, braced for impact.

"Damn it, Hana!" Scott yelled.

Hana looked up from his savior's chest and saw his angry husband.

"You saved me," he said lovingly.

He glanced down at him.

"What the hell are you thinking?"

"I was taking them to the center. I'm the only one with access to open it now."

Scott let out a loud sigh and released him.

"That's what I am here for."

"You were busy."

"Hana," Scott admonished him. He stood. "Let's go." He turned to the combat unit already back on their feet. "In formation! Move out!"

They came forward, two by three by two, with Scott in the lead and Hana close by. At the twenty foot double titanium doors, Hana placed his hand on the screen panel while an eye scanner searched his irises.

"Access confirmed. Good evening, Hana," the female A.I. said.

"Open doors."

"Opening sequence initiated."

Loud hissing and the whirring of mechanisms filled the antechamber. They could hear the inner bolts sliding until they locked into place. The doors slid open on each side and the group entered the base's core.

They walked slowly down the ramp to the main walkway and came upon what looked like chaos. Hana was taken aback by the activity. Technicians were swarming around loading cryochambers and knocking out their colleagues who tried to stop them.

"What's going on!" Hans demanded.

Before he could step closer, Scott was hit and sent

flying backwards. She could see his body folded over itself in the air before hitting the wall. Hana screamed and was being dragged away. He fought the men who had a grip on him. Celestial Mother stood ahead of him.

"I am taking you with me," she declared.

"Let go of me!" Hana screamed.

He was able to turn and see Scott slumped over. With surprising fervor, Hana fought harder, yelling and kicking. The combat unit was engaged with fighting an elite group of soldiers doing Celestial Mother's bidding. Filled with despair and anger at the alien for trying to sever her from her family, leaving them to die, Hana dropped to his knees, taking his assailants with him. With every bit of energy he could muster, he unleashed a pulse that pushed everything and everyone within fifty feet out. Some of the equipment exploded and the communication counter cracked in half.

The only one left standing was Celestial Mother. Seeing how far Hana was willing to fight, she tapped into his mind and for the first time understood. She felt guilty for trying to separate him from the only family he ever had. With one flash step, she was before Hana and hit him near the base of the neck. Hana dropped like a stone.

"Find them all and load them in the containers."

Two technicians grabbed hold of Scott and carried him to a cryochamber. The elite soldiers headed out to do her bidding. She watched a technician load Hana into an empty chamber and hook up the sensors. The man seemed to take extra care in handling him. She knew how much the staff respected Hana and how much sacrifice was made.

An elite soldier came out of a mini vortex with an unconscious man at his feet. He was holding him up from the floor by his jacket collar. Celestial Mother recognized the young man as Hana's middle son, Shawn, who was leading the fight in the docking bay.

"Make sure we meet the deadline. I want off this planet before it goes up in flames."

There was a ruckus ahead and Telia stared out into the dark abyss. Her vision zoomed in on the double doors that led into the corridor. They bowed at the seams, the center line bulging. The technicians scurried into the cryo-chamber bay right as the barrier slid across to separate it from the main hall. Telia stepped away and moved closer to the corridor. With a deafening explosion, the giant doors burst open, each side flying outwards and crashing onto the ground. A unit of thirty Relliants bled out like rats down the ramp. She flash stepped to the entryway and met them head on.

Telia and the leader met each other's gaze. She stood with her legs shoulder width apart and her arms relaxed by her sides. They kept advancing yet she did not move, her stare unwavering. The heated air bristled the fur lining the edges of her sleeveless duster. When the horde was in range, she pushed it to the side and pulled out the long-sword made special for her. Its length spanned six feet, both sides of the sharp blade glistening in the light. She turned it sideways.

With one strike, she knocked the first row to the left. The leader dodged, exposing the second row to her next swing and sent to the right. A Relliant soldier came upon her, eyes glowing with battle high. She bent her knees slightly and delivered a punch that went through his chest with a crunching sound.

The next wave advanced. She turned the sword back straight then tossed the soldier's body out of the way. The blade sliced across them. Some managed to bend back away from it, getting knicked in the neck or torso. Others weren't so lucky, being cut in half. The horde halted.

Telia sensed the leader from above and looked up to see him falling towards her wih a fist raised ready to deliver a deadly blow. She smiled at his face contorted in hatred. Lifting one arm, she brought her fingers together like a spade. He could not maneuver out of her way, him being nearly inches from her. She adjusted the angle of her arm and he landed on her pointed fingers. They imbedded deep protruding out his back. Dark, nearly black, blood spewed from his lips while his body lay slumped, impaled on her arm.

"Come. I invite you to your deaths," Telia offered.

She dropped her arm and let the leader's body slide off onto the floor. Their numbers were now half because of her and they hesitated.

"Hmph!" She smirked and turned back to the sealed off lab.

She was sure the others had already returned. It was time to go.

CASUALTIES OF WAR

Purple lights dimly shrouded the lower levels of Metropolis' main hub. In the chamber at the end of the corridor, Terence lay on the round bed in female form with one arm across her eyes. The inside was configured like a silo, three levels high. Shelves and holoscreens spiraled upwards along the walls.

Three months before, she had undergone a procedure to remove the wet ware implants. Midway, her body had shifted to female in response to extreme trauma. She was now bedridden, her body soft from her muscles not being utilized. The ample bosom was a burden, making her chest feel weighed down. They were even more cumbersome when she laid on her back. And her hips hurt. The long black silk robe with a red sash keeping it closed was the only thing she could wear that didn't chafed her sensitive skin.

She removed her arm, letting it fall to her side and stared up at the multiple feeds running on the holoscreens. The battle was fiercer than she had imagined, confirming her decision to lower Metropolis was right. The population was finally adjusting with little complaints. They understood the reason.

A sharp pain stabbed her in the temples, forcing her to rise abruptly. Her body was in no condition for that kind of motion so she struggled to roll over on her side. She let out a scream as her fingers dug into the sheets and grabbed hold.

Kevin!

She felt whatever pain he was enduring at that very moment. When the pain subsided, she looked towards the holoscreens and zeroed in on one. It flipped through different feeds until it landed on a region right outside the outskirts of the destroyed Grid Community.

"Commander!" She yelled vocally and telepathically.

Within moments, the chamber door hissed open and her second in command was in the doorway. He stood straight, both hands clasped behind his back. His disgusted expression towards her was infuriating. Due to the results of her procedure, many of the operatives who were willing to do it had backed out. He often commented on her timing.

"Send a transport unit to extract them." She pointed to the holoscreen.

"I will not jeopardize a team of our people for your one sided lust obsession."

She forced herself to sit up then leaned forward. Her eyes brightening, accenting the lines in her irises.

"You will open a pathway, send a transport ship, and go get them."

Her voice was low as she spoke through gritted teeth.

Her second in command gave her another hostile stare then sighed.

"If this goes south, it is on your hands alone."

He turned away and the door slid shut, resealing itself. Terence slumped back against the headboard and glanced back up at the holoscreen. She didn't dare zoom in for fear of what she might see. From what she could sense, he had his children with him.

Stupid!

He should have evacuated them long before this. She averted her eyes from the feed as streaks of fire rained down on the region.

Hurry!

⌒

Blood dripped from a head wound into Kevin's right eye as he held his middle daughter's body tight against him. The hole in her chest had been cauterized by the super heated round that hit her. He couldn't even cry. His mind was blank. Enemy fighters were all around and he didn't care. His remaining children formed a defense perimeter to protect him. Streaks of multicolored beams criss crossed through the air. A military plane went down close, its explosion sending a gust of hot wind that nearly knocked them to the ground.

Kevin felt his arms starting to give out so he gently laid her down. He caressed her forehead, pushing the bloody strands from her face. His eldest son walked backwards to him and knelt by his side. Dried tears mixed with dirt and blood stained his cheeks. Kevin let his arms drop to his knees.

"I'm so sorry, sweetheart," he whispered to her.

"Dad." Otto turned and locked eyes with him. "It's okay. We tried. You said we might not make it. So," his son seemed to struggle with his emotions. "You can just rest now. There's no need for you to see us all go down. We're not going out without a fight though." He smiled then. "You taught us that much."

His youngest son went flying back, the round from a pulse rifle hitting him in the abdomen. Smoke drifted from the wound as he cried out in agony. The rest of his children tightened the circle. Kevin knew he wasn't going to last long. There were at least twelve holes in him, one in his head, and the calf of his left leg was shattered.

For some reason, he thought of Terence earlier. A mountain of regret had consumed him as the fighting intensified. He wondered if he had gotten with him after the death of his wife what it would have been like. His youngest son choked on his own blood beside him.

I can't. I won't.

Relenting to his wounds and taking what Otto said to heart, he let his body fall sideways to the ground. As his eyes closed, he saw a glint of purple lights.

The transport unit sent from Metropolis sped into the battle zone accompanied by four fighter jets. They mowed down every enemy craft in their wake, clearing the path for the transport to land near Kevin and his family. The modified soldiers filed out in a star formation.

Otto reared back, not knowing what to do. Once human specimens marched towards him with glowing purple lenses in their right eye and internal mics slithering from behind their ears. One of them grabbed his youngest brother by the feet and lifted him up like a sack over his shoulder. Another dragged his father off while one carefully picked up his sister's body and carried it to the ship. When he turned back around, one of the soldiers was bent down directly in front of him.

"We must leave. Board the ship and prepare for departure."

He nodded, not sure what to make of the situation.

"Can't kick a gift horse in the mouth," his younger sister said. "Isn't that how that old saying goes?"

For the first time, he got a good look at the state she was in. She was covered in blood, half her hair singed, and there was a large gash in her left arm.

"Yeah. That's it. Come on."

They all rose to their feet and were immediately surrounded by the transport soldiers. Enemy fire was diverted towards them and the soldiers dealt with it like well oiled machines. Their targeting was pristine and got them safely on the transport. Otto made sure his siblings were strapped in before doing that himself. The transport left the battlefield the same way it showed up; in a hailstorm of laser fire.

Farther inside the transport, he could his father being hooked up to a life support system. His sister's body was laid into a cryochamber for preservation. He squeezed his eyes shut. He never wanted to see that. The way her eyes widened in shock and pain a split second before she fell, dead and smoldering.

"We are taking the long route back to avoid depletion of energy cells," the soldier said.

"Oh, okay."

He opened his eyes and found his siblings had fallen asleep. They were slumped in disarray, only the restraints keeping them from hitting the floor.

"You should also rest. We will make sure you are delivered to Metropolis as instructed."

As instructed? He frowned, then smirked. *Terence.*

His body suddenly felt heavy and he drifted off into sleep.

Terence hadn't slept since the transport left three days before. She witnessed the pick up and then the feed was lost. For the transport to make another jump through the pathways, it would have needed a second energy cell. Her second in command refused to allow it. He cited if Kevin was still alive when the transport got there and back, she should count her blessings. His wounds would be closed up on the surface but not healed.

Still in nothing except the black robe, she stared up at the holoscreens floating around the walls. As much as she hated mankind, Earth was still her home and she refused to leave it. Watching the surface being desecrated hurt her.

"Incoming transport." The A.I. announced over the intercom. "Docking at bat zero zero nine. Commencing depressurization."

Terence struggled to her knees on the bed and crawled to the end. She slid her legs over and felt her feet touch the cool tiled floor. With a hard push, she made herself stand. Pain shot through her entire body. She threw her head back and screamed. Yet, she didn't let herself fall back. She endured until it subsided. Taking a deep breath, she hit the release panel on the door and walked into the dark corridor.

At the lift, she contemplated going up. The staff had not seen her since the procedure and showing up unannounced might stir up trouble. In answer to her dilemma, the lift doors opened and her second in command stepped out.

"What do you think you're doing?" He demanded in a hostile tone.

"I need to…"

"You need to go back into your hole ad stay there until further notice," he cut her off. "No one wants to see your decrepit body on the main deck."

"How dare you!" She didn't get to finish.

"What are you playing at?"

Terence clenched her hands then released them.

"I want him brought to me."

"Oh?" Her second in commands brow shot up. "Going to nurse him back to health yourself?" He glared down at her. "Disgusting." With that, he turned and went back into the lift. "As you wish."

The lift closed and he was gone. Terence pursed her lips, trying to fight back tears of rage. She knew how fragile she was at the moment. He didn't need to tell her that. She walked back to her chamber, the pain coming in intermittent waves. By the time she was back on her bed, her body was exhausted and she doze off.

The sound of her chamber door opening woke her. She looked up at one of the view screens and saw she had been out for two hours. She slid off the bed right as two modified technicians came in carrying Kevin. She made a sharp intake of breath as her eyes roamed his features. They set him on the bed and left. Her second in command standing in the doorway tsked before turning away.

Terence stood at the foot of the bed, now alone with Kevin. She watched as his chest moved up and down. Each breath he took, labored. Not in her right mind, she climbed onto the bed and crawled over him. She sat astride him staring at his face. Her gaze roamed down his bare chest and stopped right above his pelvis.

This is wrong! She chastised herself. A second voice in her mind chimed in. *I don't care.*

She stroked his cock with delicate ease and marveled at its full length and girth. Even in his unconscious state, it didn't take much for her to arouse him. She shrugged the robe off her shoulders and let it fall behind her. Rising on her knees, she positioned herself over his erection and eased down.

"Ahh!"

The pain shocked her, getting worse as it went deeper. She placed her hands on his chest for leverage and stayed like that for a while until she caught her breath.

"You always hurt me, even now," she whispered.

Traitor.

Craig had heard that term thrown around from the start of the fighting and it was no less hurtful now as Relliant soldiers loyal to the General spat at him during combat. He took a deep breath and exhaled slowly as a group approached with eyes burning full of rage. The assault had been non stop for days. His unit was near exhaustion awaiting reinforcements. He could see the Relliant fighters coming at him were at their limits as well.

So far, he had managed not to kill any of his fellow Relliant soldiers, knowing they were merely misguided. Yet, he had no qualms about severely injuring them by his own hands. Their wounds would be treated once back on their ships to Rellia. All around him, the ground was spotted with dark red blood. From a distance, he could hear the familiar sound of Bree's combat ship approaching. It shot down one of the Relliant ships as it neared. That didn't deter the enemy from their advance.

He was surrounded within seconds, ten against one. Even though they were outmatched, his level of skills as a Command Fleet officer exceeding their combined might, he still showed them no mercy. One by one, he defeated them in hand to hand combat, sending their bodies flying out of the circle they created to trap him.

Another wave of soldiers was coming. He turned as he sent his last opponent off into the air like the rest and braced for a second round. A fiery blast erupted from behind them and their bodies scattered like confetti. Bree's ship landed, its ramp already open to let his soldiers mill out onto the battlefield.

"Took you long enough," he called out to Bree.

"You were doing fine on your own," Bree replied, yelling over the din.

"Hmph! I'm not that good, sweetheart."

Bree came up to him and gave him a soft peck on the lips.

"Your modesty is not appealing."

"Shall we?"

He nodded at the third wave of combatants filing over the hillside from the opposite direction.

"They're relentless," Bree sighed.

"Defense formation! Three by five, East!" Craig ordered his unit.

They branched out into groups of fifteen, forming an arc across the east side ahead of the enemy. Each group was divided by three sections to cover all sides: front, center, and rear. Bree's soldiers moved to form an arc the opposite direction to engage the constant barrage from the west. Craig stared in awe at the number of soldiers cresting the hill. It was as if this was their last ditch effort to slay their own.

Hundreds of Relliant soldiers came down to meet their brethren in deadly combat. Craig realized they were not only fueled by blind loyalty, but blood lust as well. Not keen on using weapons, he caved and found a longsword still gripped by an unconscious soldier on the ground. He pried it from his fingers and swung it a few times to feel its weight. His second in command turned and gave him a questioning look.

"This isn't going to go well," he said to the officer.

"No. But isn't that a little desperate?" His second in command pointed to the sword.

Craig shrugged and went into a crouched stance.

"We'll find out soon enough. Here they come."

From both sides, their forces were swallowed up by a sea of bodies. Craig was able to cut down twice as many with the sword yet he felt a sense of reluctance. When the number of enemy began to dwindle, he heard an odd noise come from the other side of the hill. At first he thought it was humming, then a strangled throttling. Right as the ship rose above the line of sight, he realized what it was. The sound of a cannon being powered up.

Bree turned to see it and gaped in horror. Craig looked around the area and knew if that weapon fired, it would take everything with it. He watched its barrel glow hot with blue light, like a giant iris in the sky.

A power he had not felt before welled up inside him. As it coursed through his body, he could tell it was ancient and somehow became familiar. His eyes glimmered a brilliant violet and he instinctively slammed his fist into the ground, causing an earthquake. It broke apart, spanning a quarter mile, to create pockets of deep crevices that his soldiers fell through. When he stood, he was in the cannon's direct path.

"Love you for eternity," he said softly to Bree.

He moved with lightning speed and shoved Bree out of the way, sending him backwards. Craig turned back to the weapon.

"No!" He heard Bree scream out in protest, the word fading in the distance as he flew.

There was nowhere for him to run. He stared down the cannon as it fired. Using his newly found power to form a shield, even knowing it would not save him, he braced for impact.

At least my body won't be destroyed, he thought as the blast hit him.

Bree watched from afar as the cannon's fire hit Craig's energy shield. The blast concaved around it and was spread apart, dissipated the damage. That didn't stop some of the rays from penetrating Craig's barrier and shooting holes through his body. Bree lay on the ground with fists clenched, trying to hold back his tears, as the streaks of light shot across the battlefield. Everything in its path above ground was obliterated, including an enemy Relliant ship that tried to evade. Bree stared wide eyed at Craig while he waited for the super heated air to cool. A shot from behind him hit the cannon's ship, knocking it from the sky. Startled, he looked up to see Gragor's ship hovering above.

Not caring anymore about the state of the area, Bree got into a crouched position and launched himself towards Craig at sonic speed, reaching him before his body hit the ground. He cradled him in his arms and began shaking from rage and sorrow. A primal yell was caught in his throat and he didn't dare unleash it. That would be the end of his will. Blood sizzled from the holes in Craig's body, the smell wafting in Bree's nostrils. He swayed back and forth, gripping Craig tighter.

Gragor dropped down from his ship's ramp and went to stand over him. The Commander didn't speak. He kept vigil whie serving as their protector from the battle still in progress. No enemy would get near them on his watch. Bree could no longer hold in his despair and let the pain out. His screams echoed through the valley, making some of Craig's soldiers climbing out of the cracks halt their ascent. Gragor let his head fall back as he stared at the burnt air, listening to Bree cry over and over.

⌒

General Tartha stared at the viewport on the bridge as it displayed images from the ground fights on Earth. The battle should not have gone on for so long, in his opinion. He started to realize how similar to his own race humans were. No matter how many were struck down, there was another swarm of them lying in wait for their turn to seek glory. He almost admired their tenacity. Seeing his own soldiers fighting against each other made his blood boil.

Gragor.

The Command Fleet was stationed nearby and true to form, had not moved to join the fray. An image caught his eye.

"Stop! Move back three frames." He commanded his helmsman.

On a mountain plateau was Darnizva sending groups of Relliant warriors to their doom with only a fighting stick and his bare hands. To his amazement, Darnizva finished off the last one then turned to look up. His gaze seemed to have met his own. Tartha's frustration had reached its limit. He stood from his seat.

"Prepare the main cannon," he ordered.

"Starting energizing sequence of main cannon," his weapons officer replied.

He didn't take his eyes off Darnizva. How much he despised the Karysilan rose to a new level and he felt his eyes twitch as they narrowed. The cannon blast would annihilate everything within hundreds of miles, the second causing a massive wave of destruction, putting an end to the battle.

"I win," Tartha said, grinning maniacally. "Fire main cannon."

"Firing first round."

A wide beam of light shot from the ship and headed straight down to Darnizva's location.

From the bridge of the Command Fleet, Commander Fravral watched in horror as the general's ship fired onto the Earth surface. He had been instructed to shoot down the Armada ship if it seemed like that was the case. This was unexpected so far into the fight. He felt if the general had any inclination to use it, he would have done so at the beginning. To unleash such power after years of combat made no sense.

Unless something angered him beyond reason.

Which meant this was a childish attempt to show might. Commander Fravral let out a sigh and shook his head. It was too late to shoot down the ship. The damage had already been done. He was sure Commander Gragor could see the cannon fire from wherever he was.

Darnizva saw the beam of fiery death scorching the air as it came towards him. He stared at it incredulous, knowing it was a result of General Tartha's feelings about him. The Relliant fleet that his own engaged with in the previous battle had been denied victory when he fled. To be so petty as to chase one fleet across the galaxy boggled his mind. He also knew a second round from the ship's cannon was imminent. That's how General Tartha operated.

Assurance of destruction.

A force hidden deep within Darnizva flared up, heating his entire body. A rage like nothing he had ever felt consumed him and his body radiated a red aura that spanned out all around him. Like a plug being yanked from its socket, his eyesight went black. There were no thoughts in his mind as his body moved on its own. His eyes glowed like two red suns, creating cone shaped beams of light. With ease, he levitated off the plateau until he was halfway up into the atmosphere. There was no way he could dodge the second onslaught but he was going to give Tartha a taste of his own brand of hate.

A bubble of energy pulsing with various shades of red enveloped his body while he arched back., his chest pushed out to its limit. As he bent forward, Darnizva unleashed a sonic yell followed by a blast of red that shot from him. The main cannon's first round entered the area and collided with it, causing a ripple of heat that spread across hundreds of miles. On impact, the two blasts combined. Darnizva's narrowed into a beam creating a ricochet that sped towards space and headed directly for General Tartha's ship right as the second round struck Darnizva back down to Earth's surface.

Soldiers on Tartha's ships scrambled to the evacuation pods. The bridge was cleared within minutes, leaving him to stare in awe at the returned attack. When he saw Darnizva turn red, he knew he was doomed. There were always rumors about what lay hidden within the Karysilan child. This was too much, for he also understood it was merely a drop of what Dranizva was truly capable of.

"General, we must go, now!"

He turned to his second in command. The soldier was wild eyed and desperate. Tartha, reluctantly walked over and followed him out to the lower bowels of the ship. He would not abandon his ship. It would be crippled but not destroyed. He thanked the Gods that Darnizva had no idea how to harness his own power.

The residuals of the second round's beam were still leaving the main ship when the red beam of death, widening along the way, struck. It ripped through the hull like a zipper and knocked the ship off kilter, forcing it to shift ninety degrees and allow the beam to resume travel. The beam streaked across other ships in its wake, hitting one of the Earth evacuee ships as it did an emergency jump, then finished its aiming sequence in the opposite direction.

Commander Fravral stood on the bridge of the Command Fleet's main ship and watched it head towards him. He let out a sigh of defeat. The crew turned to him, anxiety etched on their faces.

"Prepare for impact."

It would hit them hard. Even though it was already dissipating and still needed to travel a good distance, the blast would go straight through the hull from front to back. The ship was bound to free fall until the maintenance crew could correct it.

"Once the ship is stabilized, we will launch escape pods for any who wish to transport to the other ships. I am going to rendezvous with Commander Gragor."

Out of the corner of his eye, he saw a massive fleet appear near Earth space from a jump. He recognized the League insignia on their hulls.

You're too late.

Chapter 5: Desolation

ALLIANCE

With an entire fleet in tow, Lieutenant Sspark brought them out of the jump in time to see a huge section of Earth engulfed in red along with General Tartha's ship tilting in an awkward position. The Command Fleet was struck by the main Armada's cannon fire. It lit up from the inside all the way down its length. He stood at the helm confused, and terrified. His glittering body suit sent speckles of light around him as he changed his posture to stand straight.

What has happened?

"Full stop!" He commanded.

His communications officer taped the commlink.

"All ships, full stop!"

Each ship slowed to a crawl and halted in an arrow like formation. Sspark took a good look at the red ball spreading like a disease across the planet surface while the rest of it seared Tartha's ship to a crisp. Only one who could have caused such destruction came to mind.

Darnizva.

That made it worse than he thought. Whenever the Captain got angry, his eyes glowed a sinister shade of red. No other being did that except his father. He would have to report this to General Phalkar. He shifted his weight from one leg to other, making his bodysuit shimmer even more against the light.

The League's main fleet was a third of the way to Karysilan when the arguments heated up. General Phalkar became angered by the possible mutiny. Leaving Darnizva and his fleet to fend for themselves against General Tartha himself and a Command Fleet was like sentencing them to death. An execution as punishment for the Captain's actions. General Phalkar denied it but Ammordia confronted him. Her hostility towards him turned many to her side.

Before the second jump was to commence, Sspark, along with Admiral Goulld, volunteered to head back to Earth. He thought Phalkar would deny his request, citing the safety of his mate being of importance. That didn't happen. The general merely waved a hand and angrily told him to do as he pleased. Disappointed and hurt, Sspark took off immediately. Admiral Goulld's ship would arrive on the outskirts of the solar system in case Sspark's forces were not enough. Ammordia was not far behind. The rest of the fleet had returned home in protest.

A group of Relliant ships maneuvering towards them with weapons targeted caught his eye and he smirked. From what he could tell, the battle had not gone as General Tartha had planned. The humans were putting up a hell of a fight despite their lack of technology.

"Ready weapons," he commanded. "Looks like we'll have to fight our way to the Earth's surface." He turned to Ballamian. "Want to board one of those ships once we cripple it?"

The Cybok's eyes narrowed. He nodded.

"If you allow it," Ballamian replied.

"You don't need me to go with you, correct?" Sspark asked jokingly.

Ballamian turned and walked off the bridge. Sspark knew he was heading to the docks and would soon be leading a fighter ship to take down the closest enemy vessel. Bringing his attention back to the viewport, Sspark rubbed the bottom of his chin with one finger. He too, needed to go. Darnizva may require a rescue or something similar in his mind.

"Prepare my ship. I'm going down. A full tactical unit will accompany me along with a fighter squadron."

"Yes, Commander," his crew answered.

Wait for me, Darnizva.

DAMAGE

With his body smoldering on the ground, Darnizva managed to raise his head and see out of the one eye not swimming in his own blood. The creamy white liquid oozed out, streaming down his cheek. Both hands were scorched yet he used them with barely enough strength to claw his way towards the cliff's edge. Flat on his stomach, he made a slow progression.

The sky was blood red and he could feel the extreme heat in the air. Everything was still.

The edge seemed too far away so he stopped for a moment to rest. He needed to see what was going on below. His memory had a huge gap following the blast that came from Tartha's ship. He assumed it must have hit since the sky was blotted out and the air felt asphyxiating. Something was off about. He had never seen so much red before after a Relliant attack. Other questions arose. Why was it so silent? Had everyone died? He pushed the thought out of his mind while he mustered up more energy to continue his crawl.

Sspark located Darnizva on the plateau and sucked in his breath. Another Karysilan fighter ship was nearby and he saw Shatis Va run out towards Darnizva. She stopped a good distance from him and seemed to be waiting for something. He maneuvered his fighter into a sideways approach then landed next to hers.

His combat team followed while the other ships went to scout the area. He got out and walked over to stand beside her. They both watched Darnizva regain consciousness and resume crawling towards the ledge. Most of his uniform was gone, exposing patches of pale skin with burn scars. There were deep wounds as well, cauterized by the blast and weeping.

"Are you satisfied, Lieutenant?" She asked.

Her words were like an assault and Sspark turned to stare up at her.

"What did you say?" He snapped.

"Isn't this what you always wanted? To see Darnizva near his demise. Disappointed you weren't able to kill him personally?"

"That's not what I wanted!" He yelled.

Even as he said, he knew no one would believe that to be true. He now understood how it looked and sounded when he constantly berated Darnizva, voicing his hatred. Threatening to kill him off if he could get away with it. He turned his attention back to Darnizva now close to the edge. Shatis Va went over and lightly tapped him in the back of the neck. His body went limp. She lifted him gently from the ground and slung him over one shoulder. Turning back, she carried him to her ship. Sspark stood rooted, frowning, not sure what to do. His emotions were going haywire. Right now, his heart was breaking, and he couldn't stop the wave of hurt from crashing into him.

I never wanted this!

The leader of his combat unit came to his side.

"Lieutenant. Shall we check the perimeter for hostiles?"

Sspark felt his body start to give way, his knees buckling from sorrow. With every fiber of his being, he managed to stop the process and straighten his posture. His hands clenched and unclenched. Taking a deep breath, he turned to his squadron leader and gave his most winning smile.

"Of course. Let's see how many Relliant rats we can scurry out of the chaos and exterminate."

"Very well. Will you be joining us?"

"No. I have to make sure that other imbecile is still alive." The leader gave him a confused expression. Sspark sighed. "Lieutenant Zanzibar."

The leader did not comment and went back to his fighter ship. When the squadron took off, Sspark fell to his hands and knees, shaking. Tears flowed from his eyes despite his attempts to stop them by squeezing them shut. Against his will, a strangled cry escaped from him. He grabbed the scorched earth under his fingers and pounded it repeatedly. His shimmering white bodysuit became dirty, no longer sparkling.

Movement caught his eye and he looked up. Clamoring over the edge of the cliff was a group of Relliant soldiers. One had a handheld holoscreen with an image of Darnizva's body at the location. He realized instantly that they had come to finish him off. That angered Sspark. He had encountered on occasion some Relliants having no honor code. Rising to his feet, he stood legs wide apart with his arms at his side.

When the group leapt up and landed on the ledge, they found Sspark waiting, his right hand glowing as the silver sphere formed. The one with the holoscreen deactivated the device and stared at him.

"Where did you take that monster's body?" The Relliant asked.

Sspark smirked. The sphere elongated until it was seven feet in length then solidified into a metal rod. He spun it effortlessly, his gaze never leaving the sight of his prey.

"Oh, there's no need for you to worry about that. This is the end of line for you."

"Hmph!" The Relliant drew out two short blades. "We shall see about that."

Sspark cocked his head to one side as the enemy advanced. The image of Darnizva laying helpless in the dirt flashed in his mind. His eyes glowed white hot as he swung his sphere weapon to take out the first set of soldiers on the left. There would be no mercy from him.

⤲

Admiral Goulld received the reports from Shatis Va, and Ssparks recon group. His chest tightened with anxiety while he read each one being displayed on the screen floating before him. He had no desire to tell his mate, Ammordia, that another child of hers had been taken down by Relliant forces. There was already resentment towards Phalkar for impregnating Ammordia during the last war while Goulld was out on the battle-field. The entire militia voiced their anger which didn't faze Phalkar in the least. Their son, Jonah, was happy to have a baby brother but as he got older came to despise their general for his actions as well.

He tapped the feed and zoomed in on the red blot still spreading across Earth's surface. General Phalkar would not be getting that report. He needed to make Sspark understand the reason why they should all keep it to themselves.

The fighting had all but ceased. Humanity would survive. The frustration he encountered came from the fact that Phalkar waited too long to approve reinforcements. They should have been there sooner, or not have left at all.

"Prepare for incoming. We are moving into position."

His crew went to work as ordered. His ship would do a small jump to rendezvous with Sspark's fleet. From there, he'd be in range to scan the League ships on Earth for damage. Theirs did not have full medical bays like his ship did. Darnizva needed to be transferred from Shatis Va's. He sat in his command chair and let the straps slither from beneath and close around him. The main viewport went blank, the shields engaged to combat the solar system's sun, and the ship entered the jump.

Coming out of it, on the other side with the sun behind them, Admiral Goulld pressed himself further in his seat as the viewport opened to reveal the scene. Seeing it up close was more than he anticipated. A ring of destruction orbited the planet.

"Contact Shatis Va," he commanded his communications officer.

A ship launched from the crippled Command Fleet's flag ship. He found that curious. One ship was no threat, so he didn't order a pursuit. The problem at hand was the aftermath laid before him. He could only imagine what the surface looked like.

STATUS

Mountains with missing chunks blasted off finally succumbed from their own weight and crumbled. The ground shook from the avalanche of boulders whose diameter was equal to the size of houses. Parts of the ocean were boiling, the creatures within dead. Most of the rivers, lakes, and seas had either turned poisonous or evaporated. Areas of vegetation were wiped out. Empty fields of wasteland replaced them. What remained was probably inedible, contaminated by residuals from alien weaponry. Animals that had taken shelter were found dead in their hiding places. For the ones who were still roaming during the battle, the only thing left of them was the outline of their carcasses.

Sspark's scouts were accompanied by a small human recon group and both races seemed saddened by the devastation. The lead scout took in the appearance of the recon members. They had clearly been in battle not too long ago and seemed to be functioning beyond their limits. With the head scientists evacuated, the task of assessments went to the ones left after the fall. He felt a sense of pity for them. This was not their forte, yet they had no choice.

A hybrid male human bent down and submerged a tube in the nearby waterway. The rancid smell coming from it didn't incite much hope for consumption. He pulled it out and closed the cap before handing it to another man behind him. The tube was inserted into a small handheld device. After a few moments it beeped.

"This shit could kill you if you drank it. The levels are off the charts."

The first man looked up at his counterpart and simply nodded.

"Can I see the data?" The scout leader asked.

He took the device from him and looked at the information on the screen.

"We may have a way to neutralize it. I'm sure our scientists will have the same results."

"This world needed to be cleansed," the second man said. "Maybe now, humans will see that all those wars, all the bigotry and hate, was trivial. All for nothing."

"Your optimism is refreshing, albeit, naïve." One of the other recon members said.

"Yeah, I know."

The scout leader handed the sample analysis instrument back to the man. He understood their thinking. His commlink activated with a loud ping.

"I think," the voice on the other end said. "Lieutenant Sspark may be in trouble."

"Hmm?" A quizzical expression formed on his face. The holoscreen in his hand switched from taking footage of the scenery to a live feed of the battle on the cliff. Sspark was outnumbered twenty to one. He zoomed in, getting a closer look at his commander's face, and flinched. Then he smirked. "Our leader will be fine."

"Are you certain we don't need to intervene?"

"Oh, I am quite sure." *That crazed monster loves combat.*

The first recon man finally stood. He brushed off his already filthy and torn leggings.

"There's still fighting going on?" He asked.

"Not really. Just small instances. This war is over," the scout leader replied.

"Was it really a war?" The second man asked. "We were never going to win."

"But we did," the third member said.

"No," one of the scout soldiers answered. "Your race got extremely lucky."

He gave the scout leader a knowing look. It was true. If not for Darnizva, Earth would be uninhabitable now.

﹏

Sspark was delighted when more Relliant soldiers came to assist their downed comrades. He gleefully struck them with deadly force, watching the nearly black arcs of blood fly through the air. He had not sense of fear. And he should have. His bodysuit had already been torn open from enemy blades making gashes in his flesh. Yet, he was relentless. His mind had all but blanked out, consumed by rage.

Lavender colored slashes formed a whirlwind on the other side of the enemy and blood splattered on Sspark's face, stopping him mid swing. He stared wide eyed as the enemy soldiers before him disappeared over the ledge. Some going with severed limbs that followed them over. The rest of the enemy soldiers retreated, dragging off their dead and wounded.

Lieutenant Zanzibar stood at the ledge, looking down, watching the enemy fall. He turned to Sspark and nodded before walking past him to his fighter ship. When Sspark didn't move, he stopped.

"Come." Zanzibar said it softly.

Sspark lowered his sphere and let it fade back into his hand. He turned away from the ledge and followed Zanzibar. Hovering above them was Zanzibar's command ship. He had not noticed the behemoth show up. They both got into their fighters and flew up to the docking bay already open and ready for them. When the docking arms grabbed hold and secured the fighters, Sspark got out and stood on the platform.

"Where are we going?" He asked Zanzibar.

"Darnizva."

The name hit him like a sledgehammer. His posture faltered and he leaned against his fighter's hull. For the first time since engaging in battle, he took stock of his physical state and injuries. Zanzibar was able to catch him before he fell to the floor. He was losing consciousness.

No, no, no! I am not this weak!

He chastised himself to no avail. Everything seemed to close in on him until there was nothing but darkness. His hatred long gone.

Inside the protective bubble floating in mid air above the once great city of Los Angeles, Roland sat cross legged, watching the red death's progress. He had an idea of what Darnizva was and did not have an ounce of surprise when he unleashed such tremendous power. By the way the ball of destruction moved, he figured it would stop soon, having engulfed a third of the planet. The fall out would be just as awful as it dissipated, its residue settling to the ground.

For a moment, he pitied the humans. Then, he thought about all that he'd seen over the course of his time on the planet. No. They deserved much worse than this. He felt they got off easy. Other civilizations that had taken similar paths were eventually annihilated by their own hands or invasion. He was certain that if left alone, humanity would destroy itself in the next hundred years or so.

With his mind, he moved the bubble to a different continent on the other side of the red death. From that vantage point, he could see the tendrils reached down to the surface, etching grooves in everything they touched. Snow caps had already been obliterated from the intense heat, causing avalanches of acidic water.

Such a waste.

Early on he had stated his reluctance to fix the planet. Now he felt like changing his mind. Not immediately, of course. He wanted to let the aftermath settle before he decided what the next course of action would be. Maybe in a decade or two he could do something about the oceans. Water was essential to human life, after all.

He felt omniscient eyes bearing down on the planet and made a sideways glance up. There was no doubt who it was. He wondered if they had the same thoughts. Would they save humanity from itself?

What are you up to, Destroyer? He asked silently.

〜

Engulfed in soft ethereal light that shimmered like mist, Bryce also sat with legs crossed observing the Earth from above in space. He stared down at the chaos with a deadpan expression. Not a thought entered his mind for a long time. He too, had decided to wait until the red death finished its path of destruction. There were areas within the hot zone that were filled with humans in agony.

Darnizva.

The thought shocked him and he came out of his state of nothingness. His mind went through the archives within and found the reference that explained the phenomenon.

The Red Star.

Formed at the start of the universe and evolved into an entity by the White Star, the first of its kind. Generations of beings were created from the Red Star's seed but never a direct descendant. It was reincarnated many times over the millenias, with no memory of its true self. He cursed Phalkar for deciding to have offspring even though he knew the general had no idea why he shouldn't.

He spotted the Litigator making the rounds to every corner of the planet to assess the damage. Half the planet had evacuated, leaving too many on the surface. Most were fighters. The others were stubborn creatures who refused to abandon their home world. He understood that sentiment. Having no real home, he envied planet dwellers. Until, incidents like this happened. Only fools would throw out common sense and brave the storm.

Bryce took a deep breath and exhaled slowly. For now, he needed to decide on what to do next. Any actions taken would require the Litigator to assist in fixing it. The screams coming from Earth's surface were getting worse. He winced from the decibel level.

They're suffering.

He raised a hand over the planet and a thought came to mind. End it. All of it. Earth could be remade a few hundred years from now.

SURVIVAL

The last five evacuation ships came out of the vortex in close range of a nearby planet's stratosphere in a new solar system. Two of the ships veered off course towards the surface. One was crippled, it's rear hull breached with sparks of electrical fire spitting out.

On board the lead ship, the navigator checked the read outs from all the ships to confirm their location. He slammed a fist on the console and stared at the screen. The damaged ship and the one beside it were in front of the others acting as a tow. When the enemy blast hit it, their trajectory was knocked off course. He had no idea where they were. It would take some time to calculate how far off track from the original rendezvous point.

"I need a quick scan of that planet," he called out to a recon officer. "And catch up to those ships! We can't afford to have them crash like that."

Darnizva would never forgive me.

"Scan complete. Adjusting ship to accommodate atmosphere."

"Send us in."

The navigator sat back in his seat and braced for entry. His eyes went wide with anxiety as the ship rocked and bucked violently. As it cleared the troposphere, he saw why. The entire planet's surface was bubbling with patches of angry, flowing magma. He watched the damaged ship slam down onto a blackened terrain and break apart. The second ship followed, remaining intact except for the middle section. From above, he could see some of the ice blocks tumble out onto the ground. They started to smolder.

"Hurry! We have no idea if they'll melt here."

The pilot was able to steer the ship towards them, the two in the rear following suit. All three ships landed in a protective arc around the two downed ships. Emergency crews were already in action, erecting a breathable barrier while retrieving the wayward ice blocks. The navigator met up with the others at the center of the crash site.

Darnizva had established a hierarchy that only required the Navigator to be in control since the transport ships were not for combat. They had minimal weapons for offense only.

"What do we have?" He asked the first ship's navigator.

"Some of the ice blocks are damaged. We'll have to melt them and redo the process."

"Can those ships be repaired?" The fourth navigator asked.

The damaged ship's navigator shook his head.

"We have to wait for new transports."

"First, we need to find out where we are," the main ship's navigator said.

"And how long this planet has before it goes. If we can't get a transport ship here before that, we all perish." The fifth navigator added with frown.

A loud boom followed a giant eruption of lava spewing upwards on the outside of the barrier. They watched it dribble back down and set the already black surface ablaze.

"We can't stay here."

"Let's get the damaged cubes undone for now."

"And tell the humans what when they see this?" The second navigator exclaimed as he swept an arm across the scene before them.

"The truth," the head navigator spat. "It serves no purpose to lie."

They went back to their ships and prepared to assist in the coming tasks. The head navigator made it back to the bridge and walked over to his co navigator.

"So?" He asked.

His co navigator looked over at him.

"We are way off. I sent a communicae to the others already at the destined site. It would take about three years for them to get here with two transport ships. Another five to reach the original coordinates. Two of those for re-blocking the humans in ice and loading."

"And the planet?" He asked his head science officer.

"Five years, give or take."

There was a resounding sharp intake of air from the crew. That left no time for them to get off the planet before its demise.

"That means we'll be cutting it close."

"Understatement of the century. It could be sooner than that."

"Tell them to hurry, and why," the head navigator commanded.

He turned away, cursing inwardly. Images of the Relliant blast hitting the lead ship filled his mind. There was no way to deflect it during a jump.

They got us. They got us good.

Little by little, the unfrozen humans stumbled out of their deep sleep onto the raging planet's surface. The protective barrier didn't block the heat from the spewing lava. Within minutes, they were all sweating profusely, begging for water and crying in misery. Many slumped on cragged rocks while others looked up at the sky with longing. A handful were mesmerized by the fact that they were on another planet not of their solar system.

That level of innocence, derived from the first time of discovery, was something the head navigator remembered well. His maiden jump into battle two hundred years ago, he had never been off Karysilan. The ship had crashed onto a nearby planet similar to now and he remembered staring in awe at its strange attributes. Seeing the excited humans made him feel better.

The head navigator had explained the situation to them, and he was confronted with hostility. He found that ridiculous since it was not his fault. Humans liked to blame others regardless of facts, from his own observations. They milled around each day, trying to find things to do as they waited for salvation. He didn't have the stomach to tell them the other truth.

It had already been five years since they left Earth. Whether it had been obliterated or survived was unknown to any of them.

****END****

EXCERPT FROM

CURVE OF HUMANITY
BOOK FIVE

HOMECOMING

NEW FACTION

Dark shadows cascaded across the already dimly lit walls of the bunker. Men and women wrapped in make-shift tattered ponchos were huddled on the floor. Their faces were weary from being on a rotating watch while they waited for the last crew of explorers to come back. Every six months a group was sent out with equipment to gauge the air quality and test the soil. After five years, it appeared to have gotten better. Two years later and it was still not quite livable conditions yet. The rain that started two months earlier brought more despair, turning what soil remained black like soot. Test samples showed nothing could grow in it.

On the other side of the bunker was a small lab to do all their research on. When all the work was done, there was nothing left to do except wait for the next round of specimens. Professor Heines was the lead scientist of the small group and the only one standing with his head bowed down over the metal table. He had taken the reins due to his level head while everyone else went into a panic, scared of their chances for survival even this far underground. When the last transport landed for loading during the battle, an urge to see it through came over him. At the last moment, he backed away and headed for the nearest bunker along with the other sadists.

It all went south after they felt the impact of enemy's blast. He could tell by the way the bunker seemed to tilt nearly ninety degrees before settling back down not quite level that the ground had been lifted all around them. Anything above outside would not have survived, he was sure of that.

A click from above echoed and they all looked up to see the hatch creak open. In the beginning it would silently slide, its hydraulics working as designed. Now, it was corroded from the elements. The harsh squeal and popping grated on their senses. Muted light shone into the bunker making the swirling fine dust visible.

"We made it!" The first person to climb down the metal ring stairs exclaimed. "It's crazy looking out there."

Professor Heines stepped away from the table and met the man halfway.

"What's it like now?"

The second person coming down leapt from the third from the last ring and answered.

"The sky is shades of pink, orange, and grey. Kind of beautiful. The ground is shit though. That black stuff is everywhere. Not a hint of a plant to be found."

"That rain is nothing nice either," the last in the group said as he climbed down.

"Did you get a new sample?"

"Right here," the third replied, handing him a vial.

The rest of the people in the bunker stirred and began to rise. Professor Heines inserted the vial into the water tester and hit the process button. Everyone hovered around it, waiting for the result. Water had become scarce. What they found had to go through a ten step filter system. Even then, the water had an odd taste and some people broke out in hives. If the water was at least ten percent better in quality, they could drop down to a five step process and eliminate most of the impurities.

The machine beeped and the digital screen flashed twenty two percent improvement. They all burst out with joy, some hugging each other. Professor Heines raised his head until he was staring at the ceiling.

They would have decent water within the next few weeks.

"He's meticulous. Give him all the time he needs. He knows the deadline."

"I'm just anxious," Professor Makoto snapped.

"So am I. Let's have a little more patience."

Professor Makoto nodded.

"I hope to hear an update soon."

With that, the screen went blank and his screen saver resumed. General Perrara sighed and swung around in his chair to face the window. Night had fallen and the desert sky was full of stars. Mankind wanted so badly to reach further than their solar system but knowing what's out there, he wondered if that was the right answer. Compared to the aliens in their midst, humans were like insects. And not the resourceful kind.

Can we even win?

ABOUT THE AUTHOR

Hi there. I'm Maquel A. Jacob. I have had a passion for the written word since the age of seven, reading everything I could get my grubby little hands on which included encyclopedias and the thesaurus. At twelve, I had my first encounter with a Stephen King novel and was hooked. I then became inspired to write my own brand of fiction. Combining multiple genres to keep things interesting.

I am a HUGE Anime fan, love a great bottle of wine and rock out to heavy metal music. Green and lush Oregon is where I currently reside spinning imaginary worlds in my head and daydreaming.

For cool limited-edition Swag, updates, FREE short stories, Newsletters

...and more

Visit: http://www.majacobauthor.com/

Like Maquel A. Jacob on Facebook

Follow on Tumblr and Twitter @MaquelAJ1

Also find me on Goodreads

MAJart Works on Instagram